A Confidential Man

Wings Press, Inc.

Michael Embry

A Confidential Man

Chase Elliott heard the quick steps of someone coming behind him in the parking lot. The area was secure with a tall fence around it and guard facility at the entrance, so he wasn't worried about being accosted by a mugger, even though the building bordered an unsavory neighborhood.

"Got time for a beer?"

Chase glanced over his shoulder as Taylor Riggins sprinted closer to him.

"I think so," Chase said after glancing at his watch. "I don't have anything going on this evening."

"How about meeting me over at Pappy's?" Riggins said breathlessly.

Ten minutes later, they pulled into the parking lot behind Pappy's, the regular watering hole for reporters, lawyers and derelicts from all social classes. A lingering cigarette odor permeated the air like a burned-out house and managed to cling to clothes like an unpleasant perfume. Pappy's was a no-frills establishment, with a U-shaped bar in the middle, scattered round bar tables and stools placed in no particular order. A row of six booths lined one dark walnut-paneled wall. Neon beer signs and several dated Kentucky basketball schedule posters adorned the walls. A vintage jukebox near the entrance usually didn't come to life until later in the evening after the patrons had a few drinks under the belts, and then it was usually honky-tonk songs. As for Pappy, the bar's namesake, he passed away several years ago and the string of owners since his death continued to honor him with his moniker. Pappy would have been proud.

A busty barmaid with long coal-black hair and dressed a black blouse and tight-fitting black capris, who was probably old enough to remember Pappy, brought frosted mugs of draft beer to their table. The place was half-filled but it would be loud and packed in less than an hour later for a brief period as people made their daily stop before heading home. For some, it was practically a home away from home when not at work, and they would stay until closing.

"So what's going on?" Chase asked after taking a quick sip of beer and leaning back on the stool.

"Not a whole lot," Riggins said while surveying the room looking for familiar faces. "I need to get an opinion on something and wondered if you'd help."

What They Are Saying About
A Confidential Man

Michael Embry's honest, open, evocative prose engages readers from the opening sentence and propels readers along a storyline that leads straight to the heart. One of my must reads, but be forewarned, once you start reading *A Confidential Man,* you won't want to put it down until you finish.

--Chris Helvey,
eliminations editor for *Best New Writing 2009*
author of *Purple Adobe.*

Love, liaisons, death and deceit all find their way into the newsroom where sportswriter Chase Elliott spends his days. Admired for his reticence, Chase fears that the last secret entrusted to him may hold the key to a friend's mysterious death and may have put his own life in jeopardy as well. Michael Embry has crafted a treasure of intrigue and romance in *A Confidential* Man--a real page turner by anyone's standards.

--Cleo Roberson,
newspaper columnist and co-author of *Muhlenberg County (Images of America: Kentucky)*
and *A Mother's Cherished Memories.*

Everybody has secrets! You better be careful who you tell them to. **A Confidential Man** by Michael Embry looks at the inner workings of a major newspaper. Sports columnist Chase Elliott is the "Confidential Man." He can keep secrets and give advice. He isn't like others who love to gossip and some who are direct pipelines to management.

Some secrets are just too big. Chase struggles with his own personal responsibility with secrets revealed to him in confidence. Infidelity and fraudulent news stories become the focus of ongoing office romances and newspaper politics. What should Chase do? What can he do?

His friend, Brett Johnson, special sections editor, dies suddenly. The apparent accident spirals into a murder investigation as each piece of the puzzle is revealed. The action reaches every corner of the newspaper as you turn the pages quickly wanting to know more. Michael Embry weaves an exciting story with shocking revelations. This newspaper will never be the same.

--Peter Hurley,
Beyond the Rain

A Confidential Man

Michael Embry

A Wings ePress, Inc.

General Fiction Mainstream

Wings ePress, Inc.

Edited by: Rosalie Franklin
Copy Edited by: Leslie Hodges
Senior Editor: Leslie Hodges
Managing Editor: Karen Babcock
Executive Editor: Marilyn Kapp
Cover Artist: Pat Evans

Wings ePress Books
http://www.wingsepress.com

Copyright © 2009 by Michael Embry
ISBN 978-1-59705-617-5

Published In the United States Of America

Wings ePress Inc.
3000 N. Rock Road
Newton, KS 67114

Dedication

This novel is dedicated to my colleagues while working at The (Madisonville, Ky.) Messenger (1975-77), The Lexington Herald (1977-80), The Associated Press (1980-98), and Kentucky Monthly magazine (1998-2006).

One

Chase Elliott heard the quick steps of someone coming behind him in the parking lot. The area was secure with a tall fence around it and guard facility at the entrance, so he wasn't worried about being accosted by a mugger, even though the building bordered an unsavory neighborhood.

"Got time for a beer?"

Chase glanced over his shoulder as Taylor Riggins sprinted closer to him.

"I think so," Chase said after glancing at his watch. "I don't have anything going on this evening."

"How about meeting me over at Pappy's?" Riggins said breathlessly.

Ten minutes later, they pulled into the parking lot behind Pappy's, the regular watering hole for reporters, lawyers and derelicts from all social classes. A lingering cigarette odor permeated the air like a burned-out house and managed to cling to clothes like an unpleasant perfume. Pappy's was a no-frills establishment, with a U-shaped bar in the middle, scattered round bar tables and stools placed in no particular order. A row of six booths lined one dark walnut-paneled wall. Neon beer signs and several dated Kentucky basketball schedule posters adorned the walls. A vintage jukebox near the entrance usually didn't come to life until later in the evening after the patrons had a few drinks under the belts, and then it was usually honky-tonk songs. As for Pappy, the bar's namesake, he passed away several years ago and the string of owners since his death continued to honor him with his moniker. Pappy would have been proud.

A busty barmaid with long coal-black hair and dressed a black blouse and tight-fitting black capris, who was probably old enough to remember Pappy, brought frosted mugs of draft beer to their table. The place was half-filled but it would be loud and packed in less than an hour later for a brief period as people made their daily stop before heading home. For some, it was practically a home away from home when not at work, and they would stay until closing.

"So what's going on?" Chase asked after taking a quick sip of beer and leaning back on the stool.

"Not a whole lot," Riggins said while surveying the room looking for familiar faces. "I need to get an opinion on something and wondered if you'd help."

"Sure, but I don't know how much help I'll be."

"It's a professional thing. Just between us." A smile appeared and quickly disappeared from Riggins's angular face.

"Are you sure you want to tell me?" Chase asked with furrowed brows.

"I've known you for a long time and I've always trusted you, Chase. You manage to keep things in confidence, unlike some other people I know."

"Thanks." Chase forced a smile. "Isn't that what friends are supposed to do?"

Riggins took another swallow from his mug and looked around the room again, this time even more slowly and carefully. Chase watched Riggins for a second, and then found himself gazing about the room, for no apparent reason other than to find out what Riggins was looking for in the bar. The smoky haze made his eyes burn after a few seconds.

As Riggins was about to open his mouth, the front door opened quickly and three middle-age men in business attire came in and sat at the table next to them.

"Damn," Riggins said, a smirk revealing his annoyance by the innocent intrusion.

"What's the matter?"

"I was hoping for a little privacy."

"Do you know those guys?"

"No, but you can never be sure they don't know you or know one of your friends. You should be especially careful since your photograph appears in the paper several times a week in the sports section. You know that people read you and recognize you."

"Probably so," Chase said with a shrug. "I really don't give it that much thought."

"Because you're used to it."

"I guess so."

"People don't know me although they may recognize my byline."

"So would you prefer not telling me what you want to tell me?"

"I guess it's safe. Promise you won't tell anyone?"

"Are you sure you want to tell me?" Chase asked.

"Can't I trust you?" Riggins leaned slightly over the table and looked intently at Chase.

"Of course you can. It's just that I wonder if it's not so personal that perhaps you shouldn't tell anyone until you're comfortable with it. Is there a big hurry?"

"I just need to tell someone. And it's more professional than personal. I don't like carrying things around all the time. I need to unload on somebody and you're the person I trust the most. You're not a gossip or snitch like others around the newsroom."

"I try to mind my own business."

At that moment, a man in a pinstriped suit sitting next them glanced over his shoulder at them and then toward the bar. Riggins and Chase sat quietly. The man raised his hand to get the attention of the barmaid. A minute later, she brought a pitcher of beer and three mugs to their table. The men resumed their conversation while drinking their beers.

"So what do you want to tell me?" Chase asked softly.

"Remember that series I wrote a few months ago about the drug problem in town?"

"Yeah, it was very good. Some of the best work you've ever done."

"Thanks," Riggins said sheepishly.

"So what about it?"

"Most of it was made up."

"What?" Chase's expression went from calm to edgy. He straightened up and dropped his hands to his side. *Most of it was made up?*

"You can't tell a soul about this. I couldn't get hardly anyone to talk to me for the story so I did some research into the drug culture in some other towns and fabricated some incidents for the stories," Riggins said in hushed tone. "I know it wasn't right but I found a common thread through all drug stories that I could apply to Lexington."

"Damnit, Taylor, why in the hell did you do something stupid like that?" Chase said, shaking his head in disbelief and trying to keep from raising his voice. He was furious at his friend's disclosure but he knew it wasn't the right place to show his emotions. He fought the urge to slam his fist on the table or walk out of the bar. *I don't believe I'm hearing this!*

"I thought I would get a little more sympathy from you." Sadness crossed Riggins's face and the lines from his eyes grew deeper as he looked down at the table.

"I wish you hadn't even told me," Chase said, exasperated by the unexpected disclosure.

"Thanks a lot. I thought you were a friend."

"I am a friend but you shouldn't have unloaded this on me. What are you going to do about it now?"

"Nothing." Riggins shrugged and stared blankly at the wall.

"Nothing? Are you serious?"

"Do you think I'm going to tell the bosses, let them run a retraction, fire me and get me branded for life?" Riggins said as he raised his head and glared at Chase. "I do have a career. I do have a family to support."

Chase sat quietly for a few seconds, finishing his beer and staring across the room at nothing in particular. He then looked directly at Riggins. "I don't know what to say."

"I'm not proud of it," Riggins said, taking a deep breath. "I guess that's why I needed to tell you. It's been bugging the hell out of me ever since it was published."

"And you haven't told anyone?

"Not even my wife."

"I wish you hadn't told me."

"Are you going to tell someone?"

"I don't know what to do. This sickens me. You've been a damn good reporter all these years and you do something stupid like that."

"I had to."

"Why?"

"We've got some good, young reporters on staff and I needed to show everyone in the news department that I can still turn a good story."

"You certainly did that."

"What's that supposed to mean?" Riggins said, his voice rising as he glared at Chase. One of the men at the next table turned around and looked at Riggins for a moment, then turned back around and continued to talk to his friends.

"If you don't know what I mean, then you'll never know," Chase said.

"I never thought I'd get this much crap from you." Riggins grew silent, then took a big swallow from his mug.

A young man with long hair and paint-spattered bib overalls ambled to the jukebox and pushed in the numbers to several songs. Seconds later, the Kentucky Headhunters' "Dumas Walker" blared through the speakers. Chase and Riggins sat for a minute without speaking, sipping their beers in their self-imposed silence.

They left after finishing their beers, leaving nearly a half pitcher, and hardly saying a word to each other as they walked to their cars. "Thanks again," Riggins said before getting into his car. Chase nodded without a smile or word. He waited in his vehicle until Riggins drove out of the parking lot.

~ * ~

Chase drove home in silence, almost on auto-pilot as his mind was engulfed with Riggins's confession. He began to wonder if a person can really know someone else after listening to Riggins. The respect he had for Riggins had vanished.

After arriving at his home, Chase felt a sense of relief as he sat down on his oversized recliner, pulled the side lever and leaned back. He closed his eyes, the conversation with Riggins preying on his mind. He couldn't believe a veteran journalist could be so deceitful as to fabricate part of a story, regardless of any reason, because there was no justification for it. Reaching down to the side of the chair, he picked up the morning newspaper and Riggins's byline jumped out at him. *I still can't believe he did this.*

Chase wadded up the paper and angrily tossed it across the room, nearly knocking down a table lamp. Pulling himself out of the chair, he picked up the crinkled ball of paper and slammed it in the trash can in the kitchen. He opened the dishwasher, placed dirty dishes and silverware inside and turned it on. The humming of the dishwasher momentarily took his mind off Riggins' confession until he heard four quick knocks on the front door.

Chase could see a small, plump figure through the sheer curtains next to the front door and knew it was Bernie Robbins. He almost wished he could hide but with several lights were on, his car in the driveway, and the dishwasher running, it was too late. He opened the door. Reluctantly.

"Hi, Chase," she said with a bright smile. "I hope you don't mind me dropping by unannounced."

"Should I?" he said with a tad of sarcasm. "Do you ever call beforehand?"

"Friends shouldn't have to and you're being mean to me. May I come in?"

Chase stepped aside. Bernie marched directly to the kitchen and took a Pepsi from the refrigerator.

"Do you want one?" she said, raising the can in the air.

"No thanks," he said.

"How about a beer?"

"No thanks," he said indifferently.

She padded to the living room and sat on the couch while Chase plopped himself back in the recliner.

"Did you have a good day?" she asked after taking a sip from the can.

"It could have been better."

"Something bad happen?" An exaggerated frown spread over her pudgy face.

"I guess you could say that."

"Care to share?"

"I don't believe so."

"Okay, be that way," she said, dropping her lower lip in a mock pout.

"So how was your day?"

"Nothing out of the ordinary. I covered a city council meeting this afternoon. It was kinda boring, as usual. That's about it."

"So what brings you here?

"Don't you like me to visit?"

"Of course I do," he said, forcing a rigid smile. "But you usually have something on your mind when you drop by without any advanced warning."

"That's mean, Chase," Bernie said with a grin as she crossed her legs and leaned back on the couch. "Why are you being so hateful with me? You know I love you."

"Is that why you came by?"

"Sort of. I haven't seen you for a couple of days and I was in the neighborhood and I didn't think you'd mind me dropping by."

"I don't mind."

"But there is one thing."

"What's that?"

"I've heard some juicy newsroom gossip. Angela Cook is having an affair with one of the guys in the newsroom."

"Really?"

"Is it you?"

Chase let out a big cough and rose quickly in the recliner. He cleared his throat and shook his head.

"Are you serious?" he said with a light laugh. "Is that what you've heard?"

"Well, some people in the newsroom think that you would be the most eligible person since you're single and apparently unattached to any woman."

"I don't even know the woman. Plus, I don't have affairs with married women."

"Still waiting for me?" she asked while batting her eyelashes.

"You know it," Chase said as he slowly sat back down.

"I didn't think you'd be having anything going on with her. I just thought you'd like to know some of the loose talk going on at the paper."

"There's always some kind of wild story circulating around the newsroom. I just try to ignore it all."

"But sometimes you can be blindsided if you don't know what's going on."

"That's why I depend on trusting friends like you to keep me alerted to anything that could involve me," he said with a sigh.

"Do you know who Angela could be involved with?"

"I don't have a clue," he said, turning his head away from her and picking up a magazine off the floor. "And I could care less."

"So what are you going to be doing this week?"

"I've got two basketball games to cover and that's about it."

"When are you going to let me go to a game with you?"

"If I did that, there would be all kinds of talk in the newsroom."

"I know," she said, her blue eyes lighting up. "Wouldn't that be great?"

The phone rang and Chase answered on the second ring.

"Taylor here."

"Hi."

"Do you have company?"

"Yes, I do."

Bernie sat attentively on the couch, looking nonchalant but Chase was aware that she was trying to eavesdrop on the conversation. He turned his back to her.

"Can we talk again tomorrow?" Riggins asked.

"Sure thing."

"Thanks, Chase."

Chase put down the receiver and smiled tersely.

"Now where were we?" he asked.

"Who was that?" Bernie blurted out.

"Someone taking a survey."

"I don't think so but that's okay." Bernie shook her head while looking at the ceiling.

"It was nothing important."

"I guess it's none of my business anyway. It was probably a woman."
"You're right."
"It was a woman?" Bernie asked impatiently.
"No. It was none of your business."
Bernie shook her head and grinned. "You're mean, Chase."

Two

Chase turned on the television after Bernie left. He took off his shoes and socks, sat in the recliner, put his head back and closed his eyes. The flickering images on the TV were the only light as they danced on the bare, pale blue walls. He thought back on the day and wished that it was all a dream. Instead, it seemed more like a nightmare. Just as he was about to drift off to sleep, the phone rang. He sat in the chair for two rings before getting up to answer it. *Please don't be Taylor.*

"Did I wake you up?" Hannah Sims asked softly. "I know it's a little late."

"Nah," Chase said after clearing his throat. "I was watching TV." He found her voice soothing to his nerves.

"You sound half asleep."

"Well, I was resting my eyes," he said with a mild laugh.

"I can get back with you tomorrow."

"No, that's okay."

"Are you sure?"

"Perfectly sure. So what's up?"

"I just got home after going out with some of the girls at work for a bite to eat at one of the pubs near the office."

"Did you have a good time?"

"We always have fun. Several of them are married and have kids so they like getting away for a few hours."

"I'm sure they do," Chase said.

"Have you done anything this evening?"

"Bernie Robbins dropped by uninvited for a few minutes."

"What's going on with her?"

"Nothing much. She was just in the neighborhood and decided to stop by."

"I need to meet this woman who seems to be flirting with my guy," Hannah said with a giggle.

"You have nothing to worry about. She's only a friend."

"Well, if you say so."

"I say so. Nothing to fear. Ever."

"Can we get together later this week?"

"I've got a couple of ball games to cover but that shouldn't be a problem. Do you have a light schedule?"

"I should be in town all week but I'm not sure how light it will be. I usually get bogged down with a lot of paperwork with orders from the department stores."

"I don't see how you can go around to all those stores and stay on top of things like you do."

"I've got some good people working for me so it's not that bad. But I must admit that I need a break from it now and then."

"Maybe we could take off for a week after basketball season is over."

"That would be nice but I don't know if I can wait another two months," she said with a laugh.

"How about a long weekend?"

"That might work."

"Or would you be interested in going with me to some games?"

"Are you sure that's a good idea?"

"Why not?"

"You're always worrying about what others will say."

"It's not a big deal anymore. I want to see more of you."

"Why, thank you," she said warmly. "I'd like to see more of you as well."

Chase heard the Seth Thomas clock in the hallway chime ten times.

"Is it too late to see you tonight?" he asked. "It's only ten."

"Oh honey, I'd love to but I have a sales meeting at eight in the morning and I still have two reports to finish," she said.

"I figured it was a long shot," he said with a laugh.

"You know I would if I could."

"I know," he said with a tone of resignation.

"I guess I should be going now and finish the paperwork. I just wanted to hear your voice. I hope you sleep well tonight."

"It'd be better with you next to me," he said.

"Silly man," she said with a giggle.

"Oh well, you can't blame a guy for trying."

"Good night, Chase. Can we talk tomorrow?

"You know we can. Just call me at the office when you get a chance. I should be there late in the morning or early afternoon."

"Okay. I hope you have a great day."

"Same to you, sweetie."

Chase got undressed and went to bed. He spent a restless night as he couldn't help but think about Riggins's lies. After a several false starts, and one trip to the bathroom, he finally drifted off to sleep but awoke at five. He glanced at the alarm clock and eased out of bed. A few minutes later he stumbled to the kitchen and brewed a pot of coffee.

It was dark outside when he opened the front door and retrieved the newspaper from the porch. The houses on the street were shadowy as the only illumination came from street lights and decorative lamp posts in yards. He picked up the newspaper and glanced over the headlines as he returned to the kitchen. On the front of the city section, he noticed a small item below the fold: "Drug Series Nominated for Journalism Award." Riggins's story was among the top entries for a national award in investigative journalism. It quoted the one of the newspaper's assistant managing editors as saying that Riggins was one of the finest investigative journalists in the state and how proud the paper was for him to be considered for the award. Chase placed the paper on the table and shook his head in disbelief.

"This is unreal," he said out loud as he poured a cup of coffee. This wasn't the way he wanted to start a new day. He took his time drinking the coffee and skimming over the rest of the paper. The item about Riggins took away any appetite he had for breakfast.

Chase stood in front of the bathroom mirror after taking a shower and stared at his face momentarily, not really seeing his image. Droplets of moisture from the steamy shower rolled down the mirror. Riggins and the story in the newspaper about the journalism award consumed his thoughts. He shook his head in disbelief and finished toweling off his body. Back in the bedroom, he dressed in his standard khaki pants and white shirt. He always kept several blue ties tucked away at work and in his SUV in case he needed to upgrade his attire for dressy occasions. Several minutes later he was out the front door and on the way to the office.

As he entered the newspaper building, Riggins was standing by himself at the elevator, looking around and smiling at no one in particular.

"Good morning, Taylor," Chase said.

"Oh, hi, Chase," said Riggins, startled for a moment. "You're here early today. No game tonight?"

"There's nothing going on tonight. How about with you?"

The elevator door opened and Jordan Means, editor of the *Daily Register*, stepped out in wearing an expensive Italian-designer suit. He nodded at Chase and extended his thin arm to shake Riggins's hand.

"I got a call this morning saying that you're a strong finalist for the award," Means said in his proper New England dialect as he patted his short, kinky, pepper-gray hair to make sure every hair was in place. "Congratulations. Doesn't that make your day?"

"I guess it does," Riggins said mildly, an easy smile becoming forced as he looked at Means. "That's really wonderful."

"I've got a good feeling about this," Means said as he pointed toward the walls in the foyer with plaques and photos of some of the newspaper's awards through the years. "I'd be delighted to have you honored on these walls."

Riggins's smile grew wider as he raised his eyebrows. He cleared his throat and said, "That would surely be an honor for me and the newspaper."

"Well gentlemen," Means said abruptly, glancing at Chase and then back at Riggins, "I have to attend a journalism symposium on ethics at the university and I'll be late if I don't move on." Chase avoided making any eye contact with Riggins.

Means raised his limp hand in a short salute and stepped quickly out the front door as Chase and Riggins waited for the elevator to return. In less than a minute, they stepped inside the empty chamber and headed to the sixth floor.

"I bet you're excited," Chase said sarcastically.

"I can't believe this shit," Riggins said, looking down at the floor and slowly shaking his head.

"What are you going to do?"

"What can I do?" Riggins said, looking directly at Chase. "This thing is spinning out of control. I told them I didn't want them to submit the story in that contest in the first place but couldn't stop them. I didn't think I had a snowball's chance in hell of being a finalist."

"And now it's snowballed on you."

"Very funny, Chase. I don't need your witty remarks."

"So you don't intend to tell anyone that the story is a lie?"

"I've told you."

"You know what I mean," Chase said as the elevator opened on the sixth floor. Five people were standing outside, ready to step inside as they stepped out and walked toward the newsroom.

"Can we discuss it later?" Riggins asked quietly.

"Sure," said Chase, disappointed by Riggins's responses.

"I hope you have a good day," Riggins said wearily as they parted ways, Chase to the sports section and Riggins to the city desk.

Chase sat down and sifted through his mail. The sports department was nearly vacant except for a few clerks working on statistical information on area basketball teams.

Easing back in his chair he noticed Cole Green, his boss in the sports department, approaching his desk. Green would be difficult to miss as he was a former college football offensive lineman who had grown soft around the belly in middle age. But for many people, including some of the young staffers, he could be a fearsome and intimidating figure lumbering around the newsroom, with his creaky knees, from a legacy of injuries and surgeries from his playing days giving him a hulking presence.

"How's it going?" Green asked in his deep voice.

"I'm just trying to get a little organized around here," Chase said.

"After you get finished, why don't you come over to my office and get it organized?" Green asked with a hearty laugh as he put his large hands to his waist and adjusted his baggy pants. "I've got a stack of papers that grows higher each day."

"It can get away from you if you don't take care of it several days a week."

"You're not telling me anything I don't know. I just need to find the time to do it."

Chase picked up his pocket calendar book and opened it to the work week. "Anything going on that I should know?"

"Nothing really except the regular assortment of ball games. There are enough of those right now to max out the staff, and then you throw in the other sports that are going on. But we somehow seem to manage. We always do."

"I'm not sure what I'm going to write about this week. I should have some idea by the end of the day." Chase said.

"Well, I'll leave you to that. I've got a news meeting coming up in fifteen minutes so I have to get some things together for that. See you later."

"Have fun," Chase said with a grin.

"Yeah," Green said as he rolled his eyes and went to his office on the other side of the newsroom.

The phone rang and Chase picked it up on first ring.

"Listen Chase, I'm totally embarrassed about this whole mess. I don't want you to think that I'm proud of what I did," Riggins said, slightly above a whisper. "This is driving me insane."

"To be honest, I still can't believe you did it," Chase said.

"That's why I feel I won't get caught. I don't think anybody would believe I could do such a thing."

"What's that supposed to mean?"

"I just think that this thing will blow over."

"That's beside the point."

"No it's not," Riggins replied with a tinge of anger. "If you were in my shoes, you'd know what I mean."

"But I'm not in your shoes," Chase said, "and I'd never want to be in them."

"Chase, I confided in you because I thought you were my friend."

"There are some things friends shouldn't tell friends."

"I've got a staff meeting coming up in a few minutes. Can we meet and discuss this later?"

"Sure." Chase sighed. "At your convenience."

Chase slowly put the phone down and stood up. He looked around the office for a moment, then pushed his chair toward the desk and went to the elevator. A few minutes later he was outside the building and heading downtown at a brisk pace.

"Hey, wait up!"

Two blocks from the newspaper building, Chase turned around and saw Bernie waving her hands and practically at a run to catch him. She held an arm over her ample bosom to keep her breasts from bouncing too noticeably.

"Hi, Bern," Chase said as she came within a few steps.

"Where are you going in such a hurry?" Bernie asked, breathing heavily. "A fire?"

"I wish I could put out a fire," he said with an exasperated look. "I just needed to get out of the office for a bit so I decided to take a short walk."

"Mind if I join you?"

"That's fine."

"Sure?"

"Yes, Bern, I'm sure."

"So what's up?" Bernie asked as her short legs worked double time trying to keep up with Chase's long strides.

"Nothing, really. A friend has sort of irritated me."

"Anything I can do to help?"

"Nah, it's a personal thing."

"What do you think about Taylor Riggins?"

Chase looked down sharply at Bernie.

"What do you mean?"

"The award he's been nominated for. Isn't that cool?"

"Yeah, I guess so."

"Taylor is such a good reporter. It couldn't happen to a more deserving guy even if he can be a bit of a jerk."

"Yeah, he's deserving all right." Chase said while turning a corner and looking straight ahead.

"I wish I could come up with some kind of award-winning story."

"Just keep your eyes and ears open, they'll fall into your lap."

"Maybe I could get lucky like Taylor."

"Sometimes it takes more than luck," Chase said.

"Huh?"

"Just use your imagination."

Three

Chase sat at the bar in Pappy's and sipped on a cold mug of beer. A George Strait love ballad floated softly from the jukebox. The place was nearly empty, but he didn't mind because he didn't want all the noise and chatter. He accepted that would change in the next few hours as more people got off from work and made their way to the bar for a drink or two before heading home for the night.

He felt a gentle tap on his shoulder and turned around. Hannah stood behind him smiling

"Mind if I join you?" she asked. "You look like you could use some company."

Chase grinned and kissed her on the cheek as she eased on to the bar stool. She slightly shook her head to stir her long brunette hair off her slender neck.

"Would you like to sit at a booth?" Chase asked.

"No, this is fine," she said. The bartender came over and she ordered a margarita.

"So how was your day?" he asked.

"Very uneventful. I placed a lot of orders for companies. It was rather quiet in the office as well. How about you?"

"Much the same." He shrugged.

"Is something bothering you? You look like something very serious is on your mind," Hannah said, resting a hand on top of his.

"I've got a few things going on at work but I can handle it." Chase turned his hand over and gently squeezed hers as a taut smile crossed his face.

"If you need to bounce something off someone, you know I'm available."

"I know that and I appreciate it," he said. "It's just too early to talk about it. I hope it all passes over soon. It may not amount to anything. It has more to do with a friend than the newspaper."

Hannah patted him on the knee, and then leaned over and kissed him softly on the cheek.

Chase smiled and took another swallow of beer. He felt fortunate to have someone like Hannah because she never pressured him into disclosing things. Although a private person, Chase knew he'd eventually open up to her about personal problems but only when he felt the time was right to do so. And he knew he could always count on her for support.

"So you don't have a ball game this evening?" Hannah asked.

"No, but I've got one tomorrow night."

"Why don't you come over to my place for dinner?"

"Tonight?"

"Yes," she said coyly. "I can pick up some Chinese carryout. Would you like that?"

"Are you sure it won't be any trouble?"

"Of course not, silly. You're never any trouble for me."

"Okay then," Chase said as he took a credit card from his wallet to pay for their drinks. "Are you sure I can't pick up the food?"

"I can do it. There's a good restaurant on the way home. Just give me time to get the table set."

"Sounds like a plan," he said. "I'll leave about ten minutes after you."

Hannah slipped off the bar stool, kissed him again on the cheek and left. She turned and smiled before walking out the door. Chase couldn't help notice that several other men in the bar glanced at her shapely figure as she left.

"Who was that lovely lady?"

Chase turned to his right as Conner Rhodes from the newspaper's photo department took Hannah's bar stool and sat down. He was wearing his oversized green photographer's vest that looked more like a hunter's jacket.

"Hi, Conner," Chase said. "She's a woman I've been dating for a while."

"Nice looking gal," Conner said with an approving grin. "Not bad. Not bad at all."

"She's a wonderful woman." Chase said, unable to suppress a smile.

"A keeper?"

"Could be."

"I'd be careful because some guy may come along and snatch her up," Conner said with a chuckle.

"I'll keep that in mind."

The bartender wiped off the counter in front of Conner and placed a frosty mug of draft beer on a coaster. Conner picked it up and took a long swallow.

"Hmm. That tastes good."

"So you don't work tonight either?"

"Hell no. I've got a game tomorrow evening."

"Same here."

"Have you heard about the latest office romance?"

"Maybe," Chase said. "Who's involved this time?"

"Angela Cook."

"Oh."

"Well, I've heard that Angela Cook may be giving her lover boy some problems."

"How's that?"

"Someone told me she may go down to personnel and talk to them about possible sexual harassment."

"Damn. Where did you hear that?"

"She apparently said something to one of the gals in our department. You know how girls talk."

Chase glanced at the clock on the wall and noticed that ten minutes had passed since Hannah left.

"I need to be going," Chase said.

"So soon?"

"I have a dinner date with a friend."

"The lady that just left?"

"Yep."

"Have fun now," Conner said with a devious wink. "If you know what I mean."

"I'll see you," Chase said as he shook his head and smiled before sliding off the bar stool and heading out the front door.

Fifteen minutes later Chase pulled his SUV into Hannah's driveway. He walked to the front door of the two-story white Victorian house and knocked twice. He could see Hannah's image through the beveled glass on the door.

"Come on in," Hannah shouted. "The door's unlocked."

He stepped inside the front foyer and wandered to the dining room. Hannah was setting the plates and silverware on the table.

"Can I do anything?" he asked.

"I think I have everything ready," she said with a smile. "Just have a seat. What do you want to drink? Wine? Beer? Soft drink? Tea?"

"I believe I'll just have water," he said.

She returned to the table with two glasses of ice water and sat down next to him. They passed the small boxes of white rice, vegetables and noodles to each other and filled their plates.

"This looks good," Chase said. "Thanks for inviting me."

"You're welcome. It's nice to have someone to have dinner with."

They took their time eating while discussing world and national events of the day. Afterward, they cleared off the table and put the dishes in the dishwasher. Hannah took his hand and led him to the den and they sat down on a thick, fluffy white sofa. She reached to the coffee table and picked up the TV remote.

"Is there anything you'd like to watch?" she asked.

Chase took the remote from her hand and put it back on the coffee table.

"I'd just like to watch you," he said as he cupped her face in his hands and gently kissed her on the mouth.

Hannah smiled and snuggled close as he put his left arm around her and kissed her again, this time longer and with more passion. One hand on her waist pulled her closer. He ran his other hand over the back of her head, inhaling her intoxicating sweet scent.

"Can you spend the night?" she asked softly.

"I don't think that would be a problem," he said with a gentle smile. "You won't have to twist my arm."

"I need to get the bedroom ready," Hannah said as she sat on the edge of the sofa. "Give me a few minutes."

As she walked away, he picked up the TV remote. He held it for a few seconds, thinking twice about turning on the TV, and put it back on the coffee table. Instead he sat quietly on the sofa as the light from her bedroom filtered into the room with a faint glow. He thought about their relationship and how deep it had grown. Although they had dated for less than a year, he felt he had known her for much longer.

"I'm ready," she said from her bedroom.

Chase walked to the bedroom. She was standing next to the bed in a white satin gown with lace across the top. He stared at her momentarily and grinned.

"You're such a beautiful woman," he said. "I don't know what I've done to deserve you." He thought back to Conner's comments about her being a keeper.

Hannah blushed lightly as he approached her. She took one step into his outstretched arms. He pulled her against him and held her tightly for a few seconds before kissing her softly. Slowly lifting the gown over her head, he again clasped her waist and kissed her hard and passionately.

Hannah stepped back and slipped between the white sheets. As Chase reached over and turned out the lights on the night stand. Removing his clothes he slid in beside her. Kissing and exploring each other's bodies, they made tender love before drifting off to sleep.

The next morning, Hannah fixed a pot of coffee while Chase showered. With the coffee brewing, she joined him where they lovingly lathered each other's bodies.

"Busy day ahead?" Chase asked as they drank coffee in the kitchen

"I hope not," she said. "Didn't you say you had a ball game?"

"This evening."

"You can stay here for awhile if you want to. I need to be leaving soon."

"That's okay I need to go to the office and do a few things," he said. "I'll probably take part of the afternoon off before going to the game. I guess I should be going."

"Thank you for coming over"

"Thank you for a lovely night," He kissed her at the door and left for work.

After arriving at the office, Chase went to the cafeteria for another cup of coffee. He sat by himself looking at the newspaper when Brett Johnson walked in with a troubled look on his face. Spotting Chase at the corner table, he walked directly to him and sat down. They had been friends for several years, arriving at the newspaper about the same time. Brett had gone on from sports to become special projects editor.

"Do you mind if I join you for a few minutes?" Brett asked.

"Of course not. What's up?"

"A lady is putting the screws to me in more ways than one," Brett said in a voice just above a whisper.

"Angela Cook?"

"Yes," he said. "I can't believe the bitch."

"Bitch? What has she done?"

"I think she's going to hit me with a claim of sexual harassment."

"You've got to be kidding," Chase said while slowly shaking his head. "I've heard rumors but didn't know it was you they were talking about."

"No shit," Brett said. "She's crazy. I should have known better than to have gotten involved with her."

"What are you going to do?"

"I've tried talking to her but she's not listening. She doesn't care if she breaks up my family, ruins my career or anything."

"Have you talked to personnel or any of the editors?"

"What good is that going to do?"

"Perhaps they can give you some guidance."

"The only guidance they'd give me would be pushing my ass out the front door."

"Have you told Victoria?"

"I mentioned something to her last night."

"What did she have to say?"

"As you can imagine, she's crushed."

"She didn't kick you out of the house?"

"I didn't tell her everything. She only knows about the sexual harassment."

"Don't you think you should tell her everything?"

"Not right now," Brett said. "She'll hear about it soon enough if Angela goes through with it."

"I wish there was something I could do to help."

"Could you talk to Angela?" Brett asked pleadingly.

"What?" Chase sat up in his chair and looked directly into Brett's eyes. "Are you serious?"

"Maybe you could get her to stop this nonsense."

"Brett, I don't even know the woman," Chase said, shaking his head in disbelief.

"That would make it even better. She might listen to you."

"I don't know, Brett. I feel funny getting involved in someone's personal affairs."

"I need someone to talk some sense into her."

"I'll give it some thought."

"Thanks, Chase," Brett said. "I knew I could count on you."

"Don't count on me so soon. I said I would give it some thought. I'm not a counselor. I'm a sportswriter."

"Yeah, but people listen to you."

"Like I said, I'll give it some thought. I need to go back to my desk now and take care of a few things."

"Thanks again for listening."

Chase got up slowly and ambled to the elevator. When the door opened, Angela was standing in the rear of the elevator talking to Means. She was oblivious to Chase while Means made quick eye contact and nodded. They stepped out together on the sixth floor. Chase went to the sports department, leaving Means and Angela to talk off to the side before Means went to his office and she returned to her desk in the newsroom.

A few minutes later Angela walked past Chase and gave him a lingering smile before going to the city desk. He flashed a smile and turned his head, wondering what was going on with her. He thought she was a lovely woman, but in those sparkling dark green eyes he saw a deviousness that he really didn't want to engage.

His phone rang and he picked it up on the second ring.

"How's your day going so far?" Hannah asked brightly.

"It's been okay," Chase said. "It certainly doesn't compare to last night. How is your day?"

"About the same as yesterday. Still doing some paperwork. I got a little break and decided to give you a call."

"I'm glad you did. You're always a nice break for me."

"Are you looking forward to the ball game?"

"I guess so. I won't be back until midnight or so. Do you have any plans?"

"I'll probably sit at home and watch TV or read."

"I wish I could join you."

"I wish you could, too."

"Can we get together later this week?"

"How about Thursday?"

Chase glanced at the calendar and noticed he didn't have any games or meetings to attend.

"Sounds good to me," he said. "How about a dinner and movie?"

"That would be fun."

"I'll pick you up at six-thirty."

Four

"How was your game last night?" Hannah asked Chase as they drove to Old Italy restaurant on the east side of town. "I noticed that UK won."

"It was a big victory for them," Chase said. "They beat a good team."

"Do you ever get tired of going to the games?"

"Sometimes I do, especially late in the season. But every season brings on new players, new opponents and new games so I guess that's why I don't really get tired of them. It's kind of rejuvenation."

"I never looked at it that way but that makes sense. That's sort of like my work. Every year it seems that there are enough changes to keep things somewhat fresh and challenging."

"I guess we all do what we've got to do to keep things fresh and reinvent ourselves," Chase said. "It's not always easy, especially as we grow older. And there are people who disappoint us along the way that makes things more difficult."

Hannah touched Chase's shoulder. "I know something is bothering you," she said. "You know I'll be there for you."

"You read me too well," Chase said with a half-hearted laugh. "I'm fine but I'll remember your offer. It's only a matter of time."

Chase pulled into a half-filled parking lot. He walked around and opened her door and held her hand as she got out of the car. She draped her winter coat around her shoulders as they walked to the entrance of the restaurant. The hostess took them to a candlelit table by a window. Chase ordered a carafe of red wine.

"This is a lovely place," Hannah said. "I've only been here one other time."

"I've eaten here a few times. I think it has the best Italian food in town."

A waiter arrived with the wine and poured about an ounce each into their glasses. Chase took a sip and nodded approval to the waiter, who then filled the glasses to three-quarters.

The waiter tipped his head and smiled before stepping away.

"Do you like wine?" Chase asked.

"I love wine," Hannah said. "There are several wineries in the area that I've visited and they're producing some excellent wines."

"I've heard that. I'd like to go one of these days. I've been to some distilleries and they were interesting to see."

"Perhaps this spring we can go to a winery. They often have cheese- and wine-parties."

"We'll do that," Chase said, lifting his glass and taking another swallow. "Mark it on your calendar so I won't forget."

A few minutes later their food arrived and they sat quietly and ate, knowing they had to be leaving soon to go to a movie. By the time they finished, the restaurant was nearly filled to capacity and the quiet ambience was turning into a low din of chatter.

"I thought we'd go see the new Robert Redford movie," Chase said as they left the restaurant. "I hope that's okay with you. If there's something else you'd rather see, we can do that."

"I like his movies," Hannah said. "There's not many movies out right now that I care to see."

"I know what you mean. There always seems to be a lull before the summer season."

They arrived at the cinemaplex ten minutes before show time, bought their tickets and sat in the middle of the sparsely-filled theater. He reached over and held her hand.

"Care for any popcorn, candy or anything?" Chase asked.

"No, thank you. I'm stuffed," Hannah said. "Breadsticks do that to me."

Chase put his arm around her and shortly into the movie she inched closer and rested her head on his shoulder. He leaned over and kissed her on the forehead.

After the movie, Chase drove Hannah to her home. After pulling into her driveway, they sat in his car for a few minutes with the engine running. The Beatles' *Revolver* was playing on the compact disc player.

"I really enjoyed the evening," she said as she unfastened her seatbelt and moved closer to him.

Chase put his arm around her shoulders and kissed her gently on the mouth.

"Can you come in for a little while?" she asked with a soft smile.

"I can't stay long."

"Oh really," she purred. "Do you have other things to do?"

Chase tried to suppress a blush hat would be hidden by the darkness of the night.

He sank into the soft, cushy white couch in her living room as she moved about gracefully, putting her purse on the dark mahogany coffee table and placing her coat in the closet. Hannah flashed several pert smiles as his eyes followed her every motion.

She turned on the stereo to a soft-rock radio station. The Little River Band's "Reminiscing" played softly in the background.

"I'm going to fix myself a cup of green tea" she said. "Would you care for some?"

"That would be nice."

"I'll be back in a few minutes," Hannah said as she gently tapped his shoulder. "Don't go away." She smiled again, this one a bit more lingering before she turned and headed to the kitchen.

Chase picked up a home-improvement magazine and began mindlessly thumbing through the pages. He kept glancing toward the kitchen, anxiously awaiting her reappearance. He wriggled a bit as his thoughts centered on Hannah. Before Chase knew it, she was standing in front of him in a red robe and handing him a cup of tea.

"That was quick," he said with a smile.

"I hope you don't mind me getting out of my clothes and into something more comfortable"

"I'm not complaining." His eyes moved slowly over her slender body, imagining the softness under the long crimson garment.

Hannah sat down next to him and put her bare feet up on the coffee table as she smoothed the robe to cover her legs. Chase took a sip of the tea while his eyes focused momentarily on her painted, red toenails.

"So you're into home improvement?" he asked while laying the magazine on the coffee table and trying to gather his thoughts on things besides Hannah's sensuous presence.

"I try to do a few things around here," she said. "I don't have enough time to do what I'd like to do."

"I know what you mean. There's hardly enough time to do anything other than work. I'm not much of a handyman. I usually make things worse than they were."

"You need to take time from work to do other things."

"I agree."

"Of course, I'm telling you that and I hardly make time for myself."

"Then you should listen to your own advice," Chase with a laugh. "We all get wrapped up in our work and sometimes let the most important things in life slip away from us."

They each placed their tea cups on coasters and she snuggled up close to him. He kissed her softly and gently, and then pulled her more closely and the kiss became long and passionate. As her body turned toward him, her robe opened between her legs, revealing her nakedness. Chase placed his hand on her inner thigh and gently rubbed as they continued to kiss.

"Wouldn't it be more comfortable in the bedroom?" Hannah whispered.

Chase rose from the overstuffed couch and took her hand as she stood. He kissed her again as her robe opened fully. He cupped her right breast as they kissed, and then held her hand as he guided her to the bedroom. She pulled back the bedspread and got in bed. Chase turned off the lamp on the nightstand and removed his clothes. She lifted the white satin sheet as he slipped in beside her.

"I thought I was only going to be here for a few minutes," he said as she cuddled into his arms.

"I hope you're not in a hurry now," she cooed with her head resting on his chest.

Their wet mouths met again, long and tenderly, as they held each other tightly before making passionate love. She fell asleep with her head on his shoulder as he held her securely through the night.

Chase woke up at four forty-five and tip-toed to the kitchen. He sat down at the table as his eyes adjusted to the bright light, staring unseeing at the clock on the wall, momentarily lost in his thoughts.

"What's the matter, hon?" Hannah said, standing at the doorway in her robe.

"Good morning." Chase was startled for a moment and then smiled. "There's some things going on at the office that I'm trying to sort out. I'm sorry if I seem distracted at times. I hope I can tell you one of these days."

Hannah didn't say anything but he sensed an expression of understanding and compassion on her face.

"Can I make some coffee?"

"I'd love some. I was going to make a pot but wasn't sure where you put everything."

Chase watched as she took the coffee from the refrigerator and filters from the cabinet next to it. The coffee maker was sitting on the counter.

"I would have never looked for the coffee in the fridge," he said. "What's it doing there?"

"I learned from my mother a long time ago that it keeps it fresh, just like most foods."

"Nice thing to know."

As the coffee brewed, Hannah sat down at the table with Chase. She reached up and pulled her robe closer together at the top.

"Do you have a busy day ahead?" she asked.

"It shouldn't be anything out of the ordinary. How about you?"

"Some old stuff I've been doing the past week or so. I'm about finished. Next week I'll be in several Ohio cities for a few days. I think business will be picking up in the coming weeks."

Hannah went to the cabinet and took out two cups and two spoons and placed them on the table. She poured their coffee and sat back down at the table. Chase put a teaspoon of coffee creamer in his coffee while she drank hers black.

"If you're hungry I can fix some eggs or something," she said.

"I'm fine. I may eat some toast a little later."

"The bread is in the bread box on the counter," she said. "Jelly and butter in the fridge."

"Thanks," he said as the grandfather clock in the front foyer chimed five times

"Do you get the newspaper delivered?"

"I think it arrives around five-thirty or so."

"How did you like the movie last night?" Chase asked after taking a sip of coffee.

"I've seen Redford in better movies but it was still enjoyable. It had a nice plot and some good twists."

"I agree. His movies generally have some underlying moral message that makes you think."

"We'll have to explore that some evening," Hannah said. "It's too early in the morning for me to discuss moral issues in movies."

"You're right," Chase said. "I think I'll have some toast. Do you want any?

"I'll have one slice."

Chase took the bread out of the bread box and put three slices into the toaster while Hannah took out the margarine and grape jelly from the refrigerator and took two knives and two plates from dish drain and placed them on the table. A minute later, the toast popped up and Chase put one slice on her plate and two on his.

"No wonder you look so good," Chase said as he buttered his toast.

"What do you mean?"

"Here I am eating two slices and you one."

"I'm a light eater for breakfast," she said. "Plus, I can afford to lose a few pounds."

"I don't know where."

"If you've seen me naked, you'd know where," she blurted out.

"I have and you look awfully fit to me," Chase said with a wink.

Hannah blushed lightly.

"You know what I mean," she said. "I could tighten up in a few places. My rear end is too big."

"I guess I'll have to check that out more closely next time," Chase said as he playfully turned his head to the side to look at her backside.

"Stop that!," she said with a grin.

A moment later, they heard a thump against the front door.

"That must be the newspaper," Chase said.

"I'm sure it is," Hannah said as she stood up. "I'll got get it."

"I can do that," he said.

"No problem," she said as she got up and went to the front door. In less than a minute, she was back with the newspaper and handed it to him.

"Hey, it's your newspaper."

"I'm in no hurry to read it."

Chase unfolded the paper and glanced at the headlines on the front page.

"Anything interesting?" Hannah asked.

"There doesn't seem to be," Chase said, and then he caught a small item at the bottom of the page with the headline: *Riggins Named Assistant Managing Editor*. The story said that Riggins, a finalist for one of journalism's top prizes, was promoted to a management position. "Holy shit!"

"What's the matter?" Hannah asked.

"This guy I know was named assistant managing editor."

"He's not qualified or what?"

"It's not that. He's a bright guy and everything."

"Then why are you surprised?"

"I wish I could tell you."

Hannah's eyes dropped and she turned her head. Chase reached over and touched her hand.

"I didn't mean it that way," he said.

"Who got the promotion?" she asked.

"Taylor Riggins. I've known him for quite a while."

"I know him," Hannah said.

"Really?" Chase said with a bewildered expression.

"It was a long time ago."

An alarm clock beeped in the bedroom. Hannah left and turned it off, and then retreated to the bathroom.

"Go ahead and finish breakfast," she said from the doorway. "I'm going to shower."

"Take your time. I'll have another cup of coffee," Chase said while flipping through the newspaper pages.

Five

As Chase entered the newsroom, he saw Riggins chatting with several reporters at the city editor's desk. They briefly made eye contact as Chase went to his desk and sat down. He looked at several phone messages and quickly went through his mail to see if there was anything other than routine news releases. Clicking on his computer, he checked e-mail.

After working on a column for a couple hours, Chase picked up a company directory and found Angela's phone number. He lifted the phone and punched the first three digits.

"Are you doing anything for lunch?" Riggins said as he approached Chase's desk.

"Oh, hi, Taylor," Chase said as he put phone down. "Congratulations on the promotion."

"Thanks. It came out of the blue."

"Are you going to the cafeteria?"

"Sure, or we can go to the burger place around the corner."

"Cafeteria is fine."

They took the elevator to the cafeteria. They went through the line and got their food and sat down at table in the rear of the room.

"So the promotion wasn't expected?"

"Somehow they got word that I was thinking about leaving."

"Were you?"

"You know why," Riggins said as he looked around to make sure no one was within earshot of their conversation. "I had mentioned it to a couple of reporters and I guess the word got to Jordan. We met a couple days ago and he offered me the position."

"Any word on the award?"

"Any day now."

"Excited about it?"

"Sort of," Riggins said before taking a bite of his tuna-salad sandwich.

"I guess I would be, too."

"I just want to get it over with. Jordan and some other editors seem to think that I'll win. I think that's the big reason for the promotion."

"I just hope it doesn't come back to haunt you."

"It won't if some people keep it to themselves," Riggins said, staring steely-eyed at Chase. "Do you know what I mean?"

"I know exactly what you mean. But again, it's something you have to live with."

"I think I can handle it," Riggins said with an edge to his voice. "It would be easier if you'd stop reminding me."

Chase didn't reply.

They finished their lunch practically in silence except when co-workers would stop by their table to offer congratulations to Riggins.

"I guess I need to be going," Chase said as he pushed his chair back from the table. "I've got a few things to take care of."

"I'm counting on your support," Riggins said with a forced smile. "Don't let me down."

"Don't worry about that," Chase said as he began to walk away. "You've already done that." Riggins glared at him.

Chase returned to his desk and finished his column. He dialed Angela's extension but got a voice mail saying that she wouldn't be back in the newsroom until the next day.

After work Chase stopped at Pappy's for a beer. While he wasn't a big drinker, he found that a drink once in a while after a stressful day did help his overall outlook on life, especially after what he had heard the past few weeks. He'd given up cigarettes a few years after college so a drink was his best tonic for the blues. He just wished he could bury his thoughts for a few days.

"You look down in the dumps."

Chase looked over his shoulder and Bernie was standing next to him holding a full mug of beer.

"Hi, Bern," he said. "What brings you here?"

"I was in the neighborhood and saw your car parked out front."

"Pull up a stool and join me."

"Do you mind if we sit at a booth? These stools sit too high for me."

Chase slid off his stool and followed her to a booth in the corner, away from the juke box playing a George Jones tune, and from a few of the loud patrons gathered around the TV mounted on the wall on the opposite side.

"So what have you been up to?" Chase asked.

"Covering the same old stuff. Nothing much exciting going on. What do you think about Taylor Riggins getting the promotion?"

"I don't know. I guess he's deserving."

"Some of the reporters think it's a bunch of bull."

"Why's that?"

"They say he's lazy and a smartass. He's not very well liked anymore."

"Really?"

"They say the only thing he's produced in the past couple of years was that investigative piece that's up for the award. Some folks even say that's bogus."

Chase didn't respond for a few seconds, instead took a few slow sips of his beer. "Why would they say that?" he asked casually.

"Because some of the people mentioned in the story are questioning some of the details. The paper has received several calls about it."

"That's going to happen on most stories."

"True, but several months later?"

"Is anything going to happen?"

"I doubt it, since he got his big promotion. I know some reporters had planned to double-check some of his facts but I'm not sure what they're going to do now. They even say this promotion came about to hush up some of his critics."

"That's interesting."

"Isn't he a friend of yours?"

"We've known each other for a few years."

"I don't see how you've gotten along with him. You're such a nice guy and he's become a creep."

"I've never seen that in him," Chase said, thinking that *creep* wasn't the best description.

"He's always had a reputation of being a sneak and someone you couldn't trust. He badmouths people all the time."

"You were singing his praises the other day," Chase said with a laugh. "Are you fishing for information?"

"No," Bernie said meekly. "I'm just hearing things, that's all."

"And you feel safe telling me these things?"

"I know I can trust you. I just think you'd better watch out around him now. I'm just warning you."

"I'm not too worried, Bernie. Don't you think he would have done something by now if he was such a bad guy?"

"He's probably had no reason to since you work in different departments. Now he's part of management, so he has some power. You know how power goes to some people's heads. They can't handle it."

"I'll keep that in mind. Is there anything else I should look out for?"

"Angela Cook."

"I don't even know the lady."

"You don't want to know her. I've heard she's going to get some guy on sexual harassment because he won't leave his family for her."

"You hear all kinds of things about people."

"That's the way it is on the city desk. We hear scuttlebutt about everything."

"How much of it is true?"

"There's probably a lot of false rumors but those things usually have nuggets of truth or they wouldn't get started to begin with."

"Have you heard any rumors about me?"

"You've got a clean slate," Bernie said with a sly grin. "Want me to start one about us?"

"But it would be false."

"We could get it going with a nugget of truth at my place."

"Oh, you naughty lady," he said, shaking his head and grinning.

"You're probably the most eligible bachelor at the paper. I'm sure you know that."

"I'm sure there are some others more deserving of that honor."

"There are but those guys are just out of college and too young. You're older and much more mature"

"Oh, thanks!" he said with a laugh. "As if thirty-eight is old."

"I said 'older' sweetie, not old."

"Aren't you seeing anyone?" Chase asked.

"I've dated a few guys but nothing serious."

"I'm sure you'll find someone worthy of you."

"That's why I'm waiting for you," she said with a playful wink.

"But maybe I'm not worthy."

"Oh, you are. Don't second guess yourself."

"So do you have any plans for the evening?'

"Are you asking me out?"

"No, Bernie. That's just a question between friends."

"I'll probably stop by the Mexican carryout place on the way home and just watch TV. How about you?"

"I'll probably go home and take it easy."

"See, we could spend the evening together."

"You never give up," Chase said, slowly shaking his head.

Six

As Chase drove past the newspaper building on his way home from Pappy's, he saw Means standing in the front parking lot with Angela. It was dark outside as they stood at the periphery of a street light. All of the sudden, Angela reached up, put her arms around him and kissed him on the mouth.

"Damn!" Chase thought as his car reached a traffic light. He adjusted his rear-view mirror to watch them but they disappeared into the darkness. A moment later taillights came on two cars in the lot and they began backing out of slots. The traffic light turned green and Chase moved slowly across the intersection and headed home.

Hannah's light blue sedan was parked in front of his house when he pulled into the driveway. Chase couldn't suppress a smile. He could already feel the tension melting from his body as he watched her ease out of her car. Chase quickly stood next to her, holding her hands and then pecking her on the cheek.

"This is a nice surprise," he said as he let go of her right hand and reached up and stroked the back of her hair. "What did I do to deserve this honor?"

"I had to work a little late so I thought I'd stop by for a few minutes. I hope you don't mind," she said as he unlocked the door and they stepped inside his modest ranch home. He quickly began to pick up some newspapers and magazines that were strewn on the floor next to the couch.

"Please forgive the mess," he said.

"Don't worry about it," she said with a laugh. "If the place was immaculate, I'd worry about our relationship."

"Why's that?"

"That would mean you might have another girlfriend and she's keeping it tidy for you."

"Only a woman would think that," Chase said with a chuckle. "And yes, I do have a woman in here on occasion. She's from a maid service and comes in every few weeks and cleans up for me. Do you want to volunteer?"

"I think I'll pass on that," Hannah said. "But it looks like you'll need to give her another call."

"Funny," he said after taking her coat and hanging it on the rack next to the front door.

"I'm only kidding, honey." She jabbed him softly in the side.

"Have you had anything to eat?" he asked while surveying the room and shaking his head.

"No, but don't worry about it. I can get something later."

"I can order a pizza. I haven't had anything to eat either."

"Okay then, if it's not too much trouble."

"Any particular toppings?"

"It doesn't make me any difference, as long as it's not anchovies or sausage."

Chase placed an order for a mushroom and green pepper pizza and breadsticks and then went back to his bedroom as Hannah sat on the couch flipping through a magazine. He quickly made up his bed and picked up clothes that he had tossed in the corner and put them in the hamper in the bathroom adjoining the bedroom.

"So how was your day?" he asked as he returned to the living room.

"Much the same as it has been the past week. How was yours?"

"Same here except for some weird stuff," he said as he sat down beside her.

"What do you mean?"

"While driving home, I saw our editor in the parking lot with a reporter."

"So?"

"Well, before they left, she kissed him."

"A big, wet one?" Hannah said with a laugh.

""I don't think so. I was too far away to see. It just seemed strange."

"Were there others in the parking lot?"

"Not that I could see."

"Have they been dating?"

"I doubt it unless it's been secretive. They're both married. The gal has a couple kids."

The doorbell rang and Chase hurried over to answer it. "That must be the pizza delivery. That was quick."

When he opened the door, Bernie stood on the porch smiling broadly.

"I apologize for dropping by but you left your credit card at the bar," she said, handing him the card.

"How in the world did I do that?"

"You gave the waitress your card for the tab and then left before she came back."

"Well thanks for bringing it by."

"Do you have company?"

"Yes," Chase said as he stepped out to the front porch.

"Oh, I'm sorry."

At that moment the pizza delivery arrived. The pizza was thirteen dollars and Chase only had a ten in his wallet.

"Give me a minute and I'll get some more money," Chase said, a little red-faced.

Before he could open the door, Bernie reached into her purse and pulled out a five and gave it to the man.

"Keep the change," she said with a smile.

"Thanks Bernie," he said. "Would you care to eat pizza with us?"

"I couldn't do that," she said.

Bernie looked through the doorway and saw Hannah sitting on the couch. Chase turned around and opened the door. Bernie peeked inside.

"Hannah, I'd like for you to meet Bernie," Chase said. "I left my credit card at our watering hole and she kindly brought it to me."

"Hi, Hannah," Bernie said as she waved her hand and smiled. "My name is Bernadette but most folks call me Bernie. I work at the newspaper with Chase. It's nice to meet you."

Hannah smiled and rose from the couch. "It's nice to meet you as well. I've heard so much about you." She walked over and stood next to Chase.

"Are you sure you don't want some pizza?" Chase asked.

Bernie hesitated for a second. "I guess I can if you're sure I'm not interrupting anything." She stepped inside the house as Chase handed the pizza to Hannah. He took Bernie's coat and placed it on the rack by the door next to Hannah's. They went to the dining room as Hannah took out some plates and poured soft drinks.

They ate their pizza and talked about movies and city politics. After finishing, Bernie followed Hannah to the living room where they talked about spring fashions while Chase put the dishes in the sink. Chase joined them but thumbed through a magazine. He glanced at the wall clock[. Ten-twenty. The women continued to talk nonstop for the next thirty-five minutes.

Chase couldn't prevent a big yawn.

"I think we're boring you," Hannah said while glancing at him.

"Gee, it's past eleven," Bernie said. "I didn't realize it was so late. I need to be going. I've got a meeting to cover in the morning."

"I'm glad we got to meet," Hannah said as she rose from the couch.

"Same here," Bernie said, still sitting on the recliner. "By the way, do you play softball?"

"Not really," Hannah said. "I'm not very athletic."

"We have a softball team at the newspaper and we're always looking for new players. I thought I'd ask."

"Bernie is a pretty good player," Chase said. "She's a good fielder. No comment about her hitting."

"That's not fair," Bernie said with a laugh. "At least I don't strike out."

"I'm sure you're much better than I am," Hannah said. "Thanks for asking."

"I guess I better hit the road," Bernie said, easing out of the recliner.

Chase smiled wearily.

"I need to be going as well," Hannah said. "I have a staff meeting that I need to prepare for."

After five more minutes of chatter at the doorway, the women put on their coats.

"Thanks for coming by," Chase said to Bernie.

"Oh, I enjoyed it," she said, grinning.

"We need to do this again," Hannah said.

"Yeah," Chase said dryly.

Before he realized it, Hannah gave him a quick peck on the cheek and was out the front door. "I'll give you a call tomorrow," she said while walking hurriedly in the cold night air to her vehicle.

Chase looked down at Bernie as she zipped her coat.

"She's a really nice woman," Bernie said.

"Thanks."

"I guess I won't try to seduce you any more," she said with a wink. "But that doesn't mean I'll stop flirting."

Chase slowly shook his head and smiled. After Bernie left, he went directly to the bedroom, got undressed and was asleep in ten minutes. He woke up the early the next morning and put on a pot of coffee. While waiting for the coffee, he picked up the empty pizza box off the counter and crumpled it up, and stuffed it in the trash can.

Chase couldn't help thinking about the previous night. Or was it a lost night? He could have used some quiet time with Hannah. Then Bernie showed up.

"Oh well," he said to himself while shrugging his shoulders. "Life goes on."

After he sat down with a cup of coffee, the phone rang, startling him for a second.

"Good morning," Hannah said brightly. "I hope I didn't wake you up."

"I've been up a few minutes. "I'm just sitting here, all by my lonesome, drinking a cup of coffee."

"Oh, you poor baby," Hannah said with a giggle. "Were you wanting some company."

"I was just thinking about that when you called."

"I enjoyed last night."

"With me or Bernie?" he asked with a laugh.

"Bernie is a sweet person. It was nice to finally meet her."

"She's a character."

"You must have had something else on your mind," Hannah said coyly.

"Well, what guy wouldn't when a beautiful woman shows up at his house at night?"

"So you were disappointed about last night?

"I'm a big boy. I'll get over it," he said with a chuckle. "What are you doing up this early?"

"I have that staff meeting later and I need to go over some reports."

"I hope it goes well."

"Thanks," she said. "I need to be going now. I just wanted to give you a quick call."

"I'll try to call you tonight or tomorrow."

Chase poured a another cup of coffee, going to the front door to pick up his newspaper from the porch. A few lights were on in the neighborhood as people were getting ready for another day. He noticed two joggers in the distance. He enjoyed the early morning hours when it was dark and quiet outside. If there were any sounds, it would be an occasional bark from a dog or songbirds in an oak tree in his backyard. He would often write his column during those hours or read from a book. It wasn't until after daybreak, and he could hear traffic and the muffled chatter of children walking to school, that he would turn on the radio or television.

He took the newspaper out of the plastic wrap and the first item grabbed his attention: *Newspaper Wins Investigative Award.* The story reported that Riggins was the reporter for the prestigious award and how he spent countless hours investigating and interviewing people. It quoted Means and the newspaper's publisher, Dalton Pembroke, as well as Riggins.

Chase shook his head and put the newspaper down on the paper. He picked up his coffee and took a long sip.

"Unbelievable." He shook his head in disbelief and headed to the shower. He lost track of time as he closed his eyes while the hot spray pelted his face and chest. Chase's mind raced back to Taylor's confession and everything that had transpired since then.

"Why?" he said out loud. "Damnit! This is unreal! Is it ever going to stop?"

After getting dressed, his thoughts were consumed about Taylor's award as drove to the newspaper office. Stepping into the elevator, a piece of paper tacked to the wall above the floor buttons caught his eye. The note informed newsroom employees that there would be punch and cookies in the conference room at noon to celebrate Riggins's award.

It was ten o'clock when Chase strolled into the newsroom. Editors were already in their morning budget meeting. As Chase was reading e-mails and going through mail, the meeting ended and the editors filtered out of the conference room. Riggins marched out with Means patting him on the shoulder as they chatted. They proudly walked through the newsroom, away from Chase's desk, to Means's office and closed the door.

"I guess you know about Taylor," Green said while standing next to Chase's desk.

"Yeah, big news," Chase said.

"He deserves it," Green said. "He worked hard on that story."

"No doubt he did. I'm sure he went the extra mile and more."

"Is something the matter?"

"No, Cole," Chase said. "Just a little tired this morning."

"I hope you can make it to the conference room at noon."

"I'll try."

As the noon hour approached, newsroom staff began drifting toward the conference room. Although he didn't want to go, Chase got up and followed the others. They stood around the walls, leaving the punch and sweets untouched on the long cherry conference table. Promptly at noon, Riggins, Means and Pembroke entered the room and stood behind a lectern.

"This is a big occasion for the newspaper," Pembroke told the gathering in a folksy delivery. "While we strive each day to present the best newspaper to our readers, it is especially fulfilling when we have stories that go above and beyond the high standards we set each day.

"Taylor Riggins, with his thoughtful and penetrating piece of journalism, has taken the newspaper to new heights. He has raised that standard even higher."

There was modest applause as the publisher stepped to the side and Means stood behind the lectern.

"I agree with Mr. Pembroke," he said in his pitch-perfect delivery. "This is a proud day for our newspaper. Taylor's work is certainly one that will be difficult to duplicate but it shows us what we're capable of doing and what we need to do for award-winning journalism."

Chase looked at Riggins but didn't make eye contact. He felt uneasy and wanted to bolt from the room but knew he couldn't do it. He closed his eyes for a few seconds and took a few deep breaths to regain his composure.

"With Taylor as an assistant managing editor in charge of investigations, we'll have someone who knows firsthand what it takes to produce the kind of journalism needed to make the newspaper even better in the coming months," Means said.

Chase glanced directly across the room and noticed Angela watching attentively as Means continued with remarks. She smiled as she and Means made brief eye contact. About ten feet away from her stood Brett, unsmiling and seemingly disinterested in the proceedings.

Riggins then took his turn at the lectern, clearing his throat and pausing like a politician at a convention before speaking.

"This is a wonderful moment for me," he said. "To receive recognition for one's work is especially gratifying. I do want to thank the editors and copyeditors who worked with me and to Mr. Pembroke and Mr. Means for the support and faith they had in this story. It wasn't an easy piece to write..."

Chase lowered his head, not wanting to watch Riggins, wishing he cover his ears as well.

"I hope I can continue to be an integral and important part of the newspaper for many years to come," Riggins concluded.

Light applause broke out among the audience as the three men made their way to the punch bowl. Pembroke's secretary filled the Styrofoam cups with punch and handed each a cup as others began making their way to the table.

As several people made their way to shake Riggins's hand, Chase slipped out the door and quickly returned to his desk. The newsroom was nearly empty except for the few clerks who remained to answer telephones.

"You don't feel like celebrating?"

Chase looked around and Bernie was approaching him.

"Too much work to do," he said.

"I don't feel like celebrating and I'm not afraid to say it."

"You just better keep those thoughts to yourself. You may be working with Mr. Riggins someday."

"Don't say that," she said, rolling her eyes despairingly.

"You never know."

Seven

"Why are you doing this to me?" Brett asked Angela at the rear parking lot of the newspaper building.

"I don't think I want to talk to you," she said tersely.

"You knew before we got involved that it wouldn't last. We've got spouses and families to consider."

"I said I don't want to talk to you," she said.

"I wish you wouldn't be this way. We do have to work together in the same place."

"You don't know everything," she said, tears filled her eyes.

"What?"

Angela looked at him for a moment, turned and dashed to her car. She looked back at him as she opened the car door. Brett stood solemnly, staring at her as she backed out of the space and drove past him without even a glance.

Brett ambled to his vehicle, opened the door and sat down. He pressed his head against the steering wheel and closed his eyes. Several minutes later he was startled by a hard knock on the windshield. He looked over, saw Bernie, and rolled down the window.

"Is something wrong?" Bernie asked, leaning toward him.

"It's nothing," Brett said with a sigh.

"There has to be something. Nobody sits in the parking lot with their head against the steering wheel for no reason at all. What's up, Brett?"

"It's just a story I've been thinking about," he said while running a hand through his hair. "It's got me kind of stumped and I was just giving it some thought."

"Are you sure?" Bernie asked with raised eyebrows.

"Yes, Bern. I'm fine." Brett turned the ignition and the car hummed. "I need to be going."

"If there's anything else, please let me know. You know you can count on me. I'll help you in any way I can."

"Thanks Bern. I appreciate it." Brett smiled and backed his car out of the space as Bernie took a few steps back. She nodded as he drove away, and headed toward her car.

"Hey Bern!"

Conner sprinted to her with two cameras draped around his neck and an overstuffed camera bag drooping off his shoulder.

"Are you getting off work, too?" she asked.

"Yeah," he said. "Have you had dinner yet?"

"No. I was going to eat after I got home."

"Want to stop at Rosie's?"

"Sure," she said. "I'll meet you there."

Rosie's, a mom-and-pop restaurant with home-style food, was about a five-minute drive from the newspaper. The décor consisted of tables and chairs that didn't match, presumably purchased at yard sales and auctions, and uninspiring prints on the wall of faded flowers or washed-out city scenes. They found a table near the back. A few minutes after ordering, the waitress brought fried chicken, mashed potatoes and gravy, green beans and 32-ounce glasses of iced sweet tea.

After several minutes of chit-chat about their workday, Bernie asked, "Do you know Brett Johnson very well?"

"We're certainly not buddies but I've shot a few things that he's been involved with. He seems like a nice enough guy. Why do you ask?"

"When I left work tonight, he was sitting in his car in the parking lot."

"Any problem?" Conner asked before taking two gulps of tea as if he hadn't had any liquid intake in several days.

"He said he was thinking about a story he was working on but I don't think so."

"Why do you think that?"

"I don't think people sit in their car with their head against the steering wheel contemplating a story. He just looked like he was troubled by something."

"You're probably right." Conner chuckled. "Maybe it's that thing with Angela Cook."

"I've heard some rumors about it. That's probably it."

"It seems like she's giving him the shaft, so to speak, after he tried to break things off with her."

"I never knew she was that way," Bernie said.

"I'm told she's a sweetie to your face but she can be a real bitch behind your back."

"Really?"

"She's been known to go to editors when she feels that other reporters aren't treating her right."

"I've noticed her around Mr. Means the past few weeks."

"You're not the only one," Conner said with a sly grin.

"Do you think there's anything going on between them?"

"They seem a bit too chummy to be going over stories. I'd think he has more important things to do than worry about one of her assignments."

"That's what I thought but didn't want to read anything into it. It just looks like a lot of brown-nosing."

"Well, she's got that reputation for that so you may be right," Conner said, and added with a laugh, "A brown-nosing bitch!"

Bernie simply shook her head and sighed.

After they finished eating, they ordered coffee and slices of warm apple pie. Conner asked for two dips of vanilla ice cream.

"I really don't need this," Bernie said as she took a bite.

"Me neither but what the hell," Conner said with a laugh. "You only live once."

"Anything going on in your life?" she asked.

"Only work. How about you?"

"Same here. We lead kinda boring lives, don't we?"

"I won't argue that," Conner said as he finished off the pie with one big bite. "All work and hardly any play."

"Are you seeing anyone?"

"I've dated a few women but not many. Don't have the time. How about you?"

"I've gone out with a few lawyers and some guys who work for the city. That's about it. They weren't too exciting," she said with a shrug.

"Dated anyone at the office?"

"Never have," she said with a shrug. "I try not to mix work and romance."

"Really?"

"Yes, why?"

"Some folks thought you were interested in Chase Elliott."

Bernie slightly blushed. "Oh, we're just good friends."

"Just wondering."

After a short pause she asked, "Hey, what do you think about Taylor's award and promotion?"

"I'm happy for him," Conner said. "He's been at the paper a long time and deserves the recognition."

"Oh?"

"Some folks in the newsroom are making some wisecracks about it but they're just jealous of him," Conner said. "You know how folks are in the newspaper. They smile at your face and stab you in the back when you turn around. Always envious when someone is recognized for doing good work."

"I suppose so," Bernie said with a sigh. "I've never had that problem with my work. I guess I should win some awards. Oh well, I guess I need to get home. I've got an exciting council meeting to cover early tomorrow." She faked a yawn.

"I'm off tomorrow. I thought I'd go out to Red River Gorge and do some hiking."

"That sounds like fun. I love that place."

"Perhaps you can go with me sometime."

"Just let me know."

~ * ~

The phone rang as Chase skimmed his e-mail the following morning. "Hello?"

"Chase," Riggins said coldly. "Do you have a few minutes?"

"Sure," Chase said. "Anything important?"

"Would you mind coming to my office? I need to discuss something with you."

"I'll be there in a few minutes," Chase said. He stopped by the restroom on the way. Means was primping in front of the basin mirror.

"Good morning Chase," he said, looking at him from the mirror. "How are you this fine morning?"

"I'm doing well," Chase said as he stood in front of the urinal. "And you?"

"I can't complain. It's a lovely day."

"I agree," Chase said as went to the basin and washed and dried his hands.

"Anything going on at the university?"

"It's been relatively quiet over there the past few months."

"I know what you mean but we know it doesn't last forever. Something is probably brewing somewhere in that bastion of academic and athletic excellence."

"No doubt about that." Chase forced a smile.

"I've got a meeting coming up," Means said, taking one last look at the mirror and smiling at himself as he patted his hair in place. "I hope you have a great day."

"Same to you," Chase said as they walked out together.

Chase walked directly to Riggins's office at the end of the building. He tapped on the open door.

"Come on in," Riggins said. "Would you mind closing the door behind you?"

Chase shut the door and sat down in a chair in front of Riggins's desk. The small office had a window view of the rear parking lot and little else. The walls were barren with only outlines of frames and nail holes from the previous occupant.

"What took you so long?" Riggins asked.

"I stopped by the restroom."

"I'm in a hurry," Riggins said impatiently. "I've got a meeting coming up in a few minutes."

"I also talked with Jordan Means so that detained me a little longer," Chase said with a smile. "Sorry about that."

"Oh, okay. What did he want?"

"Nothing in particular," Chase said, unable to resist a smart-alecky smile that he knew probably irritated Riggins. "Is there something you wanted to discuss?"

"Not really discuss," Riggins said, clearing his voice. "I was just wondering what you know about Brett Johnson."

"Not a lot. Why do you ask?"

"I'm just trying to learn more about the staff. I've never really gotten to know him very well after all these years."

"Really?" Chase said with an arched eyebrow. "He's a good man. A solid journalist."

"I was looking for personal things."

"Sorry," Chase said, shrugging his shoulders. "I can't help you there."

"No talk around the office?"

"Now you know better than to ask me things like that. I'm not here that much, and when I do hear something, I don't spread it. I keep things in confidence."

"A confidential man," Riggins said.

"I guess you could say that. Perhaps even to a fault."

Riggins pushed his chair back from the desk and stood up, taking his eyes off Chase.

"I've got a meeting to attend," he said. "Thanks for coming by."

"Sorry I couldn't be of much help to you," Chase said as he stood and followed Riggins out the door.

"I'm not surprised but I thought you could provide me with something because of our friendship."

"You should know better than that."

"I suppose so." Riggins turned the corner and headed toward the conference room without looking back.

As Chase returned to the sports department, he met Green in the middle of the newsroom.

"Where have you been?" Green asked unsmiling.

"Taylor wanted to see me for a few minutes."

"Are you going to be around later?"

"I can be if you need to see me."

"I'll be back in about thirty minutes.

"I'll be at my desk."

Chase sat down at his desk and turned on his computer. He went back go his e-mail account and deleted the various spams that had slipped by the company's filter while he reflected on the meeting with Riggins. *He wants me to squeal on Brett while keeping his bogus story a big secret. Is he serious?*

He got up and went over to the water fountain and took a long sip. When he finished, Brett was standing next to him.

"Hey, how are you doing?" Chase asked.

"I don't think I'm doing too well."

"How come?"

"Can we talk about it later?"

"Sure thing. Give me a call."

Chase returned to his desk as Green was heading his way. He nodded for Chase to go to his office.

"What's up?" Chase asked as he sat down on a hard wooden chair.

"The management guys want some more hard-hitting stories from our department. They think we're being too soft."

"Don't they always say that about sports?"

"Perhaps, but we've got to do some things to show them that we aren't afraid to play hardball."

"Anything in particular?"

"They were asking if anything is going on at the university."

"It's funny you should mention that because Jordan asked me the same thing this morning."

"He did? Where did you see him?"

"Earlier, in the restroom. It was a casual chat."

"Jordan and Taylor are pushing this."

"Taylor is involved as well?"

"Yeah, I think he's trying to impress some of the folks since he got the promotion so he's cracking the whip in several places."

"Interesting."

"Why do you say that?"

"No reason," Chase said. "No reason at all."

Eight

"Are we having fun yet?" photographer Stan Riddle asked as he approached Chase near the rear of the hospitality room during the state high school basketball tournament. He lugged his photo equipment on his slight frame and placed it in the corner.

"You know it," Chase said with a laugh. "Watching all these games wears me out. I can't imagine what it's like for the players."

Riddle went to the refreshment table and returned with a soft drink and small bag of potato chips.

"Have you been here all the time?" he asked after sitting down at one of the large circular tables.

"I've watched parts of games while writing but I've been here from opening tip-off to final horn every day," Chase said. "Anything going on back at the newspaper?"

"Shit seems to be flying everywhere," Riddle said. "Ever since we won that damn award and Riggins got that promotion, it's been bad."

"I know what you mean," Chase said, shaking his head slowly. "They want more investigative pieces out of sports now."

"The shooters are involved in every project. It's like we don't have the time to do the everyday stuff that needs to be done. They want us to do our daily job and everything else on top of it. And they sure as hell don't give us more manpower to do the extra stuff. We can't even hire any freelancers. It's crazy."

"We probably do need to be doing more investigative work," Chase said. "And I think we'll be able to do it after the dust settles. Riggins is just trying to make his mark, so everybody is in an uproar over it."

"You're probably right but I think they're just going about it in the wrong way."

"No doubt about that," Chase commented as he leaned back in his chair and stretched his arms outward. "But isn't that the way they usually do things at the paper, going head first without much planning?"

"Another good point. We've been through it before in other projects."

"Like I said, I think what they're trying to do is get everyone focused on investigative stories."

"How well do you know Riggins?"

"I've known him for several years. We came to the paper about the same time."

"Has he always been such an asshole?"

"What do you mean?"

"He's been badgering the hell out of people. It's like he's alienated himself from the staff and is kissing up to Means and Pembroke."

"Well, he used to be a nice guy," Chase said with a chuckle. "I'm sure he's been under a lot of pressure, especially since winning the award."

"I've been on a few assignments with him in the past and he seemed like an okay guy. He didn't talk a lot but he was okay. You know what I mean? I even worked on that award-winning story with him."

"You did? What did you think about it?"

"I thought it was a good piece of writing but I'm not sure about the reporting. Something just didn't seem right. I don't know what it was but everything didn't seem to add up."

"That's interesting."

"Others have said the same thing but no one could pinpoint what exactly wasn't right. Have you heard anything like that?"

"Being in sports, I wouldn't hear very much about those things."

"I guess not," Riddle said as he finished eating the chips. The horn blared in the arena, signaling the restart of the game.

"I guess it's time to get back to work," Riddle said as went over to pick up his gear. "Another half of basketball at its best."

Chase laughed. "You're getting cynical in your old age."

"I'll just be glad when all this basketball season is over and I can start doing something else."

"Oh well, you can look forward to some investigative stuff," Chase said with a wily grin.

"Don't remind me," Riddle said, shaking his head as he headed out toward the equipment.

The last game of the day ended at almost eleven. Chase had already filed his column and feature story and answered questions from the copy desk. He was home by eleven-thirty. He went through his mail and listened to his answering machine. One call from Hannah, wanting him to call her when he got a chance.

He took a soft drink from the refrigerator and turned on the television, eased back into the recliner and flipped through the channels. Local news was already over. He checked the all-news channels but there was nothing but talking heads giving their opinions about things he could care less about.

Chase looked back over his mail and opened a piece he had thought was junk. It didn't have a return address. There was one sheet of paper, unsigned It was typewritten and said:

Dear Mr. Elliott:

I think your newspaper needs to examine Mr. Riggins' story. There are some false attributions in it and some misleading information. I thought I would bring this to your attention. I hope you can do something about it. Thank you.

Chase studied the letter again and again, trying to figure out who would have sent it to him. He wondered why they sent it to him rather than to someone in the newsroom or one of the editors.

He picked up the letter again the next morning as he drank his coffee in the kitchen, trying to see if there were any clues as to who had sent it. Nothing led him to suspect anyone.

Chase lay the letter down and put some bread in the toaster. Pouring another cup of coffee, he took the toast out and put margarine and apple jelly on the two slices. He glanced back at the letter on the table, but nothing was recognizable. He was hoping for some hint or clue. Nothing. Putting it aside, he stepped out on the front porch and picked up his morning newspaper. A small item at the bottom of page three in the city section snagged his attention: *Sexual Harassment Claimed at Newspaper*.

The story mentioned that a female employee at the paper had filed a complaint against special projects editor Brett Johnson. It quoted Means as saying that there would be an internal investigation and that the paper strived to have a workplace free of sexual harassment. The story also said that Johnson had been placed on paid suspension.

"My goodness!" Chase said out loud. "This is ridiculous."

He put the newspaper down on the coffee table, leaned back in the chair and closed his eyes. *How can they do this?* The phone ringing startled him. He let it ring several times, thinking it could be Riggins and not wanting to deal with him so early in the day. He reluctantly picked up the receiver.

"Hello?"

"Chase, this is Brett. Did you see the newspaper this morning?"

"Unfortunately. I'm sorry about what's happened."

"I can't believe Angela is doing this to me."

"What are you going to do?"

"I don't know what I can do. She's wrecking my life. Victoria has already left and taken the kids to her parents' home in Ohio. This is unbelievable. My reputation is shot and I'm on suspension."

"Have you got a lawyer?"

"I don't know how that would help."

"It might prevent the paper from railroading you."

"What do you mean?"

"Did you sexually harass her?"

"You know I didn't. It was a mutual affair. She threw this at me when I wouldn't continue it."

"Have you told anyone at the paper?"

"Not really."

"Are they going to have a hearing or anything of that nature?"

"I'm supposed to meet Means and Pembroke on Tuesday at eleven."

"Take an attorney with you. First of all, if you didn't sexually harass her, you may only get a reprimand but the lawyer should be able to protect you, otherwise they may even try to fire you on the spot without minimal benefits. If you're ready to leave the paper, the attorney may be able to get you a nice termination package that can help you while you get your life back in order."

"I'll do that."

"What's going to happen between Victoria and you?" Chase asked.

"Your guess is as good as mine at this point. She's taking this pretty damn hard, and I don't blame her. I was an idiot."

"How are you handling everything?"

"Before I called, I wasn't sure what I'd do. I didn't even know if I felt like living any more. This is so humiliating."

"As I said, get yourself a lawyer and discuss the options you might have."

"Thanks Chase. You've been a true friend."

"I don't know if I was that much help but let me know if there's anything else I do."

After hanging up, Chase took a hot shower and dressed. He had the championship game of the tournament to go to later in the evening, so he decided to stay at the house and do some research on the game.

He arrived at the arena two hours before tip-off and strolled into the hospitality area. Green, Riddle and Harry Waxler, the high school beat writer sat drinking coffee.

"Evening, gentlemen," Chase said as he approached the table. "Ready for the big game?"

"I know I am," said Waxler, who had attended all the games, the long hours and lack of sleep showing on his face. "And I know I'll be glad when it's over. My butt is dragging."

"You need to take a few days off next week," Green suggested.

"I think I will," Waxler said. "I have the all-state teams to take care of but I've already got a good start on them."

"What are you going to write about, Chase?" Green asked.

"That classic phrase - the thrill of victory and the agony of defeat - as it pertains to the game. I'll keep it from being trite."

"Please do," Green said. "I hope we have a good game to write about."

"Did you guys see the thing about Brett Johnson in the paper?" Riddle asked. "I wonder who the woman is."

"I'm not at liberty to say," Green said.

"I think I have an idea," Waxler said with a laugh. "Where have you been?"

"Who is it?" Riddle asked.

"My guess is that it's Angela Cook," Waxler said. "I've seen them around together the past year."

"Really?" Riddle said. "I must have been on Mars. I don't recall anything unusual between them."

"I always thought they were a little too friendly," Waxler said. "Have you noticed them, Chase?"

"Uh, not really," Chase said before taking a sip of coffee. "I really don't notice those kinds of things."

"I think I'm going out to the press table," Green said as he stood up. "I'll see you guys a little later."

After Green left the hospitality room, Riddle laughed and said, "I don't believe Cole wants to comment on it."

"I can't say I don't blame him," Chase said. "He's part of management."

"So you think Brett was screwing Angela?" Riddle asked Waxler.

"I didn't see him do anything but they just acted kind of funny together, like a couple of lovebirds," Waxler said.

"That's interesting," Riddle said. "I think more of that goes on than we realize."

"Perhaps," Chase said with a shrug as he rose from his seat. "I think it's about time to go to the floor. The teams will be warming up pretty soon."

"Yeah, we need to go," Waxler said with a laugh. "We sound like some gossipy hens here."

Nine

Chase crawled out of bed late Sunday morning, tired from covering the basketball game the previous night. He didn't leave the arena until past midnight, and then went with Waxler and several out-of-town writers and photographers to one of the local watering holes for beers before going home.

He stepped out onto the porch and picked up the newspaper. A misty rain chilled the air. He didn't really care that the weather was far from ideal because he had no intentions of leaving the house that day. His plans were to vegetate and take it easy.

Chase closed the front door and strolled back to the kitchen to put on a pot of coffee. Moments later there was a knock on the front door. He found Hannah standing there holding a small white box.

"Come on it," Chase said as he opened the door. He kissed her on the cheek as she stepped into the house. He took her coat and hung it on the coat rack.

"I took the liberty of stopping by the bakery and buying a half-dozen doughnuts."

"That's great," he said, grinning. "I could use a sugar rush this morning. Would you care for some coffee?"

"I sure would," she said. "I need to take the chill out of my body. It's colder than what it looks outside."

Chase opened the cabinet, took out a cup for Hannah and poured coffee to near the brim.

"So what have you been up to this weekend?" Chase asked as he sat down across from her.

"Nothing much. I finished my reports and had a few meetings on Friday."

"Are you going back on the road now?"

"I'm going to Fort Wayne and Toledo about mid-week. How about you?"

"I don't have any immediate plans," he said before taking a bite from a chocolate-covered doughnut.

"I read about the sexual-harassment complaint in the paper yesterday," she said. "Do you know the individuals?"

"Unfortunately I do."

"Is anything going to happen?"

"I assume something will. The guy's wife has already left him. I don't know if they can repair the marriage."

"How about the woman?"

"I really don't know her. She works on the news side."

"Are you saying they had an affair?"

"From what I know," he said after sipping coffee. "I think it was simply an office romance that went sour."

"Those things happen. Is she married as well?"

"Yup."

"So what are you going to do today?" she asked.

"I don't plan to do anything. How about you?"

"Nothing planned."

"Then why don't you stay here with me and do nothing all day?" he said with a wink.

"But don't you think we'd end up doing something?" she said, a sparkle in her eyes.

"Perhaps," he said. "But we'd be doing it together."

Hannah rose from her chair and stepped toward Chase, who opened his arms as she sat down on his lap. They kissed softly and tenderly.

"I've missed you the past few days," she cooed while resting her head on his shoulder.

"I've missed you as well," he said. "I'm glad you came over this morning."

Hannah got up from his lap and Chase stood next to her. They kissed again, and he took her hand and led her to the bedroom. The bed was unmade and his clothes were tossed in the corner.

"I apologize for the mess," he said.

"No need to apologize," she said. "You weren't expecting me and it is early."

As Chase smoothed the sheets on the bed and puffed the pillows, Hannah slipped out of her jeans and pullover sweater. She stood next to him in a black bra and bikini panty. He wrapped his arms around her and pulled her close to his body, kissing her on the neck and shoulder as he unsnapped her bra. A few seconds later, they had removed all their clothes and were snuggling under the covers. The phone rang.

"Damn!" said Chase. "Hello?"

"Bernie here."

"What is it Bernie?" he asked impatiently.

"Am I calling you at a bad time?"

"Don't worry about that," he said as he glanced at Hannah. "What is it?"

"Brett Johnson was taken to the hospital this morning."

"What happened?" Chase said as he sat up in the bed.

"I'm not really sure," she said. "They said he was apparently intoxicated and fell down and struck his head."

"Are you serious?"

"That's what I heard. They found him unconscious on his living room floor this morning."

"Who found him?"

"His wife and father-in-law. They were at the house to pick up some of her belongings and found him on the floor."

"It's so hard to believe something like that could happen."

"I thought you'd want to know."

"Thanks for calling, Bern. By the way, what hospital is he at?"

"They took him to St. Benedict's."

"Thanks again."

"I'll let you know if I hear anything else."

"I'll do the same for you."

After Chase put down the receiver, he looked at Hannah and shook his head slowly. "The guy we were talking about at the newspaper apparently got drunk, fell down and seriously injured himself."

"That's what I could gather from your conversation. Is he going to be all right?"

"I don't know. They took him to St. Benedict's."

"Do you want to go over there now?"

"I think I'll go a little later," Chase said. "His wife is with him and I'm sure he doesn't want or need visitors."

Chase got back under the covers and Hannah cuddled up next to him as he put his arm around her. They lay still until dozing off to sleep.

Several hours later Chase gently pulled Hannah toward him. They held each other for a few minutes, kissing and touching before Hannah rose on top of him. They made tender love until she collapsed into his arms.

"I love making love to you," Chase said softly.

"And I love making love to you," Hannah said, leaving a wet kiss on his neck.

Chase gently squeezed her as she rested her head under his chin. They lay quietly for several minutes, sharing a few kisses before getting up and taking a hot shower. They toweled each other off after getting out of the shower and dressed.

"Would you like to do something this evening?" Chase asked in the living room.

"I'd love to but I really need to be going," she said. "I've got a few things I need to take care of before work. I'll try to call you tomorrow."

"I'll be expecting it," he said before giving her a soft kiss as she stepped outside and walked to her car. He stood at the door until her car had pulled out of the driveway and was out of sight, already missing her.

He headed straight to the telephone and called Bernie but she didn't answer. He then called the hospital to find out Brett's condition but the receptionist wouldn't disclose it because of patient-confidentiality policy. He turned on the television, hoping to find some information about Brett but there was no mention of him on any of the channels. He called the newspaper's city desk and was told that there had been no update on Brett's condition but it was believed that he was doing fine. He was informed that Riggins had put the clamps on any story until there had been a review by the newspaper.

~ * ~

When Chase arrived at the newspaper on Monday morning the editors were in their daily budget meeting. A few reporters were sitting at their desks, most of them talking on the telephone. A company-wide message flashed on the newspaper computers about Brett's death. No details were given, except for a fund being started for his two children. A roaring silence swept the newsroom.

Chase sat motionless, staring at his computer screen, not believing what he had just read. He glanced down to Brett's desk. A funereal atmosphere already permeated the newsroom. Brett's desk looked as it always did. Papers were scattered on top, several books stacked on one corner. Chase wondered who would go through the drawers and remove personal belongings and return them to the family. *Maybe there would be some clue as to the reason behind his death.*

"Can you believe it?" Riddle said as walked up to Chase's desk. "I'm totally puzzled by it. I've talked to several of the reporters and they don't understand it either."

"I'm sure he was upset by the item in the paper," Chase said glumly

"But enough to drink yourself to death?"

"Some people can't handle the embarrassment and humiliation, I guess." Chase recalled his last conversation with Brett.

"Could be but I doubt it." Riddle argued with a knowing expression.

"Why do you say that?"

"I was told by one of the reporters that some editors didn't want to run that item but they were overruled."

"Are you serious?"

"That's what I was told."

"Who insisted on running the story?"

"Taylor Riggins."

"Riggins?" Chase asked wide-eyed. "Are you serious?"

"That's what they told me," Riddle said, nodding his head. "He said our people shouldn't be excluded from news stories."

"I can understand that to some extent but..."

"Some of the editors argued that it was only preliminary and there was no need to rush anything into print."

"That's what I was going to say. It's strictly someone's word against another's."

"And most folks don't even think it was sexual harassment."

"I've heard the same." Chase slowly shook his head. "I can't believe this has happened."

While the newsroom slowly returned to the job of gathering news, it wasn't business as usual for several hours as a mild hush engulfed the surroundings whenever the noise level reached a distracting hum. Most of the reporters couldn't help glancing at Brett's desk as they walked past it.

Later in the afternoon a man and woman in business attire walked over to the copy desk and spoke with one of the editors, who pointed toward Brett's desk. The editor picked up the telephone and a minute later Riggins walked hurriedly into the newsroom and shook their hands.

"I'm Gene Bennett and this is Marcia Slone. We're from the detective unit," he said to Riggins. "We'd like to go through Mr. Johnson's desk."

"Do you have a search warrant?" Riggins asked.

"Yes we do, Mr. Riggins," Bennett said, handing over the court order to Riggins.

"Just follow me," Riggins said as he led them to Brett's desk.

The detectives put on clear rubber gloves and took their time going over the items on the top of the desk as Riggins stood several feet away and closely watched. They pulled out the drawers and slowly began sorting through pads, pencils, envelopes and scribbles on sheets of paper, putting several items in a large plastic bag, as well as reporter's notepads.

"Anything there I can help you with?" Riggins asked.

"No sir," Bennett said without looking at Riggins.

Several reporters with desks close to Brett's desk stopped working and watched the detectives conduct their methodical investigation. Occasionally a phone would ring to break the silence.

"Mr. Riggins, we'd like to talk to some of the reporters as part of the investigation," Bennett said.

"That shouldn't be a problem."

Bennett interviewed several reporters seated near Brett's desk as his partner continued to sort through Brett's belongings. Riggins leaned closer while keeping an eye on what Slone was examining. After twenty minutes, Bennett finished with the reporters and Slone closed the drawers to the desk.

"Did you find anything?" Riggins asked.

"We'll let you know," Bennett said with a quick smile, before nodding to the reporters and walking out of the newsroom with Slone a step behind him.

"I wonder if they found anything," a news clerk asked Chase.

"Who knows?"

"Mr. Riggins doesn't appear happy."

Riggins, looking grim-faced in a dark blue suit, white shirt and bright red-and-blue tie, talked intently to three reporters at Brett's desk.

"Yeah, I wonder what's going through his mind?" Chase said, almost to himself.

Ten

Bennett and Slone took Brett's belongings from the plastic bag and sorted them out on a table in the evidence room. They each picked up a notebook and began flipping through the pages.

"How in the world could he read these scribbles?" Bennett asked, shaking his head. "It's almost undecipherable."

"I'm sure it's his personal shorthand," Slone said. "At least the notebooks are dated on the covers so we have an idea what was going on about that time."

"I think the main thing to look for is names, phone numbers, addresses and see if there is any kind of correlation."

"There even seems to be abbreviations for that. Here's a DN with 555-1106. I guess that's a person's initials and phone number."

"Why don't you give it a shot?"

Slone picked up the phone and dialed the number. After two rings an answering machine came on: "You have reached the office of Don Nader. He is not available at the present time. Please leave a name, number and short message and he'll get back with you."

"Good guess." Slone said. "Don Nader, whomever that is. Do you think we should call every number in the notebooks?"

"I don't see any other way around it," Bennett said. "Someone may be able to give us a clue as to Mr. Johnson's death."

"If that's what drinking does."

"You don't believe he was so distraught over his marriage and the story in the newspaper that he got drunk and fell?"

"It may have happened," Slone said with a shrug. "But something just seems fishy to me. It was almost too clean."

"I've wondered about that as well. There should have been some other signs but it just seems to have happened out of the clear blue."

"That's another thing. You'd think there would have been some bottles strewn about the house or other signs of a drunken stupor, such as belongings thrown around or broken."

"All we know is that he drank too much whiskey, collapsed and struck his head."

"And isn't that strange as well?" Slone asked.

"Probably so. They usually go to pass out in bed or on a couch."

"Don't you think we need to go back to the house and run some more fingerprints and look for anything else?"

"It probably wouldn't hurt," Bennett said. "I think everyone has assumed that it was an accidental death. I'm just worried that any other evidence has been erased or tampered with."

"I believe only his wife and father-in-law have been in the house."

"Well, let's send forensics back out there and see if they can turn up anything."

Bennett picked up the telephone and called the forensics unit and asked for an additional investigation. Slone continued going through the notepads. As she came across an initial and phone number, she made a call. They had all been contacts or subjects of stories Johnson had written in the past year.

"It seems the names and phone numbers correlate," Slone said.

"I just find it hard to believe that he'd drink himself silly over an affair," Bennett said, almost to himself. "Most of his co-workers said he was a thick-skinned guy. It just seems out of character for him. And they said he really didn't drink much."

"Maybe forensics will give us some more leads to work on," Slone said as she turned another page in the notebook. "I wonder what this means?"

"What?"

"This entry. It has "*TR*, then *OT*? *MD*? *RG*? *RL*? There aren't any phone numbers."

"Any idea when it was written?"

"My guess would be in the past three months."

"Well, keep that out and we'll follow up on it. Maybe someone at the newspaper knows what it means."

"Let's go through all the notebooks and see if we find similar notations, then go back and talk to some of the reporters," Slone said.

"When is Angela Cook expected back?"

"She's supposedly with her family in Florida and will be back Sunday. We've already confirmed that she was out of town when Mr. Johnson died."

"Maybe she'll give us the information we need," Bennett said, arching his eyebrows. "She did hit him with the sexual harassment."

"We need to get some more information on her as well."

~ * ~

Two days later, Rev. Joseph Flanders stood at the pulpit at Community Christian Church, overlooking the family and friends at Brett Johnson's funeral. The final mourners viewed Johnson's body as the organist played a soft and solemn "Amazing Grace." Several flower arrangements surrounded the bronze casket.

Johnson's elderly parents wept quietly while Victoria Johnson, on an opposite pew with her two children and her parents, sat stoically and stared straight ahead. Her parents comforted the children, seven-year-old Marcy and ten-year-old Jody. Most of the newsroom was in attendance. Means and Riggins sat on the second row behind Brett's parents. Chase and Bernie sat midway in the small church. Bennett and Slone were on the back row, observing everyone they could. The church grew silent when the organist played the final note. Flanders cleared his throat.

"We are here to mourn the passing of Mr. Brett Johnson," the minister bellowed, stirring the audience to attention. "It is always a time of sadness when someone leaves us, especially so when it comes so unexpectedly. Mr. Johnson was a fine husband, a good father and a respected journalist..."

Victoria dropped her head and wiped away a tear that had trickled down her cheek. Bernie and several others from the newsroom held tissues and sobbed. Means and Riggins looked directly at the minister, unmoving and showing no emotion.

"...Mr. Johnson had his faults as all we humans do but he tried to overcome them to assist others. He volunteered in various organizations and gave freely of his time to help others..."

Chase looked around at those in front of him. He noticed Conner and several photographers a couple of rows behind Means. He glanced quickly to each side, but didn't recognize anyone other than those from the newsroom. He wasn't expecting to see Angela but thought there might be a chance she would attend. As Chase surveyed the room, Bennett was watching Chase's head movements.

"...And let us not forget the professionalism that Mr. Johnson brought to journalism. He was always seeking truth and accuracy in his reporting, traits that made him a respected member of the community," Flanders said in a strong and powerful voice as he concluded the eulogy. The organist softly played "How Great Thou Art" as the mourners filed one more time past the casket and offered their condolences to Brett's families.

As Chase and Bernie walked across the parking lot, Bennett came up to them.

"Sir, I'm Gene Bennett with the police," he said politely. "I assume you knew Mr. Johnson?"

"Yes sir, I did," Chase said. "We worked together at the newspaper for several years."

"Aren't you in the sports department?" Bennett asked.

"I'm a sports columnist. I'm Chase Elliott."

"I thought you looked familiar." They shook hands.

"Is there anything you want to know?"

Bennett said, "If you don't mind, I'd like to call you later this week and ask a few questions."

"Feel free to call me at the office or at my home," Chase said, taking out a business card from his shirt pocket and handing it to him.

"I'll be getting in touch with you shortly," Bennett said, tipping his head slightly and walking away.

Chase and Bernie ambled to his car. He opened the passenger door for her and went around to his side. She reached over and unlocked his door.

"That was odd seeing a detective at the funeral," Bernie said.

"Maybe they don't believe it was an accident," Chase said as he slowly backed his car out of the space and left the parking lot.

"What do you think?" Bernie asked.

"I've had some doubts about it."

"Me, too," Bernie said. "I just find it hard to believe that he would hit his head against a coffee table and die from it."

"They said he hit his temple so that could explain it. I believe they called it a subdural hematoma."

"Maybe the police will find why it happened."

"We'll have to see," Chase said as he drove out of the parking lot.

Eleven

"It's sure nice seeing you again," Chase said to Hannah inside the small French café. "It seems like ages."

"I know what you mean," she said while reaching over to gently touch his hand on the table. "I've missed you, too."

"How was your trip to Fort Wayne and Toledo?" he asked.

"It was okay. Nothing to write home about."

Chase smiled as he turned over his hand and clutched hers. They stared at each other for a moment, and were startled when the waiter returned to take their orders. After the waiter left, they took a sip of red wine.

"I attended Brett Johnson's funeral earlier today," Chase said. "It's still hard to believe he's gone."

"I'm sure it must be difficult for a lot of people."

"I had a detective stop me in the parking lot after the funeral. He wants to ask me some questions."

"I thought his death was accidental?"

"I guess they're looking at it as a possible homicide."

"Have they questioned others at the newspaper?"

"They were in the office a few days ago."

"What can you tell them?"

"I really have no idea," Chase said, shrugging his shoulders. "I'd known Brett for several years but I don't know who could have murdered him, if that's what happened."

"Not even the woman who filed the sexual-harassment claim?"

"What reason would she have for killing him? She'd already ruined his life."

"I suppose you're right."

"Anyway, I heard she was out of town when it happened."

The waiter returned with their food. They sat quietly for several minutes as they ate their meal.

"This is very good," Hannah said. "This is one of my favorite restaurants."

"Mine, too," Chase said. "It's a little pricey but well worth it."

Angela suddenly entered the restaurant and looked around. She glimpsed at Chase and forced a smile. He nodded. Seconds later, she was gone.

"Who was that?" Hannah asked.

"The woman who claimed she was being sexually harassed."

Hannah raised her eyebrows. "Oh. I think she was looking for someone."

"Or she may have shown up to meet someone and saw me and decided to leave," Chase said.

"Didn't you tell me that she's married?"

"Yes, but that isn't an issue with her."

"So Brett Johnson wasn't the only person she's been with?"

"I'm really not sure," Chase said. "I have my suspicions."

"With someone else at the paper?"

"Perhaps," he said with grin.

"You're not going to tell me, are you?"

"I don't spread rumors. If I knew something for a fact, I'd tell you but at this point I'll keep it to myself."

"You really are a really a private person," Hannah said. "Did you know that?"

"I've been told that. I just like to protect a person's privacy. I guess I want to treat others as I would want to be treated."

"Do you have any deep, dark secrets?" Hannah said with a sly grin.

"I'm not telling," Chase said with a wink.

After finishing their dinner, they walked to a neighborhood park three blocks away. They sat on a park bench and watched several children on the swings. Chase put his arm around her and squeezed her gently on the shoulder.

"I really enjoy spending time with you," he said.

"Thank you," she said as her blue eyes sparkled under the lights. "I enjoy being with you as well."

"How long have we known each other?"

"You've already forgotten?" she said with a mock anger, jabbing him in the side.

"Times flies when you're having a good time," he said.

"I've known you for six years and we've been dating for two years."

"Do you ever want to go out with others?"

"Why do you ask me that? Are you getting tired of going out with me?"

"I'm just asking, honey," he said. "I know it must be frustrating dating a newspaperman."

"I'm not complaining," she said. "If I didn't like it, I'd tell you."

Chase kissed her softly on the cheek and pulled her closer.

"Are you ready to go now?" he asked. "It's getting a little cooler."

"If you're ready to leave. I'm comfortable sitting here with your arm around me."

He patted her shoulder and they sat for another ten minutes, watching the night sky fill with stars and a half moon ascend over the trees before strolling hand-in-hand to Chase's car.

"Do you have any other plans for the night?" Hannah asked as they drove to her house.

"Not really," he said.

"Would you like to keep me company tonight?" she asked with a smile.

"I think I could handle that."

Chase took a long way to her house, driving slowly through several neighborhoods while they listened to an Air Supply on the CD player. Her house was dark when he pulled into the driveway.

"Wait a minute before we get out," he said.

"What is it?"

Chase moved over and kissed her passionately.

"There's something about kissing a beautiful woman in a car," he said.

"I never realized you were such a romantic," Hannah cooed.

"I guess you learned something new about me tonight."

"I like these kinds of surprises."

They got out of the car and walked into the house. Chase ambled to the living room while Hannah went to the bedroom. Several minutes later, she came out in a black negligee and sat down next to him. His eyes widened.

"You sure got my attention," he said, grinning. "What a sexy outfit."

"You like it?"

"You look ravishing."

"You know how to make a girl feel sexy."

"You are sexy, sweetie."

Hannah rose from the couch and took Chase's hand and pulled him up. She reached over and turned off the lamp, then unbuttoned his shirt and took it off. She unsnapped his pants as he kicked off his shoes, lowering them enough for him to step out of them. Chase raised each leg and took off his socks before following her to the bedroom. Hannah jumped quickly in the bed and Chase followed, wrapping his arms around her and pulling her slender body close to him. Moments later, he slipped off her negligee and kissed her softly and tenderly. Before long, they were one and lost in their passionate embrace.

Chase awoke early the next morning. While Hannah slept, he took a quick shower and dressed. In the kitchen he made a pot of coffee. Several minutes later, he looked at the doorway and Hannah stood there trying to suppress a yawn.

"You must have been quiet this morning," she said. "I didn't hear a thing."

"You must have been tired because you didn't move," he said as he poured coffee into their cups.

"Why are you up so early?"

"I need to stop by the office and do a few things. I prefer going early in the morning before too many of the brass show up."

"Can I fix you any breakfast?"

"Coffee is fine."

After drinking two cups, Chase drove to office. He had a message on his voice mail from Bennett, asking for an interview. Two hours later, as he stood next to his desk talking to Green, Bennett arrived. He came up and shook hands with both men, before Green retreated to his office.

"Thank you for letting me drop by on such short notice," Bennett said. "I only have a few questions."

"Let's go to the interview room," Chase said, sensing others in the newsroom watching them. "We'll have more privacy."

"That would be fine," Bennett said as he followed Chase to a small room that contained only a table and four chairs. Chase closed the door.

"Care for any coffee?"

"No, thank you."

"So what can I do for you?" Chase asked as they sat down on the green plastic cushioned chairs.

"How well did you know Mr. Johnson?"

"I've known him for more than ten years although I wouldn't say we were buddies. We were friends."

"Had he seemed distraught or disturbed by anything?"

"Of course, there was the sexual-harassment thing. I knew that upset him."

"Did he discuss it with you?"

"We talked about it."

"What did he say?"

"He wanted to break things off with the woman. I guess when he told her, that's when she supposedly filed the complaint."

"How serious was this affair?"

"To be honest, I really don't know. I didn't even know anything about it until late. I believe others in the newsroom had heard rumors.

I'm so out of the loop at times in that I'm probably the last person to hear things," Chase said with a nervous chuckle.

"How well do you know Angela Cook?"

"I don't know her at all," Chase said. "I don't know if I've ever spoken to her."

"Was Mr. Johnson working on any big assignments?"

"I really don't know," Chase said. "You'd have to talk to one of the editors."

Three quick. hard knocks shook the door.

Chase, startled for a moment, opened the door. Riggins stepped inside, quickly closing the door behind him.

"Good morning Mr. Bennett," he said with a forced smile.

"I hate to ask this but do you think you could clear it with me before you come into the newsroom and interview our reporters?" Riggins said harshly. "We find it a bit disruptive and we could set up something downstairs to accommodate your requests."

"I'm sorry if I've caused any problems," Bennett said, looking more like an executive than a detective in his dark charcoal suit and shiny black shoes.

"It's probably my fault, Taylor," Chase said. "Mr. Bennett called me and I invited him here. I didn't think it would be a problem."

"If you could check with me first, Mr. Bennett, I think it will work better," Riggins said without acknowledging Chase. He opened the door and left without another word.

"I'm sorry if I caused you any problems," Bennett said. "Is he usually this way?"

"I'm surprised," Chase said. "I didn't think it would be such a big deal. He's new in his position."

"Trying to assert some authority?"

"Your guess is as good as mine," Chase said, shrugging his shoulders. "Could be."

"I don't have anything else to ask at the moment. I suppose I'll go through Mr. Riggins the next time I need to get in touch with you."

Chase took a business card out of his front shirt pocket and wrote down his home number on the back and handed the card to Bennett. "You can call me at home."

Bennett uncrossed his long legs and stood. He towered over Chase by at least a head. He firmly shook Chase's hand and opened the door. "Thanks again."

As Bennett headed toward the elevator, Chase returned to his desk. A few seconds later, Riggins was standing next to him.

"What did he want?" Riggins asked.

"What you would think?"

"That's not what I asked," he said with a glint in his eyes.

Chase paused a moment, and took a deep breath.

"He wanted to know how well I knew Brett and if he seemed troubled by anything."

"And what did you tell him?"

"I told him he was upset about the sexual-harassment complaint."

"Is that all?"

"I believe so."

"From now on, don't invite any police officers into the newsroom without first consulting with me. Do you understand?"

"No problem," Chase said, staring coldly at Riggins.

Riggins turned around and walked through the sparsely-filled newsroom toward his office.

A few minutes later Chase opened his e-mail and noticed a system-wide message to all newsroom employees from Riggins, announcing that they must send police interview requests through him. Chase shook his head.

"How did the interview go?" Green asked.

"Just some basic stuff."

"I guess they don't think Brett's death was an accident?"

"I'm not sure. I think they're looking at any possibilities before closing the case."

"What do you think happened?"

"As far as I know it was an accident. I don't know why there would be foul play."

"Even with the sexual-harassment stuff?"

"What would be the motive?"

"Good point." Green shrugged his big shoulders and headed to the break room.

Twelve

As Chase channel surfed from his easy chair, flipping from one station to another while hardly noticing what was on the TV screen, he heard soft tapping on his front door. He eased out of the chair and went to the door, and peeked through the peep hole. Bernie and Conner stood nearly head to head, and staring back at him. Chase opened the door, let them in the house, and they sat down on the couch. He returned to his chair and turned off the TV.

"So what brings you here this evening?" Chase asked.

"I hope you don't mind us dropping by," Bernie said. "We went out to eat after work and were discussing everything going on at the paper."

"We wanted to get your feelings on what is going on to make sure we're not the only ones who feel that there've been some things going on," Conner said.

"I'm sure you're not the only ones who notice the changed atmosphere. It does seem a bit oppressive," Chase said with a whimsical look.

"Because of Taylor Riggins?" Bernie asked.

"Well, there does seem to be a connection between what has been going on and Riggins's promotion," Chase said with a grin. "Of course, when anyone moves into a new position there is going to be some resistance. Perhaps he's simply doing what the bosses want and he's taking the heat."

"I suppose you could be right," Conner said with jutted jaw. "But it's just his attitude and arrogance. I don't recall him being such a smartass and know-it-all when he was just a plain reporter. He's pissing me off."

"Well, sometimes power corrupts," Chase said with a soft laugh.

"Did you see that e-mail about clearing things with him before talking to the police?" Bernie said.

"That came about because Detective Bennett came around to see me this morning," Chase said. "Taylor wasn't happy about seeing him in the newspaper without prior notice."

"What did Bennett want?" Conner asked.

"Some more questions about Brett Johnson," Chase said.

"You know, I'm beginning to think there was something fishy about his death," Bernie said. "I know accidents happen but this one was so coincidental."

"I guess you could say that," Chase said, "but I wouldn't go jumping to any conclusions until we know everything."

"Yeah," Conner said. "But I wonder if that will ever happen."

"Has Angela Cook been around the newsroom?" Chase asked.

"She was there today," Bernie said. "She was acting as if nothing had happened."

"I saw her in the cafeteria drinking coffee with Jordan Means," Conner said.

"Maybe she's working on a big story," Chase said.

"If she is, it's a secret to everyone in the newsroom," Bernie said.

"I guess the sexual-harassment thing is moot," Chase said.

"That's funny, too," Conner said. "You would think that she would bring something against the newspaper for creating a climate for sexual harassment."

"I guess we'll have to wait and see," Chase said. "Do you guys want something to drink?"

"No, we have to be going," Bernie said. "I appreciate you talking to us tonight."

"No problem," Chase said. "I'm glad you came over. If you hear anything else, feel free to call me."

After they left, Chase sat in the easy chair and turned on the TV. In a matter of minutes, after closing his eyes, he drifted off to sleep. He was awakened two hours later by the ringing of the telephone.

"Chase Elliott speaking," he said groggily.

"Am I calling at a bad time?"

It took a couple seconds for Chase to realize it was Riggins on the other end.

"That's okay," Chase said. "I dozed off in the chair."

"I apologize," Riggins said. "I was thinking about our conversation today and wanted to clear things up. We've been friends for a long time, Chase."

"Yes, we have."

"I'm just trying to get a handle on what's going on in the newsroom. It's been a rather loose organization the past few years and I'm trying to rein things into a cohesive unit."

"Okay."

"So what I said today wasn't to be taken personally. I hope you understand that."

"I'm sure you've got to do what you think is right."

"And I'm not telling you not to talk to the police. We just can't have them barging in the newsroom any time they please without notification. I don't want to set any precedent."

"I don't believe they've ever done that in the past. They have some reason to do it since Brett Johnson died."

"We're just laying some ground rules with them now so it won't get out of hand in the future."

"I hope it works."

"I hope my promotion doesn't end our friendship," Riggins said. "I want you to know you can count on me to stand behind you."

"I appreciate that, Taylor."

"And if you ever hear any rumors or gossip spreading through the newsroom, I'd appreciate it if you would let me know. I want to stop things in the bud before they get out of hand. And you can trust me not to let tell others that you confided in me."

"Why, thank you Taylor," Chase said, slowly shaking his head in amazement. "But you know I don't spread rumors."

"I know," Riggins said, clearing his throat. "But just in case you hear something you think I ought to know. It'll be just between us."

"I'll keep that in mind."

"Again, I apologize for calling at this hour. I'll see you at work. Good night."

Chase put down the receiver. He wondered what was going through Riggins's head. He was sounding a bit paranoid and power hungry. He tried to think of what could have transformed him from a calm reporter to a cunning editor. Perhaps it came with the territory, he thought.

~ * ~

The next morning, while sitting at her desk in the detective unit, Slone said, "These notes by Brett Johnson are very interesting. Lots of scribbles and lots of abbreviations. I guess everyone has their own version of shorthand."

"No doubt," Bennett said, sitting at the chair next to her desk. "Have you got any good leads?"

"The page with the TR. I wonder if that stands for Taylor Riggins?"

"It could stand for a lot of things but that might be a good start."

"Do you think I should go question him now?"

"I don't think so. He's a bit on the confrontational side right now. Did I tell you that he wants us to go through him before questioning reporters at the newspaper?"

"How come?"

"Your guess is as good as mine. I guess it's a First Amendment thing."

"Have you told the chief?"

"Yeah," Bennett said. "He thought it was odd. The newspaper seems to think it's okay to send reporters here anytime of the day but turnaround isn't fair play."

"I wish forensics could come up with something definitive about Johnson's death other than a blow to the head."

"Give them a little more time. I'm sure if there is any foul play, they'll find it."

"I thought I'd get in touch with Angela Cook. Should I call Riggins?"

"Why don't you call her at the newspaper and set something up away from the newsroom? Wait on Riggins."

"I'll do that now," she said, picking up the phone and dialing the newsroom. Bennett picked up the crime report on Johnson and looked over it. A few minutes later, Slone said, "I just finished talking to Ms. Cook. I'm going to meet her at three at the coffee house several blocks from the paper."

"Good luck."

~ * ~

Slone arrived at the coffee house about ten minutes early. There were a few students scattered about the tables, drinking coffee while studying and chatting. Several elderly women were gabbing softly near the front window. Slone found a table against the right wall, which was decorated with art work from area artists.

A few minutes later, Angela strolled in and looked around. Slone stood up at her table and raised her index finger to get her attention. Angela smiled and walked over to the table. They shook hands and sat down.

"I'm sorry if I'm late," Angela said.

"No, you're right on time. I got here a little early."

They both ordered cinnamon cappuccinos and talked about the weather until their drinks arrived.

"I need to ask you some questions about Brett Johnson," Slone said as the smile left her face.

"I'll try to help as much as I can," Angela said. "Wasn't it an accident?"

"That's what it appears to be but we need to make sure. If you don't mind, I'd like to get straight to the point."

"That's what I was expecting," Angela said timidly.

"I understand you had an affair with Mr. Johnson. How long did it last?"

"Probably about five or six months. We'd known each other for several years though."

"Did he seem depressed lately?"

"I guess so," Angela said. "Our relationship was beginning to sour. I'm not sure how happy he was at work either."

"What was going on at work?"

"I think there was some tension among some of the reporters and editors. That seems to have a ripple effect in a newsroom."

"I understand you had filed a sexual-harassment complaint against him."

"I did," she said.

"Why?"

"I thought that would be the only way to end the affair. We had gone hot and cold about leaving our families. I decided I wanted to save my marriage."

"And he didn't feel the same way about his?"

"I think he did."

"But wasn't that kind of extreme to file the harassment charge?"

"Looking back, I guess it was. I just didn't think everyone would find out. That was stupid of me to think that."

"Do you think Mr. Johnson could have been murdered? Did he have any enemies at the newspaper?"

"I always thought he was pretty well liked by everyone," Angela said, wiping away a tear from her eye.

"He never had words with anyone?"

"I remember Taylor Riggins and him arguing over some story but that's about it."

"You don't know what it was about?"

"I'm not really sure. I think it had something to do with sources. You know that Brett was in charge of special sections in the news department?"

"Were there any stories that Mr. Johnson was working on that could have provoked someone to hurt him?"

"Not really," Angela said. "He usually oversaw enterprise stories. I believe Taylor wanted more investigative stories."

As they finished their cappuccinos, Means came in with a young man and woman. He glanced at Angela, smiled and walked to her table. He introduced his companions as student interns at the newspaper who would be working during the summer.

Means looked at Slone, and when he wasn't formally introduced, reached out and shook her hand.

"I'm Jordan Means," he said cordially. "I'm the editor of the *Daily Register*."

"Hi," Slone said. "Marcia Slone with the police department."

Means's right eyebrow arched as he tried to keep a smile on his face.

"She has some questions about Mr. Johnson's death," Angela interjected quickly.

"Oh, I see," Means said. "Well, if you need anything from the newspaper, you'll have our full cooperation."

"Thank you," Slone said. "I appreciate that."

Means smiled and directed the students to a table near the rear of the building.

"I hope I didn't cause you any problems," Slone said softly to Angela. "There shouldn't be."

"I've heard that Mr. Riggins wants all interviews to go through him."

"He's a control freak," Angela said with a nervous laugh.

"I appreciate your time. I'd like to get back with you if something else comes up."

"Feel free to call me anytime," Angela said. "Although Brett and I had a falling out, I still cared a lot for him."

Thirteen

"Were you able to get any good information from Ms. Cook?" Bennett asked Slone after she returned to the police department.

"No, not really," she said. "She provided me with some information about their affair, but I didn't sense that there's really any connection between that and his death."

"I was hoping we could get some good leads from her."

"I'll go back and check my notes and see if there's anything there. Oh, Jordan Means showed up while we were talking. He said the newspaper would cooperate in whatever way it could."

"I wonder if he passed that on to Riggins," Bennett said with a laugh.

"Don't you think it's about time we went back and talked to Mrs. Johnson?"

"I'll go by her house today. She should be able to give us some insights as to what was going on with her husband."

"I'm going to go back over some of Mr. Johnson's notebooks," Slone said. "Maybe I'm missing something."

"That's a good idea. We need to find out what all those initials mean."

"I did find out that Riggins won some big journalism award several weeks ago."

"Perhaps you should find out what it was for and read the stories."

"I'll do that."

Bennett left the department and drove across town to interview Victoria Johnson. A car was parked in the driveway of the modest split-level brick home. He walked up to the front door and rang the doorbell. A few seconds later she opened the door slightly.

"Ms. Johnson, I'm Detective Bennett and I was wondering if I could ask you a few questions?" He opened his wallet and showed identification.

She cautiously opened the door and allowed him to step into the living room. He stood just inside the doorway until she motioned for him to sit down on the couch covered with a white bed spread.

"I apologize for dropping by unannounced but I've called a few times since the funeral and there's been no answer."

"I was at my parents' house in Toledo," she said. "My kids are there right now. Could I get you something to drink?"

"No, thank you," Bennett said with a smile.

"Please pardon my appearance," she said, brushing her hands over her blue jeans. "I've been trying to clean and sort through some things."

"I ask that you don't throw anything away that may pertain to your husband."

"Why?"

"We're treating this as a possible homicide."

"I thought it was accidental?"

"It very well may have been accidental but we want to make sure before we close the file."

"Oh, okay," she said as she tugged at the sleeves of an old blue sweatshirt. "What do you want to know?"

"Had your husband complained about anything at work?"

"He seldom talked about work when he was at home," she said. "He said he didn't want to bring problems at work home with him."

"Was he having any problems with other employees?"

"Oh, he would complain about an editor or reporter now and then, but it never seemed to be very serious. It was usually about how a story was edited or the angle they wanted him to take on it. Some reporters don't like their stories edited."

"Did he mention names?"

"I don't know if I can be much help there but I'll try," she said. "I never spent much time at the newspaper. I don't recall the last time I was ever in that building. He would mention Sarah Perkins, the city editor, but he got along with her very well."

"Any other names?"

"Oh yes, there was Taylor Riggins. We've both known him for a while. Brett would say Riggins had been on his case a lot. I don't know what it was about."

"I hate to bring this up..."

"Angela Cook?"

"Yes," Bennett said.

"He was only screwing her," Victoria said bitterly.

"Nothing else?"

"He thought he was hiding it from me but a wife knows when her husband is messing around."

"Were you going to separate or divorce?"

"We were going to try to work things out," she said. "I knew it was a mid-life thing with him, and that young hussy was making a fool out of him. He was basically a good man and good father. I think he realized how foolish he looked. Do you know what I mean?"

"Yes, ma'am," Bennett said, nodding affirmatively. "I believe so. Why were you out of town?"

"I needed some breathing room," she said. "Brett told me to go to my parents for a few days. He needed some time alone to gather his thoughts and bearings about us. We had decided to get some counseling after I returned and try to repair our marriage, if it was possible."

Victoria stood and tugged at her jeans that had crinkled at the knees from sitting down.

"Excuse me, I need to get a glass of water," she said. "Are you sure you don't want something to drink?"

"I'm fine, Mrs. Johnson."

"Please call me Victoria."

He looked across the living room while she was in the kitchen. There were several photos on a table, one of the family in happier times, if the smiles could be an indication. She returned with glass of ice water and sat down.

"I was giving some more thought about his work," she said after taking a small sip. "I remember that he used the word bogus a lot when describing the one person."

"Riggins?"

"Yes. He would keep saying the guy was bogus."

"And nothing else?"

"That's all he would say."

"So there was some animosity toward that person?"

"Definitely," she said before taking a sip of water. "That was about the only times I ever saw him upset about work. He was such an easy-going person. He seldom complained about work unless it interfered with vacation plans or the children's activities. But we all knew that came along with the territory. Isn't that the way it is for you?"

"We don't have a steady schedule either," Bennett said with an easy smile.

"I wish I could be of more help."

"I think you've helped us some. I would ask that you sort through your husband's belongings and put them in a box so we can see if there is anything that could help us with the investigation."

"There was one other thing."

"What is that Mrs. Johnson, er, Victoria?"

"I never understood why they said he smelled of whisky."

"Why?"

"He never drank whisky," she said. "He preferred beer."

Bennett got up from the couch and shook Victoria's hand.

"I appreciate you taking the time this afternoon to answer my questions," he said. "I know it has to be difficult. I'll be getting back in touch with you."

Bennett returned to the police department. As he walked toward his office, he noticed Slone in the break room drinking a soda. He poured a cup of coffee and sat down at her table.

"This is getting a bit more confusing," Bennett said. "Mrs. Johnson told me that her husband didn't drink whisky and there was a definite smell of it on his clothes."

"I'll call the lab today and see if they found anything in the toxicology report."

"I'd also like for them to tell us what brand of whisky was on the clothes, if that's possible and it's not too late."

"If he didn't have whisky in his system, then that really points to a homicide," Slone said. "Did you find out anything else from her?"

"Apparently there was some animosity Mr. Johnson had toward Riggins. Mr. Johnson referred to Riggins as bogus on several occasions. She also knew about the affair with Cook. Believe it or not, they were going to try and reconcile."

"I think I'd better do some more research on Mr. Riggins," Slone said. "Were we able to get much from him earlier?"

"We really haven't interviewed him but I believe we should soon. I'd rather wait a few more days until we get the lab reports and see if you've been able to dig anything else up from Johnson's notes."

"I've been reading Riggins's award-winning story," Slone said. "I must admit that it's very good. There's a lot more of a drug problem here than I imagined."

"Perhaps you need to talk to some other reporters about the story. They may be able to give you some good leads on it."

"I'll do that," Slone said as she finished her soft drink.

They returned to their desks and began sifting through reports. The phone rang on Slone's desk and she picked it up on the second ring.

"Hello, this is Detective Slone," she said.

"Detective Slone, I'm Taylor Riggins at the newspaper."

"Yes, sir, what can I do for you?"

"I understand that you interviewed Angela Cook," he said.

"That's correct."

"I thought we had an agreement that your office would go through me for interviews."

"I don't believe so, Mr. Riggins. That only pertained to interviews we would do in your newsroom."

"Oh," Riggins said, then clearing his throat.

"We'll certainly get in touch with you for any interviews at the newspaper. In fact, I would like to interview reporters who had a personal relationship with Mr. Johnson. Could you help me with that?"

"It depends on what you mean by personal."

"I mean those who knew him outside the newspaper, those who would socialize with him. You know, like going out for a drink after work or taking part in some activities away from the newspaper."

"I'll give it some thought and come up with some names and get back with you. When would you like to do this?"

"Oh, as soon as possible Mr. Riggins," she said brightly. "We'd like to wrap this up as soon as possible."

"I would ask that you try to refrain from talking to my reporters outside the newsroom. But I'll see what I can do because we'd like to get this over with so we can move on here at the newspaper."

"Mr. Riggins, we have an ongoing investigation and we need to talk to people regardless of where we interview them. Now I'll certainly try to talk to as many as I can at the newspaper but if I need to interview them in other places, I'll do that."

"Have you made much progress in your investigation?" Riggins asked.

"I believe we have some good leads now," she said.

"Can you disclose any of it to me?"

"I'd rather not at this time. There are just a few things we are following up on at this time."

"That's interesting," Riggins said. "Let me know if I can help in any way."

"Thank you for calling, Mr. Riggins," she said to cut off any more questions. "I'll look forward to hearing from you about the interviews. I may have a few names for you as well."

After she put down the receiver, she looked over at Bennett and shook her head and laughed.

"I assume that was our Mr. Riggins," Bennett said.

"He seems a bit concerned about the investigation. He wants us to go through him on everything."

"I heard you set the record straight with him."

"I don't think he liked it but that's the way it goes."

"I must admit that I don't care much about working with him with the interviews at the newsroom."

"I agree but I feel that keeps the door open with them," she said. "I think the reporters are going to feel too threatened and stifled to say anything at the newspaper but they may open up later when away from there. Reporters are always looking for leaks. Maybe we can find some leaks at the newspaper."

"Yep, we can play their game, but on our terms."

~ * ~

Riggins rose from his desk and went to the window. A steady rain beat down on the pavement and lightning flashed brilliantly in the distance. He stared out the window for several minutes until he heard a few knocks on his door.

"Come on in," he said, raising his voice.

Means opened the door and stepped inside. He closed the door behind him and sat down on the small couch across from Riggins's desk.

"We're really getting a storm," Riggins said.

"Yes, we're under a tornado watch right now."

Riggins sat down at his desk. He locked his fingers in front of him and faced Means. "I talked with the one of the detectives earlier."

"And what do they have to say?" Means asked.

"It seems like they're pursing some new leads on Johnson's death."

"Any idea what they are?"

"She wouldn't tell me."

"I guess we need to get someone here to see what they're up to." Means said.

"Do you think we should do our own investigation?" Riggins asked.

"I believe that perhaps we should but we need to have the right person doing it. Any suggestions?"

"How about Bernadette Robbins?"

"That's not a bad choice," Means said. "She's never done any investigative or crime reporting so she should fit the bill for us."

"I'll call her in the office a little later," Riggins said. "At least it'll give the impression that we're doing something about it."

"I also asked the detective to try to coordinate some of their interviews through me. She seemed somewhat agreeable."

"I told them yesterday that we would cooperate with them."

"Where was that?" said Riggins, a bit surprised by the revelation.

"I ran across a detective interviewing Angela Cook at the coffee house down the street," Means said.

"Did she tell them anything?"

"Not really," Means said. "It was mostly about her relationship with Johnson."

"I wonder how long this investigation is going to take?"

"Those things are difficult to gauge. If they come up with something that leads them to think there was a homicide, it may take a while."

"Let's hope they find that it was an accident," Riggins said. "I'd hate to see this thing drag on and on."

Fourteen

"They want you to do what?" Chase asked, raising his eyebrows.

"They want me to investigate and report on Brett's death," Bernie said as they sat in a corner booth at Pappy's bar. "Riggins called me into his office today and told me they thought the paper needed to be more aggressive about the death of one of its employees."

"Well, that does make sense. We really haven't done anything about it. And the police seem to believe it is more than an accident."

"But why did he pick me? I've never done any crime investigations. I've always covered boring meetings at city hall."

"Maybe they think you're a solid reporter and you'll do a good job."

"You think so?" she said, suddenly bright-eyed.

"You're a good reporter. There's no reason you can't do a good job on this. Reporting is reporting, regardless of what it is."

"Riggins wants a daily update on my progress," she said. "I've never had to do that before."

"Do you start tomorrow?"

"I guess so," she said as gloomy look began to reappear. "I'm still not looking forward to it."

"Oh, don't be silly. You'll do fine."

"I just don't like the idea of working with Riggins. I used to like him but now he gives me the creeps."

"Maybe he can give you some guidance on the story since he used to work the police beat."

"I think I'll talk to Jeffrey Wong. He's been on the police beat for several years."

"He's a good reporter. He should be able to give you lots of good tips."

"Do you know that Riggins wants me to do this solo?"

"I guess he doesn't want the newsroom stretched too thin."

"It sure as hell is thin with me on the story," she said with nervous laughter.

The barmaid came over and took their drink orders and returned two minutes later with a frosty mug of beer for Chase and a strawberry daiquiri for Bernie. She took a quick sip and forced a smile.

"How can you drink those things this time of day?" Chase asked.

"Because they're good," she said after taking another sip from the straw. "I don't see how you can ever drink beer. It's nasty tasting."

Conner came up to their booth and slid in next to Bernie.

"How are you guys doing?" he asked. "Anything going on?"

"We're just discussing my new assignment," Bernie said.

"What's that?"

"Investigating Brett's death."

"Are you serious?"

"Very serious," she said with a frown.

Chase shook his head and laughed. "She's been fretting about it. I told her she'll do just fine on it."

"I know you will," Conner said, patting her on the shoulder. "But it may be a little difficult because you knew Brett."

"It's going to be difficult because I've never done it before and even more because I have to work with Riggins on it."

"Oh shit," Conner said, shaking his head. "Are you serious?"

"I just hope I don't have to spend a lot of time on it," she said.

"I know a few cops so I'll see if they can help you any," Conner said.

"I'd appreciate anything you can do for me."

"I'll help you in any way I can. You can count on me. Just let me know how things are going and I'll do whatever I can to help you."

"That's awfully sweet of you," Bernie said.

Conner got up from the booth and went over to the bar and ordered a beer. As he stood at the counter, Riggins walked in through the front door. He stood inside for a moment, looked around, and saw Chase and Bernie. He smiled as he walked toward them, then sat next to Bernie.

"Hi," he said. "I hope you don't mind if I join you. I thought I'd stop by for a drink before heading home. I haven't been here in a while. Same old dump."

"But it's our dump," Chase said before glancing at Bernie. Conner returned to the table with a beer, and noticing his place was taken, sat next to Chase.

"Hi, Conner," Riggins said.

"How are you?" Conner said.

"I'm fine," Riggins said. "I can see that the service hasn't changed since I was last here. It's still bad."

Riggins waved at the barmaid, who came over to the table and took his order for a Manhattan and refills for the others.

"So how's everybody doing?" Riggins asked.

"Always busy," Chase said.

They sat in tense silence until the barmaid returned with their drinks. A John Michael Montgomery song played on the jukebox.

"How do you like your new job?" Conner asked Riggins.

"It's a challenge," he said. "I've got a lot to do to whip the newsroom into shape."

"Really?" Chase said. "I thought we had a pretty good staff."

"Without a doubt," Riggins said as he glanced at each person. "It's been way too soft the past few years. Except for my story, we haven't had a good, solid piece of investigative journalism in a long time. The young reporters we have need to get their feet wet with solid assignment instead of writing all this fluff. And I think we need some discipline in the newsroom. People just seem to do what they want to do."

Bernie sat quietly and sipped on her first daiquiri, glancing occasionally at Chase and Conner as if trying to communicate with her eyes.

"I don't know about the newsroom but I know the shooters are stretched to the limit," Conner said. "We could add several positions and still be busy."

"I'm sure that may be the case," Riggins said. "I've heard the same complaints in the newsroom, but more than anything it's time management. We're just not efficient anymore. We have some people who stay busy and others who sit on their ass a lot."

"I wish you success," Chase said with a pursed smile.

"Hey, bud," Riggins said with a smirk. "Sports isn't excluded from this. And neither is the features department. There's just too much wasted time and effort everywhere."

Chase nodded and took a swallow from his second mug of beer.

Riggins took a long sip from his Manhattan, looked at his watch and abruptly got up from the booth.

"I hate to leave you good folks but I promised the better half I'd be home at a decent hour tonight," he said. "You've got to keep the little lady happy, if you know what I mean."

He grinned and winked at Bernie. She forced a smile with the straw tucked tightly between her lips.

"I'll see you folks tomorrow," Riggins said as he turned around and left.

"Good riddance," Conner said quietly.

"What a creep," Bernie said, slowly shaking her head.

Chase laughed out loud and took another swallow of beer from his mug.

"I admit the guy has changed," he said. "It's funny what a little bit of power will do to someone."

A minute later, Riggins returned to their table, startling everyone for a moment.

"I almost forgot," he said as he placed a twenty-dollar bill on the table. "I ordered the drinks and forgot to pay for them. See you later."

They watched him leave again.

"See, he's not such a bad guy," Chase said with a chuckle.

Fifteen

"We got some reports back from the lab," Slone told Bennett when he strolled into the office carrying a large Styrofoam cup of coffee.

"Any surprises?" he asked as he sat down at his desk.

"It appears Mr. Johnson didn't have anything to drink," she said, raising her eyebrows. "It also appears that there was a light bruise on his left upper arm."

"So he could have been shoved, and then someone poured whisky on him to make it appear he had been drinking and stumbled?"

"That's a theory," she said. "I guess we have something to work on now."

"I wonder if they can tell us the brand of whisky that was on his clothes?"

"That's what they're testing now."

"What are you going to do today?"

"I'm going to drop by the newspaper a little later," Slone said. "I ordered some back copies of Riggins's award-winning stories and they're ready for pick up. How about you?"

"I think I'm going to go back over to Johnson's house and snoop around a little. Maybe there is something our people missed."

Bennett finished his coffee and made a phone call to Victoria Johnson. She told him to come over in about an hour. Slone left a few minutes later to go to the newspaper.

When Bennett arrived at Victoria's house, she was waiting in the living room with the front door open. She was looking at some newspaper clippings Brett had saved. Bennett knocked on the front door and she told him to come in.

"I'll try not to keep you long," he said. "Just a few questions, and I'd like to look around the house a bit."

"If anyone did anything to Brett, I want to find out who did it," she said.

"Have you given much thought to that possibility?" Bennett said as he sat down on a French chair to one side of the couch.

"Other than Brett being upset with Taylor Riggins, I really don't know who he could have had problems with," she said. "I guess that young hussy would be another person, but other than those two, he never really mentioned anyone else."

"Did you notice anything out of place when you returned?"

"Not really," she said. "It was pretty much the way I left it."

"Nothing like a break-in or anything like that?"

"Mr. Bennett, I've already gone through all of that before," she said, a little frustrated. "There was nothing suspicious. The only thing was the whisky smell on his clothes, and like I told you before, he didn't drink whisky."

"So you have no whisky in the house?"

"I never said that," she said. "We have a small liquor cabinet in the den."

"May I look at it?"

"Sure," she said as she stood and led him down a few steps to the den. She opened the liquor cabinet and moved aside. "Here's our little stash."

Bennett smiled and looked over the bottles without touching them. He reached into his coat pocket and took out a pair of rubber gloves and slipped them on his hands and reached in and pulled out three bottles of whisky and set them on the bar.

"Are you a whisky drinker?" he asked.

"I don't drink that much," she said. "We tried to keep a little of something for anyone who would visit. Brett liked beer but sometimes would drink gin or vodka. I guess I'd drink bourbon and sometimes a little rum. We also kept some wine and beer."

"Did you have many people over?"

"Not really, with his schedule," she said.

"Recall any of the whisky drinkers?"

"No," she said. "Brett would come down here and prepare the drinks or the guys would fix their own while the women were upstairs. I never paid much attention as to what people were drinking."

"I'd like to take these bottles down to the lab and have them checked for fingerprints," Bennett said.

"That's fine," she said. "For all I care you can keep them."

"I'll bring them back when the investigation is completed."

"I wish I could be of more help to you," she said.

"Don't worry about it. All I ask is that if you think of something that could relate to your husband's death, that you give me a call."

"I'll do that," she said. "Maybe I'll come across something while I'm going through his clothes."

"Anything that looks suspicious or out of place, let me know."

"I'll do that."

Bennett left her house with the three bottles in a large brown grocery sack. Several minutes after he drove away, Riggins pulled into her driveway in his new silver SUV. He knocked twice on the front door before Victoria answered.

"Hello Vicki," he said, standing on the porch.

"Hello," she said coldly.

"I was in the neighborhood and thought I'd dropped by to see how you're doing. Do you mind if I come in for a few minutes?"

She propped open the door and he stepped inside. He followed her to the couch.

"I guess things are going well, considering," she said, not making eye contact.

"If I or the newspaper can do anything, please let us know," he said. "We, er, I thought an awful lot of Brett. I really miss him. He was a good newspaperman and I treasured his advice."

Victoria looked at him for a few seconds without saying a word, and then glanced off to the large picture window across from them.

"The police hope they have some new leads."

"Oh really?" Riggins said, turning his head slightly. "Anything in particular?"

"A detective was here just a few minutes before you arrived."

"What did he tell you, if you don't mind me asking?"

"He didn't say much. He did take some bottles of whisky back with him."

"Why did he do that?"

"He said he was going to have them checked for fingerprints."

"I want to let you know that the newspaper has put a reporter on the story," he said. "Do you know Bernadette Robbins?"

"Yes, I've heard the name. Brett mentioned her on several stories."

"She's a fine reporter. We're going to have her look into the case and maybe she can come up with something. You'll probably hear from her."

"I'll remember that."

"And I hope that you tell her everything you know," he said. "Maybe the stories will flush out who was behind this."

"You don't think it could have been an accident?" she asked.

"Well, er, it could have been," he said, a bit flustered. "I thought it was an accident. You just never know. Only time will tell."

"I just want to get this over with and get my life back to some degree of normalcy. I want my children to have normal lives, if that's possible."

"That's what we want as well for you," Riggins said while getting up from the couch. "And you just let us know if there is anything we can do. You can call me anytime."

Victoria remained seated on the couch. Riggins took a step over and took her hand in his, patting the top of hers and smiled.

Sixteen

Chase poured a soft drink, sat down at the kitchen table and opened mail.

He went through the envelopes one by one, tearing up the credit-card offers and setting aside the bills. He couldn't recall the last time he received a letter since e-mail came into his life. At the bottom of the pile was a printed enveloped addressed to C. Elliott without a return address.

Taking a sip from his glass, he opened the envelope. Inside was a single sheet of paper that read: "There's more than meets the eye in the newsroom. Don't overlook anyone."

Chase read over the note again. He shook his head, wondering who was sending the anonymous notes and why they were sending them to him. What was he supposed to do about it? Go to the police? Tell management at the newspaper? He neatly folded the letter and put it back in the envelope. *Don't overlook anyone.*

Chase got up and went to the living room and sat down in the easy chair. He pulled the lever on the side and the chair went back into a reclining position. He closed his eyes and before long he was asleep even though it was early evening.

Two hours later he was awakened by a knocking on the front door. He eased up groggily from the chair and opened the door. Hannah stood there with a sweet smile.

"Did I wake you up?" she asked as she stepped inside. Chase took her coat and kissed her softly on the cheek.

"I must admit that you did," he said with a laugh. "I crashed on the chair for some reason."

"Are you feeling all right?" she asked with a look of concern.

"Just one of those days," he said as they sat down next to each other on the couch. "I'm fine. Some days you get home and there's nothing on TV, so you just crash."

"I've done that as well."

"So how was your day?"

"Rather routine. I was in the office most of the day."

"So what made you decide to come over?

"Are you unhappy I did?"

"I don't mean it that way," he said, patting her hand. "I'm glad you're here."

"I went to the mall and decided to drive by. I saw the lights on so decided to stop."

"Well, I'm glad you did," he said, and pecked her on the cheek.

"I can go if you want me to."

"Is something the matter?"

"I'm fine."

"Hannah, something is wrong. What is it?"

"Sometimes I wonder about us."

"What about us?"

"Are we ever going to have more than what we have now?"

"Is there something wrong with what we have?"

"I'm happy but I'd like to have more," she said as a tear trickled down her cheek.

Chase reached over and gently wiped the tear away with his thumb, then kissed the wetness on her face.

"I don't know what to tell you," he said. "I never realized you wanted more from our relationship."

"Sometimes I wonder if you really enjoy being with me and that's the reason we don't see each other more often."

"I think the reason we don't see each other is our work. I'd love to see you about every day."

"About every day?"

"I mean every day," he said with a slight blush. "You know what I mean. We've got crazy schedules, and if we were married, we wouldn't see each other every day."

"I guess you're right," she said. "Maybe it would be best if we simply stayed the way we are. Why mess up a good thing. Right?"

"Well, I didn't say that," he said. "We can always do things to see each other more often. Such as moving in with each other"

"I guess that would be an option."

"I'd be willing to give it a try."

"How about marriage?"

"Marriage?"

"Isn't t that about the same thing, except with commitment?"

"I suppose so," Chase said sheepishly.

"Are you afraid of marriage?"

"I've never been married so I really don't know."

"I've never been married either but I don't think it's so scary."

"I guess we can discuss that as well."

"I should be going home," Hannah said as she rose from the couch, unsmiling.

"Are you angry?"

"No, it's getting late and we both have to work tomorrow."

"You're welcome to spend the night."

"Oh, that's okay," she said as she began putting on her coat. "I have a busy day ahead of me and I need a good night's sleep. Plus I have a meeting and I need to have something to wear."

"Okay," Chase said as he slightly shrugged his shoulders. "I understand. Can I see you tomorrow night?"

"Give me a call at work," she said while opening the door.

Chase bent over to kiss her but she slightly turned her head and his mouth found her upper cheek.

"Good night, Chase," she said as she walked out the door.

"Good night, sweetheart."

After she left, Chase picked up a Richard Ford novel and spent the next two hours reading. Before going to bed, he turned on the TV and caught the local news. He slept soundly until awakened by a booming thunderstorm at six. He took his time getting dressed and eating breakfast before venturing outside to go to work.

Chase waited in his car in the newspaper parking lot, hoping the rain would lighten up and he could make a dash to the building. He left the radio on and listened to the news on an NPR station, noticing several people walking by with umbrellas in the downpour and not staying dry as the wind whipped the rain. There was a slight tap on the passenger-side window and he reached over and unlocked the door.

Bernie opened the door quickly and unfolded her black umbrella. She quickly got inside the car.

"Why are you sitting out here?" she asked.

"No umbrella."

"Do you want to go in with me?"

"Perhaps after the rain lets up a little."

"You lose more umbrellas than anyone I know."

"Occupational hazard for me, I guess."

"This new assignment isn't much fun."

"You don't enjoy crime reporting?"

"Not when it involves a friend."

"That would be a little rough."

"I'm beginning to gain a new appreciation of police work. It's difficult finding information."

"Are they cooperating?"

"I guess as much as they can," she said. "They're still gathering evidence and information and don't want to disclose too much."

"How are your interviews coming along?"

"Would you believe Riggins told me not to interview anyone at the newspaper?"

"Are you serious?"

"He said he wants it to be totally independent of the police."

"So who are you interviewing?"

"I've read some of Brett's projects the past few months and came up with a list of names."

"That's a good idea."

"I hope so," Bernie said, raising her eyebrows.

"Any other restrictions from Riggins?"

"He wants daily reports on my progress."

"Damn."

"I wish I could get out of it."

"Has he offered you any tips or suggestions?"

"You know, that's what has really surprised me. He sees himself as this top-notch investigative reporter and he hasn't helped me in one single way."

"Have you asked him?"

"Yeah, but he only says that I need to approach it like any other story. I've been covering meetings most of my career. There's hardly any comparison between the two other than talking to people and taking good notes."

"And you can't get any help from reporters?"

"Well, I've had some talk to me about Brett for background."

"Have you learned anything from them?"

"I know Brett was very depressed."

"Why was that?"

"Now this is totally off the record because I don't want Riggins on my rear end but they've told me Riggins was on his case all the time after his promotion," Bernie said. "He would berate him in front of reporters, call him at home at all hours and question him about Angela Cook. And I've heard Riggins has a drinking problem."

"That's news to me."

"Several reporters have told me that he calls the office at night and it's apparent that he's had one too many."

"Why does he call?"

"He just wants to know what's going on."

"Don't they have other editors who handle those things?"

"I thought so," she said. "They seem to be getting a bit peeved about him as well."

"And they don't say anything?"

"Well, they believe he has Means on his side. Some say that Means has given him the green light to unofficially run the newsroom."

"That's strange. I wasn't aware of that either."

"I know it is because Means used to spend so much time in the newsroom. It seems like he doesn't really care that much anymore."

The rain subsided to a light mist and they walked around the small puddles of water on the way to the building. They went up the elevator together to the newsroom.

"Thanks for listening to me," Bernie said before the elevator door opened.

"Any time," Chase said. "I don't know how much help I can be."

"You know it's always good to be able to bounce things off someone."

"You know where to reach me."

When the door opened, Riggins stepped to the side so Bernie and Chase could get off.

"Good morning," he said. "It looks like you guys brought some rain in with you."

"It was really coming down hard," Chase said.

"I know," Riggins said. "We've already got some flash-flood warnings out."

"Maybe it'll clear up soon."

"Not too soon," Riggins said with a grin. "We want to get some kind of story out of it."

"Oh," Chase said without expression. "I never thought about that."

"Bernie, please stop by my office later this morning," Riggins said as he got into the elevator.

"Sure," she said.

The elevator door closed and Chase and Bernie walked toward the newsroom.

"I guess he wants his daily report?" Chase asked.

"I don't know," Bernie said. "I usually just send him an e-mail on those things."

"Maybe he has some leads for you"

"Right," she said with a sarcastic laugh.

Seventeen

"We're having a meeting at four this afternoon in the conference room with Riggins," Green told Chase when he arrived at the office. "I'm sorry for the short notice but he only informed me yesterday. Do you have anything going on at that time?"

"My schedule is free," Chase said unenthused.

"Is anything the matter?"

"No, everything is fine. What's it about?"

"He wants to discuss more hard-hitting stories."

"Okay."

Green looked at him for a moment, then walked away to talk to another sportswriter. Chase opened his e-mail account and didn't see anything urgent.

"What are you doing for lunch today?"

Chase turned and Conner was coming up behind his desk.

"No plans."

"Care to go with me to one of the greasy spoons?"

"Sure thing," Chase said. "What time?"

"How about eleven-thirty? I've got a few things to do in the lab first."

"I'll be waiting."

"See you in about forty-five minutes then," Conner said as he headed to the photo department.

Chase made two telephone calls for a column he was working on before Conner returned. They decided on Sally's Diner, a six-table restaurant four blocks from the newspaper building.

"How's everything been going for you?" Chase asked as they walked to the restaurant.

"It's been busy but not too bad."

"Has Riggins invaded your department yet?"

"Not yet but I'm sure it's only a matter of time. He's got most of the newsroom in an uproar."

Chase laughed. "I guess he'll have the sports department that way after today. We meet him at four."

"I don't know what it is about him but he really turns people off."

"I don't understand it."

They arrived at Sally's and sat down at a table near the tiny counter. The yellow walls were unadorned except for a large red round clock over the grill that advertised a regional bread company.

After the waitress brought them silverware and ice water in scratched plastic tumblers, they resumed their conversation.

"What surprises me is that Riggins seems to have complete power to do as he pleases," Conner said. "You would think Means or someone would put some reins on him."

"I know what you mean. It's odd that they would allow someone to do this."

"I know Bernie hates it. He's making her a nervous wreck."

"I understand that he's not helping her either."

"Hell no," Conner said with a raised voice. "He wants all these daily reports and then criticizes her when she doesn't have much. She's not an investigative reporter. There are others he could have chosen for that assignment instead of her."

"It must be hard on her."

"Hell, he's had her in tears several times and you know that she's not a person to cry." Chase sensed Conner was getting hot under the collar and changed the subject.

"I'd like to get as far away from Riggins as I could," Conner said. "Even for a few days."

"Any vacation coming up?" Chase asked with a smile.

Chase began munching on a salad while Conner sank his teeth into a thick, greasy hamburger.

"Have you heard much lately about Brett's death?" Conner asked after a minute of silence.

"Only what I hear from Bernie," Chase said. "And that's not much."

"I figured you'd hear something from Cole or other editors since you're the big-time columnist."

"They don't tell me anything," Chase said, then took a swallow of water.

"You probably wouldn't say anything if they did," Conner said with a laugh.

"You might be right."

After finishing lunch, they returned to the newspaper building. The newsroom was half full as reporters and copyeditors began working on stories for the next day's edition. Chase checked his e-mail again and had a note from Angela, asking to see him after work. He replied that he could see her at six or whatever time would be convenient for her. He wondered why she would want to see him. He spent the rest of the time until the meeting with Riggins working on his column.

Twelve members of the sports staff were in the conference room, seated at the large oval table when Riggins entered the room. He looked around momentarily at each of the writers and thanked them for being there at short notice.

"We need to be more vigilant in our coverage," he said. "Too much of our coverage is strictly game results. We need to be doing more in getting behind the game stories. We know there is corruption in everything but we treat sports as if it were some fantasy world."

"Isn't it an escape?" a staffer interjected.

"Let me finish," Riggins said, stern-faced as the room grew silent.

"I'm not saying that the games aren't important to our readers. I'm saying that the sports report needs more substance. And I'm not talking about puff pieces on people. I want you to start looking behind the scenes instead of blowing smoke up someone's ass. Start digging into the business of sports and see what the motives are. Check into people's backgrounds and see if they're as lily-white as we portray them every day. Ask tough questions."

Riggins looked around the room and said, "Any questions or comments now?"

Everyone sat silent.

"You don't have anything to say?" Riggins asked. "How about you, Cole?"

Green cleared his throat. "I'm going to be meeting with some people the next few days and come up with an outline on what we should be doing."

"That should have been in place before but it's better late than never," Riggins said.

"Sometimes it's difficult to stay on things with all the games going on."

"That's an excuse," Riggins said. "I really don't want to hear those. I've met with most of the other departments and I've heard the same thing. It's all time management. From this point on we're not going to allow excuses for not doing our jobs right."

Green sat still and didn't respond.

"If we don't have any more comments or questions, I guess this meeting is adjourned," Riggins said, who rose from his chair and walked out of the hushed room.

Chase glanced at Green and they made eye contact. Green slightly shook his head and got up from his chair. As the sports staffers left the room, Green and Chase lingered at the rear of the room.

"This is going to be tough," Chase said.

"We'll make do," Green said. "We'll just have to focus on other things."

"Let me know if I can help in any way."

"As Riggins said, it's all time management. We just need to be doing things differently."

"But he didn't need to dress you down in front of the staff."

"Shit happens," Green said. "I can handle it."

"I know you can. I'm just offering some support."

"If I need any help, I'll ask for it," Green said without looking at Chase and going directly to his office. Chase stood and watched him walk away in disbelief. *I was only trying to help.*

The next afternoon Chase stopped at the university's athletic office to discuss funding of minor sports. While it was something he had done in the past, he thought he could put a different spin on the story to make it appear more hard-edged. He had been in the business long enough to know that there was more than one way to tell a story and while objectivity was always the goal, it still boiled down to the reporter's subjective view of the situation.

He spent two hours with the official, taking copious notes and getting some leads on other people to interview. It was nearly five o'clock when he left the university. Traffic was already clogging the Lexington streets, something he wanted to avoid. He decided to pull off at Sally's Diner for a quick meal. Halfway through, several reporters from the news staff came in and sat at a table next to him. His back was to them so they didn't recognize him.

"I don't know how much longer I'm going to stay," a female reporter said. "It's almost intolerable."

"I know what you mean," a male reporter said. "This guy runs the newsroom like the Gestapo."

"He's taken all the fun out of the job," another male reporter said.

Chase ate slowly as he listened to their diatribes.

"I still believe that story was total bullshit," the first male reporter said. "I wish I could prove it."

"Why don't you do some investigation of your own?" the woman said.

"How would I ever find the time when he has been doing all sorts of shit."

"Maybe we all could do some investigation, kind of like a team effort," she said.

"I bet we could get several other reporters to help us. We're not the only ones unhappy with the bastard."

"I think if we get too many involved it may get leaked about what we're doing and all of our asses will be in the frying pan."

"Yeah, but we need some help," she said. "We can't go this alone."

Their food orders arrived and they continued to talk about the newsroom situation. Chase, who didn't normally drink coffee at night, ordered a cup and sipped slowly while he continued to eavesdrop on the conversation.

"You know, I didn't like Riggins when he was a reporter," the woman said. "There was always something sneaky and shady about him."

"I thought he was okay but not very friendly. He seemed to be suspicious of everyone."

"And that story he wrote. In his entire career he hasn't done anything of note and then wins a big award. Something just isn't right."

"Sometimes it takes awhile to do anything in this business. If I can play devil's advocate, maybe he did some good things before we got here and never entered the stories in contests because he didn't want to."

"Oh, that could be the case but I doubt it. He's got too much of an ego not to try to do things."

"Maybe he was afraid of not winning and didn't try anything?"

"You sure defend him a lot," one of the men said to the woman.

"I just don't want to say he's guilty until we get some stuff on him."

"And what do you think about the paper putting Bernie on Brett Johnson's story?"

"Total bullshit."

"Why?"

"She's not an investigative reporter and they won't let her interview anyone at the paper. How can she succeed? Everything is stacked against her."

"All they've got her doing, in the name of journalism, is digging up stuff and passing it on to management."

"I think there's something fishy about that as well. That doesn't make any sense."

"I'd just be careful what I say around her because you never know what she will say to the asshole."

"Riggins?"

"How many assholes are there?"

"Actually, I could name several but I guess he's the biggest one," a man said with a chuckle.

"But if she can't interview you, why are you worried about what you say?" the woman asked.

"I'm talking about casual conversation in the newsroom."

"So you think it's best to keep her in the dark about what we plan to do?"

"I say keep everyone in the dark. We don't want to get our asses fired."

The reporters ordered desserts and their conversation drifted off to other topics. Chase ordered another cup of coffee and a slice of apple pie. What he had hoped would be a 20-minute dinner had lasted more than an hour. When the reporters finally got up to leave, he breathed a sigh of relief. He slightly turned his head toward the wall when one reporter took a step in his direction. A second later, they were walking toward the counter to leave. Chase turned around when he heard the door open and close. He looked out the window and watched them go to their cars.

Chase picked up his check and went to the register. He looked at the clock over the grill and saw that it was five-fifty. He remembered that he had agreed to meet Angela at six but they hadn't sct at meeting place. He took out his cell phone and called the newsroom and asked to speak to her. He hoped no one would recognize his voice.

"Hello," Angela said.

"This is Chase Elliott. I'm sorry for calling so late. I got caught up in a meeting and some other things."

"That's all right. I understand."

"Do you still want to meet me?"

"I can't tonight but perhaps in the next day or two?"

"How about tomorrow morning? I could meet you for breakfast."

"I guess that would work."

"Do you have any preferences?"

"How about your house?"

"My house?"

"Wouldn't that be the safest place?"

"I'm not so sure about that."

"I just don't want to go to a public place where someone could see us."

"Do you know where I live?"
"Yes."
"Well, I'll see you at nine then. Coffee and donuts?"
"Coffee will be fine."

Eighteen

Chase woke up earlier than usual, trying to get his home tidy before Angela arrived. He picked up several magazines and placed them neatly on the coffee table and put the dirty dishes in the dishwasher. Shortly before nine, the doorbell rang. Angela stood at the door wearing a conservative gray pantsuit and her hair neatly pulled back in a bun.

"Good morning," Chase said as he smiled and opened the door. "Come on in."

"Hi," she said softly. She stepped inside, looked around for a moment and then walked over to the couch and sat down.

"Can I get you anything?" Chase asked. "I have a fresh pot of coffee."

"That would be nice. Black please."

Chase went to the kitchen and poured two cups of coffee and returned to the living room. He handed her a cup and then sat down on the recliner.

"So how's everything for you at work?" he asked.

"I'm staying busy. Covering the thoroughbred industry, there's always something going on."

"I can imagine. I occasionally attend the sales and the big races."

Angela took a small sip of coffee and smiled.

"I wanted to talk to you about Brett Johnson," she said. "I hope you don't mind. I knew you and Brett were friends, and from listening to people in the newsroom, I felt I could talk to you."

"Brett and I were friends but I'm not sure how much I can help you. Is there anything in particular?"

"First of all, I'm sure you heard about our relationship?"

"Yes, I knew about it but not much of the details."

"We decided to part ways when we knew we couldn't leave our families."

"Didn't you file a sexual-harassment claim against him?"

"Sorta," she said. "I don't know how that started. I simply told him I didn't want to see him anymore and I think someone must have overheard me and started spreading the rumor. I think I had jokingly said something to one of the reporters that I would do something like that but I wasn't referring to Brett."

"You know gossip and rumors can be dangerous."

"But that's really not the reason why I want to talk to you," she said.

"Go ahead."

"This is difficult."

"Take your time," Chase said reassuringly.

Angela took another sip of coffee and coolly looked at Chase with her piercing emerald eyes.

"I have concerns about Brett's death," she said.

"Really. What are they?"

"It's just from some things I've heard. Nothing specific but innuendo."

"From anyone in particular"

"Well," she said with a pause, "Means and Riggins have made some comments about Brett's death that makes me wonder what really happened."

"What did they say?"

"Would you please not tell anyone you heard it from me?"

"Yes."

"Well, Jordan once said that Brett knew too much and that he was glad that he was no longer around."

"Knew too much about what?"

"I think it was about the award but I'm not totally sure."

"Did he say anything else about it?"

"Not really, only that the newspaper had worked hard for the award and he wasn't going to let anyone take it away."

"That's all?"

"That was it."

"How about Taylor?"

"You know, I really despise that man," she said angrily. "I think he's evil."

"Why do you say that?"

"Because I've watched how he treats people. He's mean."

"So what did he have to say about Brett?"

"I think he's the one who started the sexual-harassment stuff about Brett and me," she said. "I think he even mentioned something to human resources about it."

"So Riggins was behind it?"

"I didn't want to do it," Angela said. "They called me into the office and told me everything would be confidential and nobody would get hurt."

"They?"

"Riggins and Means."

"Did you ever ask them to set the record straight?"

"I tried to but Riggins said that he would tell my husband about the affair."

"Your husband doesn't know? He doesn't read the newspaper?"

"No, and I don't want him to know. He never associated the story with me. There's no telling what he would do."

"I understand. What does he do?"

"He's a university professor. He has a Ph.D. and thinks he knows it all. It's almost embarrassing to be married to him because of his condescending attitude toward others but he does make a good living for me and the children."

"Anything else about Taylor?"

"Taylor said Brett didn't show him the proper respect and he wasn't going to put up with it."

"Did he make any threats about Brett?"

"I didn't hear anything like that but I know there was anger in his voice when he talked about Brett."

"Why haven't you told the police?" Chase asked.

"Because I would get in deep trouble with my husband."

"I'm sure they would keep it confidential."

"You know nothing is ever confidential. Eventually, everything comes out in the open if you open your mouth."

"So why are you telling me these things?"

"I needed to tell someone and I felt I could trust you."

"And you don't think I'll tell someone else?"

"Actually, I'm hoping you do but not to implicate me."

"So what am I supposed to say if someone asks?"

"Just tell them that it's something you heard around the newsroom."

"So you want me to tell the police?"

"I don't mind as long as you don't mention my name."

"You haven't been interviewed by them?"

"I talked to one of the detectives and that's it."

"Did you know that Bernie Robbins is covering Brett's death?"

"Yes," Angela said with a grin. "Isn't that a joke?"

"Why do you say that?"

"Come on now. You know as well as I do that she's not qualified to do that story. They put her in that position to dig up information and pass it along to them."

"Who?"

"Riggins and Means."

"How do you know?"

"Because I overheard them talking about it."

"Where?"

"At lunch the other day."

"I didn't realize you were that cozy with them."

"Jordan and I are good friends. He envisions himself as being part of the horsey set, and because I cover the thoroughbred industry, he likes me."

"Really?" Chase said, recalling the meeting in the parking lot between them.

"The other day Jordan and I were having lunch and Taylor showed up. They talked about Bernie and what they were doing."

"And they discussed it in front of you?"

"They didn't say much about it. I don't think they thought I was paying any attention."

"Interesting."

"So you don't breathe a word of this to anyone because they'll know where it came from."

"We'll see."

"All I ask is that you don't tell anyone you heard it from me."

"I do believe you need to talk to the police again."

"Someday, perhaps."

Angela glanced at her watch and stood quickly.

"I've got an interview at a horse farm in thirty minutes and I need to be going. I appreciate you letting me come over and talk to you," she said as she began moving toward the front door.

"If you need to talk about it some more, you know how to reach me."

Chase walked her to the door and watched her leave in her car. He returned to the kitchen and drank another cup of coffee. Instead of going to the office, he went to the university and talked to other people about athletic policies. Before leaving the university, he called Green and told him he wouldn't be in the office until the next day.

After talking to Green, he called Hannah and asked her out to dinner. She wasn't busy and agreed to meet him at an Italian restaurant at six. She arrived about twenty minutes late as he waited in the bar. She had an exasperated look on her face when they made eye contact.

"I apologize for being late," she said as they waited to be seated. "I had a call from one of the suppliers and couldn't get off the phone."

"No problem," Chase said. "That happens to me all the time."

The waiter took them to a table in the far corner. They ordered a carafe of white wine and alfredo fettuccine.

"What's the matter?" Hannah asked over dinner.

"Oh, it's nothing," Chase said with a slight smile.

"You just seem preoccupied about something. Do you want to talk about it?"

"There's nothing the matter."

"Is it about what I said about our relationship?"

"I've been thinking about that."

Hannah picked up her glass of white wine and took a sip. She put the glass down and reached over and touched Chase's hand.

"I probably shouldn't have said anything. I was in one of those moods. I hope you understand."

"You made a lot of sense."

"I think we have something good between us and maybe by asking for too much it could spoil everything."

"I'd never want that to happen."

"Really?" she said with a bright smile.

"I don't want to lose what we have but I think it will become better over time if we let it."

"I think you're right. There's no reason to rush things."

"You're a special woman," Chase said as he took her hand in his and squeezed. "I probably don't show you enough how much I care for you."

"You're not the most outward in your emotions but I do sense you care for me. I hope you feel the same from me."

"I do," he said warmly. "And I probably don't say this enough but I do love you."

Hannah smiled as her eyes welled with tears.

"That's something I don't hear enough," she said. "But when I do, I know you mean it."

"That's just me," he said. "I'd rather show it through my actions than words."

After finishing dinner, Chase took her home. He walked her to the front door and kissed her passionately, just outside the periphery of the porch light.

"I wish you could stay," she said.

"We've both got busy days tomorrow. Will you call me tomorrow night from Columbus?"

"It will probably be late but I will."

Chase kissed her again, then went to his car and drove home. It was nine forty-five and the phone was ringing as he was unlocking the front door. He hurriedly opened the door and answered the phone.

"This is Chase."

"Hello Chase."

It was Riggins on the other end.

"Hi, Taylor. You're calling awfully late."

"I called earlier but you weren't in. Where have you been tonight?

"I was out with a friend for dinner."

"And you didn't get laid?"

"I beg your pardon?"

"Oh nothing, I'm only kidding," Riggins said with a slight slur.

"So did you need something?"

"I was just sitting here this evening and wondering if you've got any good stories coming up."

"I'm making some preliminary calls on a few things."

"You really need to be more aggressive, Chase," Riggins said, his voice growing a bit louder. "I want to see more depth to your stories. You need to set the standard in the sports department."

"Well Taylor, I am a sports columnist. I'm not an investigative reporter."

"I don't give a shit what you are or who you think you are. You need more meat to your stories."

"Is everything okay?"

"I'm fine. I just want the staff to start thinking hard-edge stories. And for you, some hard-edge columns."

"I'll certainly make an effort to get more hard-edge in my writing," Chase said, wanting to end the conversation.

"I'll be watching your stuff in the coming weeks."

"Is there anything else, Taylor?"

"No."

"Good night then."

Riggins hung up the phone without saying another word. Chase looked at the receiver for a few seconds, shook his head in disbelief, and put it down. He went to the refrigerator and took out a soft drink. There was a knock on his front door. He wasn't sure if he should answer it or not but after a few seconds walked over and opened it.

"I know it's late but I hope you don't mind me dropping by," Bernie said as she stepped inside the front foyer.

"That's okay," he said. "Can I get you something to drink?"

"I'll take a cola," she said while following him to the kitchen. She sat down at the kitchen table as he took out a can and handed it to her.

"So what's up with you this evening?"

"I think I'm going nuts," she said as tears welled in her eyes. "I'm not making any progress on it and Riggins is bothering me all the time. And now some of the reporters won't speak to me because they think I'm a spy or something."

"I don't envy you. I know it has to be difficult."

"I don't know what to do anymore."

"Have you talked to Victoria Johnson? Any of the neighbors?"

"I interviewed a few of the neighbors but they don't know anything. I haven't been able to reach Mrs. Johnson. I think she's tired of it all and wants to get it over with."

"How about the police?"

"I haven't gotten much from them either," Bernie said with a flustered look. "They're still investigating and that's about all they tell me. And then Taylor says I should get on them more about what they've found. I can't make the police tell me things."

"Tell them you need some assistance because an editor is pressuring you. They may give you some tidbits or feed you some info that they want to see in the paper."

"I just don't know how to go about doing it. I've never done this before."

"Just pester them."

"I'll see what I can do."

"How is everything else with you?" Chase asked after he finished his soft drink.

"Nothing much else. My life is miserable and boring," she said with a big sigh.

"You need to get out and do something."

"By myself?"

"You can find someone."

"Who?"

"How about Conner?"

"He's okay but he so wrapped up in photography. That's all he wants to do. And when we are together, he only wants to know about what I'm working on."

"There's no one at city hall or the other places you cover?"

"To be honest, I don't want to be around those people on a social basis."

"Then you need to go someplace where you can meet people."

"Where?"

"I don't know," Chase said. "How about church?"

"Church?"

"What's wrong with that?"

"Those people are too goody-goody."

"Then join a club or something at the library."

"Why don't you show any interest in me?"

"I do," Chase said. "I think we're good friends."

"Yeah," she said with a frown. "Only friends."

"What's wrong with that?

"Oh nothing."

Chase looked over at the clock on the microwave and it was almost eleven. She noticed where he was looking and stood up.

"Oh Chase, I'm sorry. I didn't realize it was this late."

"That's okay," he said with a caring smile.

"I'll take your advice on the story. I'll bug the crap out of the police," she said with a laugh.

Chase walked her to the front door. She turned around and gave him a hug and soft kiss on the neck. He held her for a few seconds, and gave her a tender squeeze.

"You'll do fine," he said reassuredly. "If you need anything, don't hesitate to ask me."

"Thanks Chase. You're a good friend."

Nineteen

"Do you have anything new in the Johnson case?" Bernie asked Slone as she sat at her gray, metal desk in the police station.

"Not really," Slone said with a shrug. "We're at kind of a standstill right now. We're talking to neighbors and people at the newspaper but we haven't come up with much. We hope to get a break soon."

"Anything from the lab?

"Oh, I forgot. It appears there may have been a scant amount of alcohol in Mr. Johnson's blood but nothing to suggest that he was intoxicated on the night of his death."

"When did you find that out?"

"That came back late yesterday afternoon."

"Can I quote you on the blood-alcohol report?"

"Certainly," Slone said.

"How important is that?"

"This is only speculation but I would say that Mr. Johnson's fall wasn't because of intoxication. That's not to say he didn't trip over something and strike his head against the table."

"Thanks Marcia," Bernie said. "You've been a big help. One of my editors has been on my back about this, so now I can go back to the office with something to report."

Slone smiled and picked up her coffee cup and took a long sip.

"We're not holding anything back from you," she said. "We want to get to the bottom of this as quickly as we can."

Bernie stood up and closed her notepad.

"I've got to go back to the office and give my daily report to Mr. Riggins," she said with a chuckle.

"Taylor Riggins is the one who you report to on this?"

"Yeah. Every day I have to give him a status report. I run everything by him."

"That's interesting. Is that the way a newspaper normally operates?"

"Somewhat," Bernie said. "Editors want to keep apprised of things on sensitive stories."

"So this is considered sensitive?"

"I guess so since it involved one of our reporters."

"Oh, I see. It's not your regular crime?"

"It might be for some of our readers but everyone in the newsroom is interested in it because they knew Brett," Bernie said. "Well, I need to be going. I'll try to call later this afternoon and see if there's anything new."

"I can't promise anything, but you can call Gene or me for any updates."

As Bernie left the office, a smile beamed on her pudgy face and there was a bounce in her walk. Ten minutes later she pulled her car into the newspaper parking lot and headed to the newsroom.

Bernie walked to Riggins's office but he wasn't in. She went on to her desk and typed a short note to him about the blood-alcohol test.

"How's it going today?"

"Oh, hi, Conner," she said looking up at Conner and smiling. "I'm doing well. How about you?

"I've got an assignment to go to a little later this morning. I should be off at a decent hour today. Would you like to go out to eat after work?"

"Sure," she said. "But can you give me a call around four-thirty or so to make sure that I'll be out of here at a decent hour?"

"No problem," he said. "How are things going with the Johnson story?"

"It hasn't been easy but I got some news this morning from the police."

"What was that?"

"Don't tell anyone but Brett had only a trace of alcohol in his system."

"Is that so?"

"Well, he wasn't drunk when he fell."

"They think something else happened?"

"It still could have been an accident."

"That's good news. I hope you start getting some more good leads like that."

"Me, too," she said with a grin. "It would keep Riggins off my butt."

"You know that I'll let you know if I hear anything."

"I appreciate that," she said. "I think I'm going to drive over to Johnson's house and see if his wife or any neighbors are around since Riggins isn't here this morning."

"I saw him earlier but he left after the news meeting."

Bernie picked up her purse and shouted to an assistant city editor that she was going over to Johnson's house and would be back in the afternoon. Several heads turned in the newsroom toward her. "Sorry," she said meekly.

As she drove through the Johnson's neighborhood, there was hardly any traffic and very few people to be seen. School was in session and most of the houses appeared empty. As she came closer to Johnson's house, she saw a green sedan in the driveway, parked behind the Johnson's red van. She slowed down and decided against stopping. The front living room curtain was open but the sun's glare on the picture window prevented her from seeing anything inside. She drove to the next intersection and turned around, again driving slowly past the house. This time the front door began to open and she tapped on the accelerator.

Bernie, her heart racing, drove several blocks and pulled into a vacant parking lot. She could see the green sedan back out of the driveway, but instead of going in her direction, went the opposite way.

She waited a few minutes and drove to the Johnson's house and parked in the driveway. She went to the front door and knocked and Victoria Johnson answered a few seconds later.

"Hello Mrs. Johnson. I'm Bernadette Robbins from the newspaper."

"Yes," she said flatly. "I've been expecting you."

"Do you mind if I ask you a few questions?"

"I'm really in a hurry now," she said. "I have a doctor's appointment and I'm running a little late."

"Uh, it would only take a few minutes."

"Five minutes," Victoria said impatiently as she opened the door.

Bernie took a notepad and a pen out of her oversized purse.

"Mrs. Johnson, the police told me this morning that your husband's blood-alcohol content was very low."

"Really?"

"Yes, ma'am," Bernie said. "They don't believe he was intoxicated."

"I don't know what to say," she said a bit flustered.

"I was wondering if you had any idea about what happened."

"Ms. Robbins..."

"You can call me Bernie."

"Uh, Bernie, I've been through all of this with the police. I wasn't home when it happened and I don't know. I wish I could be of more help."

"I know this must be difficult for you. It's difficult for me because I knew Brett."

"I do need to be going, Bernie," Victoria said, glancing at her watch. "Is there anything else?"

"Do you mind if I get back with you on occasion?"

"All I ask is that you don't ask questions in front of the children. As you can imagine, it has been very hard on them."

"I understand," Bernie said as she got up. "I'll keep that in mind."

"I'm sorry I can't be of much help now but I do have to go."

~ * ~

Conner and Bernie met at Fellini's Italian restaurant after work. She was already seated at a table when he arrived. He spotted her on the left side, already sipping on a glass of white wine.

"Hi," he said. "You look lovely tonight."

Bernie blushed and gazed down at her low-cut yellow spring dress. She looked up and smiled.

"This is an old dress," she said. "I don't wear it that often."

"Well, you should," he said as he sat down across from her. "I wish I had worn a tie or something now."

"You look just fine," she said. "I hope you don't mind me ordering a glass a wine. I got here about fifteen minutes ago."

"No problem," he said. "I could use a glass of wine as well."

A waiter came to their table and Conner ordered a bottle of the wine she was drinking. The waiter returned two minutes later and poured him a glass and refilled Bernie's. He took their orders for baked spaghetti.

"So how was your day?" Bernie asked.

"I finished my stuff around five-thirty or so," he said. "It was a routine shoot at one of the elementary schools. Some students were receiving some kind of governor's award for academic achievement. So how was your day?"

"It was kind of bizarre," Bernie said. "I drove over to Victoria Johnson's house and there was a green sedan in the driveway."

"Jordan Means drives a green Buick."

"Really? I thought the car looked familiar so I didn't stop."

"So you don't know if it was him or not"

"Well, I tried to play spy and parked my car a few blocks away but when the car left her house, it went in the opposite direction."

"Did you go see Mrs. Johnson?"

"I spoke with her for a few minutes. I didn't get much out of her. She had a doctor's appointment so was in a hurry to leave."

"Was she cooperative?"

"I guess so. She said I could get back with her."

"So what did Taylor think about your report today?"

"I have no idea," Bernie said after drinking some wine. "I went back to the office and didn't see him. I don't think he was in all day."

"That was good for you."

"No kidding. He really makes my skin crawl anymore. I can't stand to be around him."

"That's the word around the newsroom. He's really alienated himself from the rest of the staff. Even the other editors aren't that friendly with him because he's been sticking his nose in their business."

"That's something I don't understand. I thought he was only supposed to be leading investigative efforts."

"He seems to think that every story in every department should be investigative. We may have to rename the paper the *Investigative Journal*," Conner said with a laugh. "But I want you to know that you can always count on me if you have any problems. I may not be able to do a lot but I can be a sounding board for you.'

"I appreciate that, Conner. It's always nice to be able to bounce things off people, especially this story since I feel so much in the dark."

Their meals arrived and they chatted about other things in between bites of food and sips of wine. They finished the bottle of wine and were there for nearly two hours as they lost track of time. Bernie looked at her watch and noticed it was past nine o'clock.

"Oh, I really need to be going," she said. "I've got work in the morning."

"I've enjoyed our evening," Conner said.

"Me, too," she said sweetly.

"We need to do this again."

"I hope we can."

The waiter brought over the check and Conner picked it up.

"You don't need to do that," Bernie said. "Let me pay half of it."

"How about we just take turns? I'll pay this time and you can do it next time."

"I guess that sounds fair," she said. "But I really don't mind going Dutch. Please don't think it's an assault on your manhood."

"I'm past that," Conner said with a lighthearted wink.

Conner paid with a credit card and they left. They stood in the restaurant parking lot under the unseasonably warm spring sky filled with stars and a three-quarter moon.

"It is beautiful out here tonight," Bernie said as a shooting star streaked across the southern sky. "It almost makes you not want to go home."

"We can go to a few more places if you like," Conner said.

"I'd love to and probably would if this was a weekend night."

Conner put his arm around her and was poised to kiss her on the mouth but she turned her head and his lips pressed hard against her cheek. She put her arms around him and gave him a quick hug, then let go and stepped back.

"I had a nice time," she said with a quick smile. "I need to be going home."

Conner paused for a moment. "I hope to see you at work tomorrow."

Bernie arrived home twenty minutes later. She was slightly lightheaded from the wine. She put on a light knee-length gown and went to the living room, where she sat down on the couch and curled her legs underneath her and picked up a women's magazine. Moments later, the phone rang.

"Oh, hi, Chase," she said brightly. "This is a surprise."

"I had tried to call earlier but you weren't home," he said. "I was wondering how your day went."

"It was great," she said. "I got some information from the police and even talked to Victoria Johnson. I believe I'm making some headway now."

"I'm glad," he said.

"So what are you doing tonight?"

"I've been watching TV and reading. How about you?"

"Conner and I went out to dinner at Fellini's"

"Did you have a nice time?"

"It was very relaxing and enjoyable."

"I like Conner," Chase said. "He's a nice guy."

"I like him too. He's easy to talk to."

"So what have you got planned tomorrow?"

"I'll just be making more calls and trying to talk to some of the people in Johnson's neighborhood."

"You might even check some of the stories Brett was involved in the past month and talk to some of those people. Perhaps they could give you some help."

"That's a great idea. Thanks Chase."

"I guess I need to be getting off here now. It's getting late."

"I really appreciate you calling," she said.

Twenty

Chase sat at his desk, pecking out a column on his computer. He was totally absorbed in what he was doing and completely oblivious to what was going on around him. It was late afternoon and the newsroom was filling up as copy editors were laying out the pages and reporters were working on their stories for the next day's paper.

Chase finished his column and gave it a once-over before sending it to the copy desk, then he leaned back in his chair and observed the activity in the newsroom. There was a humming drone from one end of the newsroom to the other.

"Hi, Chase," came a soft voice from his rear.

Chase rose up erect in his chair, turned around and saw Angela approaching his desk.

"Hello Angela," he said. "How are you?"

"I'm doing fine. I just finished a story and was getting ready to go home."

"I'll be heading out as well in a few minutes."

"Oh really? Any plans?"

"I'll probably go home and relax," he said with a smile.

"Are you expecting any company?"

"Not to my knowledge. It should be a quiet evening at my humble abode."

"I need to be going," she said. "I hope you have a nice evening. Bye."

"Take care," he said as he watched her walk toward the city desk. He couldn't help but stare for a few seconds as she seemingly glided away with little or no motion in her hips.

"You'd better be careful."

Chase looked to his side. Green was standing there shaking his head and his hands on his hips.

Chase blushed lightly. "It doesn't hurt to look once in awhile, does it?"

"As they say, look all you want but don't touch, especially her. She's trouble and you know it."

"That's what I've been told."

"Believe everything you've heard, Chase. She's trouble. Make that double-trouble."

"Thanks for the advice, Cole, but to be honest, I have no interest in her."

"I know you don't. I'm just giving you a hard time," Green said with a soft chuckle.

"I guess I need to be heading home," Chase said as he neatly stacked some papers on his desk. "My column is finished and in the hands of our crack copy desk."

"I'll probably be around for another hour or so to make sure everything is moving along smoothly."

"I hope you don't have to stay too late," Chase said as he stood up and pushed his chair under the desk.

"You have a nice evening," Green said as he walked away toward the copy desk.

Chase stopped at a Chinese carryout restaurant on the way home. As he sat in the kitchen eating his food and glancing through a magazine, the doorbell rang. When he opened the front door, Angela was standing on the porch.

"Oh, hi, Angela," Chase said. "I didn't expect to see you. Is there something wrong?"

"Do you mind if I come in?"

Chase looked around the outside for a moment and opened the front door.

"Is something the matter?" she asked.

"No," he said a bit flustered. "Come on in. I was eating dinner."

"I'm sorry," she said. "I came at a bad time."

"I'm eating some Chinese. Do you care for any? They always give you more than you can eat."

"That would be nice," she said as he led her to the kitchen. He took out another plate and poured her a soft drink. She dished out some rice and vegetable stir fry on her plate.

"So what brings you over tonight?"

"I left the office and drove around for a little bit and didn't want to go home so I decided to stop by."

"I'm sure you had another reason."

"Not really," she said. "You're a nice guy and easy to talk to."

"Don't you have children?"

"I have two," she said. "They're six and four. Little boys."

"Where are they?"

"At my mom's house. She watches them for me."

"That must be convenient."

"Oh, it is. She loves to keep the boys. I only have to call her and tell her I'll be late and she never complains."

The phone rang and Chase answered it on the second ring.

"Hello Chase," Hannah said. "Are you busy tonight?"

"Not really," he said.

"Did you buy a red sports car?"

"Huh?"

"I drove by on the way home from work and saw a red sports car in your driveway."

"A friend from the newsroom dropped by."

"Do I know him?"

"No," he said.

Angela could hear his comments and smiled coyly as she watched him lean against the wall.

"I was hoping to see you but I guess we can do it another night."

"I can come over a little later if you'd like."

"No, that's okay. I need to get to bed early. I've got a busy day ahead of me tomorrow."

"Let's try to do something."

"I'll give you a call tomorrow," she said. "Bye."

"Good night," Chase said as he hung up the phone.

"Who was that?" Angela asked.

"A friend of mine," Chase said as he returned to the table.

"Woman?"

"Yes."

"I guess I should have called instead of dropping by unannounced."

"That's okay. Others do it as well."

"Women?"

"Men and women."

"You must be a popular guy."

"I wouldn't say that. Just friends of mine."

"I'd like to be your friend."

"You would?" Chase said as a silly smile crossed his face. He ran his fingers through his short brown hair.

"You don't want another friend?"

"We can be friends," he said.

Angela got up from the table and Chase immediately stood and picked up the dirty dishes and put them in the sink. She walked over next to him, slightly pressing her breasts against him. He moved away slightly.

"Is something the matter?" she cooed softly.

"I just need to put this stuff away."

"Can't that wait?"

"What time do you have to pick up your kids?"

"Anytime I please."

Chase cleared his throat and began wiping off the kitchen table. He took long, slow sweeping motions as he tried to gather his thoughts. "That's convenient," he muttered.

"I can spend the night if you want me to."

"Huh?"

"I said I can stay overnight."

"I don't think that's very advisable. We hardly know each other."

"But we could learn a lot about each other if I spent the night."

"You know what I mean."

Angela gave him a disdainful look and shook her head.

"If you don't want me to then I'd better go," she said.

"I do have a few things to do this evening before going to bed."

"Work things?"

"Yep," Chase said.

"I don't want to keep you from them," she said as she went to the front door. "Thanks again for the dinner. We have to do it again soon. Real soon."

"Just give me some advance notice."

Angela opened the front door, smiled seductively, and left.

Chase shook his head in disbelief as he walked over and locked the door behind her. He pulled back the curtain slightly and watched get into her sports car and drive away. Chase picked up the telephone and called Hannah's house to tell her about Angela's visit but there was no an answer.

~ * ~

A gentle rain awakened Chase the next morning with a rhythmic tapping on the window. He glanced sleepy-eyed at the clock and noticed he had overslept by nearly an hour. He groaned and lay in bed for another ten minutes before mounting enough energy to lift off the covers and finally get up. After putting on a pot of coffee in the kitchen, Chase took a hot shower and felt somewhat re-energized to face a new day.

Sitting at the kitchen table and sipping on coffee he thought about Angela's visit. He felt badly that he wasn't forthcoming to Hannah but would tell her later on in the day what happened. After finishing the coffee, he got up and went to the bedroom to dress. As he was about to step out the front door, Angela pulled into the driveway.

"Good morning," she said cheerfully as she walked up to his house holding a white sack. "I was hoping you'd still be here. I was in the neighborhood and bought some pastries."

Chase forced a smile and opened the door wider so she could come into the house.

"I just turned off the coffee but it should still be warm," he said.

"We can put it in the microwave," she said as she made her way to the kitchen as he remained standing at the door almost in disbelief of seeing her again. "I hope you like Bavarian crèmes."

Chase closed the door and followed her to the kitchen. "They're fine. I'm not much of a doughnut eater."

"I thought all newspapermen liked doughnuts. That's why most of them are so out of shape."

"Do I look out of shape?" he asked, looking down at his stomach.

"I said most newspapermen," she said. "You're not in that group. You look rather fit."

"Thank you," he said sardonically.

Angela opened the cabinet doors until she found the one that contained coffee cups. She took down two, filled them with coffee and put them in the microwave for one minute. The coffee was steaming hot when she took them out and placed them on the table.

"So do you have a busy day planned?" she asked.

"I was getting ready to go into the office," he said. "I'm not really sure what's on the agenda at this point. How about you?"

"I'm supposed to meet with Taylor Riggins later this morning about an investigative assignment," she said. "I'm sorta looking forward to it. It should be fun."

"Fun?"

"Oh yes," she said cheerfully. "Even though he can be an ass, I'm sure I can learn a lot from him."

"I'm sure you can," Chase said, trying to keep a straight face.

"You know, we're really fortunate to have someone of Taylor's ability at the newspaper. He can make us become a better newspaper because of his experience. He could have gone to practically any newspaper in the country after he won that award but decided to stay with us."

"I never thought of it that way," Chase said, and then took a bite from the pastry.

"Don't you and Taylor go a long ways back?"

"We've known each other for several years."

"It's sad about him and his wife."

"What's that?" Chase asked with a puzzled look.

"They're getting a divorce. I thought everyone knew that."

"That's news to me."

"They've been married for nearly twenty years, I think, and several children."

"I believe they have three kids."

"I guess that shows what this business can do to a family."

"I suppose so."

"How come you've never been married?"

"How do you know that?"

"I've been asking around," Angela said with a wink.

"Oh really," he said. "I've been too busy to settle down."

"Don't you have a girlfriend?"

"What do you think?"

"Uh, I've heard you've been dating a woman for several years."

"You heard right."

"Is she the jealous type?"

"I don't believe so."

"So she doesn't mind women flirting with you?"

"I didn't say that."

"That's interesting. I know I'd be a jealous if you were my man and women were flirting with you."

"So if I may ask, why did you come over this morning? I know it couldn't have been to know about my private life."

"Like I said, I was just in the area and thought you wouldn't mind. I hope you don't."

"It's okay but I wish you would call or give me some notice beforehand. I may not have been here."

"I'll try to remember that."

Chase breathed a sigh of relief when Angela walked out of the front door. *No more visits! Please!*

Twenty-one

Chase sensed a buzz in the newsroom. There seemed to be more activity and noise as people were moving back and forth from desks.

"What in the world is going on?" he asked Charlie Thomas, a student intern.

"I'm not really sure, Mr. Elliott," he said. "Mr. Riggins is back this morning. I've heard there've been some changes but I'm probably the last person to know about those things."

Chase walked to the middle of the newsroom and saw Bernie sitting at her desk and went over to her.

"Hey Bern," he said.

"Hi, Chase," she said glumly.

"What's the matter?"

"They've promoted Taylor Riggins to managing editor."

"Damn," he said. "What happened to Ed Rogers?"

"We're really not sure if he got pushed aside, fired or demoted. He hasn't been in this morning."

"How about Taylor? Is he here?"

"Jordan made the announcement about twenty minutes ago with Taylor at his side. I guess they're in a meeting now."

"Did they give any explanation?"

"They said they wanted a new direction in the newsroom with more hard-edged stories."

"This is such a lovely place to work," Chase said, shaking his head and returning to his desk. "I mean a hard-edged place to work."

"Hey Chase, can you come to my office in a few minutes?" Green asked.

"I'll be right there."

As Green was talking to another sports writer, Chase sorted through some of the mail on his desk. He opened a handwritten envelope. On a small sheet of white paper the note read: "TR is on a rampage. Watch your back. Don't sit and watch. Do something."

Chase stared at the note for a few seconds until Green beckoned. "Ready?"

Chase followed Green into his office and shut the door behind him. Green sat down in his high-back swivel chair and leaned back.

"Chase, I need for you to do some hard-hitting pieces," he said. "Some folks around here are saying that you're too soft."

"Some folks?"

"Well..."

"Taylor Riggins?"

"Yes," Green said as he leaned forward and crossed his arms across the desk. "He doesn't think you're going after people hard enough."

"Well Cole, as a columnist I thought the newspaper wanted my observations and opinions on sporting events."

"It used to be that way."

"Has he made similar demands on other members of the staff?"

"No one in particular."

"I'm the only person he's specifically mentioned?"

"Yes, but I wouldn't read too much into that. You're the most visible person on the staff so it's natural that you would be mentioned. You know he'd like the entire department to go after more meaty stories."

"I'll see what I can do," Chase said.

"I'd like for you to get something out soon so it will take some of the heat off."

"Has he been pressuring you?"

"He's been pressuring everybody."

"I'll try to get something to you in the next day or so."

"Chase, I just want to let you know that I don't have a problem with your work. I've been very pleased with your performance. I'm sure some of these things will pass after he gets settled into the job. You know there's always a difficult transition when there's change around here."

"I understand Cole," Chase said with a smile. "I don't take it personally. I set the highest standards for myself so anything he does really doesn't bother me. The only thing is that I know him too well."

"We've all known him for a long time so it's kind of unsettling to see him in such a different light. I would have never guessed it."

"There are some reasons for it, I'm sure."

"All I can say is stay on top of things and don't be a target. I can only do so much to protect my staff."

"I guess I'd better get back to work," Chase said as he stood up. "I appreciate you being up front with me."

"Haven't I always been, with you and the others?"

"Always."

Chase returned to his desk and picked up the note and read it again. He wondered who could be sending him the notes. He found himself getting a bit angry at the way Riggins was going after him. He knew it was personal.

Chase left the sports department and drove to the campus. He interviewed several officials about funding for minor sports. He also talked to the coaches and several players to get their opinions on what was happening in their programs. He spent the rest of the afternoon on the phone with the conference and national organizations to get statistics to compare and contrast the university's programs.

He finished late in the afternoon and decided to go on home. As he approached his house, he noticed Angela's red sports car in his driveway. She was standing at the front door of the house, her back to him. He stopped his car and backed up out of her sight and waited. A minute later, she backed out of the driveway and drove away. Chase decided that it wasn't safe to go home so he went to the supermarket and bought a few groceries.

After he got home and put the groceries away, he put a frozen pizza into the oven. The phone rang and he answered on the third ring.

"This is Chase Elliott."

"Mr. Elliott, this is Gene Bennett. I apologize for calling. I hope I haven't interrupted supper or anything."

"I've got a pizza in the oven, so I'm okay right now."

"This will only take a minute or so."

"What do you need?"

"Have you noticed anything suspicious in the newsroom?"

"Not really," Chase said. "We've had some turnover in the newsroom but that's not unusual."

"I understand Mr. Riggins received a big promotion."

"That's correct. You've got good sources," Chase said with a laugh.

"Have you seen any change in his demeanor?"

"I don't see him very often so I can't really say."

"You don't sense anything?"

"I guess he's more assertive and aggressive. I guess that comes with the new job."

"Do you know Mrs. Riggins? I believe her name is Sheila."

"I've known her for about as long as I've known Taylor."

"Good friends?"

"I wouldn't say good friends but I guess we're friends. Why?"

"Just checking some leads. Did you know she had filed for divorce?"

"I just learned that the other day."

"Surprised?"

"I would say so. They've been married for nearly 20 years."

"Has he been fooling around?"

"I have no idea."

"No rumors about it in the newsroom?"

"I haven't heard anything. Like I've told you, I'm usually one of the last to hear about things."

"I appreciate you taking the time to answer my questions."

"I wish I could be of more help."

"Every little bit helps."

"Do you mind if I ask if you're getting any closer to finding out Johnson's death?"

"There's not much to report at this time."

"Please don't hesitate to get back with me because Brett was a friend."

"I'll do that, Mr. Elliott. I hope you have a nice evening. Enjoy your pizza."

"Oh, one other thing," Chase said.

"What is that?"

"I hate to repeat this but I heard that Taylor and Jordan Means weren't exactly upset when Brett died," Chase said, recalling his conversation with Angela. "I heard that Taylor didn't think Brett showed him the proper amount of respect."

"Who told you that?" Bennett asked.

"It's just a rumor I heard floating around the newsroom," Chase said. "I don't ever put much credence into those things but thought I'd pass it on to you. Maybe someone else could verify it to you?"

"I appreciate the information," Bennett said. "Anything else come to mind?"

"That's about it," Chase said.

After hanging up the phone and eating half the pizza, Chase picked up the telephone book and found Riggins's home phone number. He dialed the number, hoping that Sheila would answer.

"Hello," a man's voice answered.

"Is this the Riggins's residence?" Chase asked.

"Is this you, Chase?"

Chase rolled his eyes and slowly shook his head. It was Riggins on the other end.

"Hello Chase" he said. "What are you doing calling here at this hour?"

"Uh, I didn't see you at work and wanted to congratulate you on your promotion."

"Thank you, Chase."

"I wish you the best of luck."

"Anything else?"

"That's all," Chase said. "I'll see you at work."

"Thanks again," Riggins said coldly and hung up the phone. Chase put down the receiver.

"Damn!" Chase said to himself. "I can't believe he answered the phone. Just my luck!"

A few minutes later, his phone rang. He picked it up on the second ring.

"Is it safe to come over?" Hannah asked.

"What do you mean? Of course it is," Chase said. "You are always welcome here."

"I'm about five minutes from your house. Have you eaten supper?"

"I've got about half of a pizza that I can put in the microwave."

"I'll see you in a few minutes."

Chase put down the phone and began to tidy up the living room, stacking magazines on the coffee table and grabbing old newspapers to toss in the trash can. He went back to the bedroom and quickly made the bed and put soiled clothes in the hamper. Before he knew it, Hannah was at the front door ringing the doorbell.

"Hi, there," he said as he opened the door. He kissed her gently on the cheek as she stepped into the house.

Hannah walked over to the couch and sat down. She put her head back on the cushion and closed her eyes for a few seconds.

"Rough day at work?" Chase asked.

"Just a long day," she said. "Two meetings and some reports to take care of. My eyes are tired and my neck is stiff. And I've got a slight headache."

Chase walked around the back of the couch and began massaging her neck and shoulders.

"Oh, that feels good," she said softly. "Don't ever stop."

"I'll do my best but I won't be able to do it forever," he said with a light chuckle.

"So you had no company tonight?"

"What's that suppose to mean?"

"Where's the little red sports car?"

"I guess it's with the owner."

"Who is she?"

"She?"

"Now Chase, don't go around in circles with me. You know I don't like that."

"It was Angela Cook from the newspaper."

"Why do I know her name?"

"She had the affair with Brett Johnson."

"That's right."

"She was asking me about the case."

"Why you?"

"Because Brett and I were friends, I would assume."

"So she decided to spend the night?"

"What?" Chase's hands left her shoulders and he walked around and sat on the couch.

"That little red sports car was in your driveway the next morning."

"She dropped by unannounced the next morning with some pastries."

"Am I supposed to believe that?"

"Do I sense some jealousy this evening?"

"Chase, what am I to think?" Hannah said, turning her head toward Chase. "Yes, there may be a degree of jealousy. What would you think if you saw the same car in my driveway one evening and the next morning?"

"I suppose you're right."

"I am right" she said sternly. "There's no suppose about it."

"I wish you'd stopped by."

"That would have been great," she said, rolling her eyes.

"She would have left if you had showed up."

"If you say so."

"So what are your plans this evening?"

"Nothing really."

"Oh, you just wanted to confront me," he said with a boyish grin.

"Well, perhaps," she said.

Chase lifted her chin with his hand and gently kissed her firm mouth.

"Where is your car?"

"In your driveway. Why?"

"Why don't you leave it parked there all night?"

"Oh, you would like that?" she asked coyly.

"Do you have any plans for the morning?"

"I've got a late meeting in the morning."

"Do you think you can spend the night?"

"I think I can handle that."

Chase put his arm around her and she cuddled next to him. She tilted her head and he kissed her long and passionately. After their mouths parted, she tucked her head under his chin and closed her eyes. They sat quietly for a few minutes before Chase realized that she had dozed off to sleep. She was finally startled by the ringing of the phone. She sat up and rubbed her eyes.

"We'll let it ring," Chase said.

The phone rang six times before it stopped. It was ten forty-five. Chase wondered who would be calling at that hour but remained on the couch with Hannah in his arms. After a few more minutes, they got up and went to the bedroom. He pulled back the sheets as she put on one of his T-shirts that reached her mid-thigh. She quickly got into bed and pulled up the covers.

"I'll be right back," Chase said as he went to the kitchen. He looked at the caller I.D. and saw that it was Riggins's home number. He was tempted to call back but it was nearly eleven and he wasn't in the mood to spar with Riggins.

Chase turned off the lights in the living room and kitchen and returned to the bedroom. He took off his clothes, turned off the lamp on the nightstand, and slipped under the covers wearing his boxer shorts. Moments later, Hannah turned over and snuggled close to him with her head on his shoulder. He realized there wouldn't be any lovemaking as she drifted off to sleep in his arms.

Before he knew it, he heard some noise coming from the kitchen. Hannah was no longer in bed with him and the clock on the nightstand read five-fifty. He got out of bed and put on the khaki slacks he wore the day before and went into the kitchen.

Hannah was still in the T-shirt as she prepared a pot of coffee.

"Good morning," she said brightly. "I'm sorry for waking you up."

"Oh, that's okay," he said with a sleepy smile. "You're a lovely sight to behold in the morning."

Hannah came over, wrapped her arms around him and kissed him. She rested her head against his chest for a few seconds.

"So what do you want for breakfast?" she asked while taking a step back.

"I guess you would be out of the question," he said.

"Don't be silly," she said, smiling. "You need a good breakfast to start the day. It gives you energy."

"I think your body could jumpstart me."

"Silly man," she said. "You need a good breakfast."

"Okay, I think I'll have a bowl of cereal," he said in mock defeat.

"Are you sure?" she asked. "I can fix some bacon and eggs and toast. How about pancakes?"

"I'm more of a light eater in the morning."

Chase took down a box of multi-grain cereal and a bowl from the cabinet while Hannah got the milk from the refrigerator.

"What other cereal do you have?" she asked.

"There's some toasted oats," he said. "I also have some oatmeal."

"I'll take the toasted oats. Do you have any bananas?"

"Nope."

"Well, I guess I can eat them without bananas."

They sat and ate the cereal and then drank their coffee. The only sounds outside was an occasional car driving by or the barking of a dog.

"Who called last night?" she asked.

"It was Taylor Riggins's number"

"Shouldn't you have called him back?"

"I was with you and this is my time."

"I don't want you getting into trouble with him."

"Don't worry about it."

The clock in the living room chimed seven times. It was beginning to get lighter outside.

"I guess it would be asking too much to go back in bed?" Chase asked.

"Are you still sleepy?" she teased.

"Now what do you think?"

"I wish we could but I've really got to get to my house and get showered and dressed for the meeting."

"I understand," he said, pushing out his lower lip.

"Oh, don't be so sad," she said as reached over and kissed him on the forehead. "Does that make you feel better?"

"Oh, immensely," he said with a wink.

"It's either all or nothing with men," she said.

"Hey, that's not fair. Didn't I let you sleep last night?"

"I'm just teasing, honey."

Chase reached over and kissed her softly on the mouth.

"I really do need to be going." Hannah stood up and carried her bowl and cup to the sink.

"I guess I need to get ready for work as well."

Hannah went back to the bedroom and put on her clothes while Chase turned on the shower in the bathroom.

"I wish you could join me in the shower," he called out.

"Next time, dear," she said. She kissed him again, then headed to the front door. "I'll lock the door behind me. Have a great day."

Hannah noticed a red sports car driving by as she walked to her car. The driver looked straight ahead as Hannah tried to catch of glimpse. She couldn't suppress a smile as the car disappeared down the street.

Chase took a quick shower and shaved. He got dressed, then went to the front door and picked up the newspaper on the porch. It was still early so he went back to the kitchen and poured another cup of coffee and read the newspaper.

Twenty-two

Chase went to the office and made the remaining telephone calls he needed for the story about funding for minor sports. While waiting for some faxes containing statistical information, he headed the cafeteria for a cup of coffee. Bernie came in and sat down with him. Her eyes were red and she forced a smile when he looked at her.

"What's the matter?" Chase asked.

"What do you think?"

"Your crime story?"

"Good guess," she said as she wiped her nose with a paper napkin. "It's impossible. I can't talk to people here about it, the neighbors don't know anything, and the police haven't made much progress. And on top of that, I have to report to a son of a bitch."

"I feel for you."

"He just finished meeting with me," she said, her eyes watering. "He told me he wasn't happy with my work. What does he expect? I may even lose my job over this."

"I think you're going to have to do your own thing," Chase said. "You're going to have to do what you think is right to get the story."

"You mean talking to people in the newsroom?"

"That's what I would do."

"But they may be afraid to be quoted."

"Use them as sources and background and protect their confidentiality like you would anyone else."

"But what if Taylor asks about the information?"

"Just tell him that you're protecting your sources and you'd rather not disclose the names. He should understand that."

"But what if he insists on names?"

"We'll cross that bridge when we get to it."

"I think I'll take your advice and do that," Bernie said, a smile slowly crossing her face. "What have I got to lose?"

"I'll try to help you on it. I'll talk to some of the reporters who knew Brett and see if I can get them to tell you something. And if they don't want to tell you, maybe they'll tell me and I can pass the information on to you."

"Would you do that for me?"

"Of course but we've got to be careful. I don't want either of us getting in trouble over this."

"You can count on me. I won't breathe a word to anybody that you doing this."

Riggins and Means walked into the cafeteria and sat down at one of the rear tables. Riggins caught Chase's eye and nodded. Bernie glanced in Riggins's direction and blushed lightly.

"I need to be going," she said. "I see that Satan has arrived."

"Just be cool," Chase said. "If you get up and leave, he'll suspect something is going on between us."

"You're right," she said. "I'll sit here a little longer. So what have you been up to lately?"

"I'm working on a story about college funding for minor sports. It's one of those hard-edged stories."

Bernie laughed. "I can't wait to read it."

"I hope to write it this afternoon. I just came down here for a break while waiting for some faxes."

"Do you think it's safe for me to leave now?" Bernie asked. "I don't like being in the same room with him."

"It's probably safe to go now."

"I'll see you later then," Bernie said as she stood up. "Have a good day."

After Bernie left the cafeteria, Chase sat for a few more minutes reading the business section of the newspaper. He finished his coffee and got up to leave.

"Chase, can you come over here for a minute?" Riggins asked while motioning with his hand.

Chase dropped his paper cup in the trash receptacle and went to their table.

"I was just wondering how you're coming along on the funding story. Cole told me you've had some interviews."

"I hope to finish it today."

"That's great," Riggins said, glancing at Means with an approving smile. "Our readers will appreciate it."

"Anything else going on?" Means asked Chase.

"Nothing big comes to mind," Chase said.

"Well, we need to think in those terms," Means said. "We have to lead the way in the community."

"No doubt about that," Chase said with a smile.

"Well, I'll let you get back to writing," Riggins said.

Chase nodded at both men and returned to the sports department. The faxes had arrived and were sitting on top of his desk. He perused the numbers and took out a green highlighter to mark significant ones that would be used in his story.

His phone rang and he picked it up.

"This is Sheila Riggins."

"It's nice to hear from you."

"Did you call the house last night?"

"Yes, I did."

"Was there something you wanted?"

"To be honest, I was surprised Taylor answered the phone. I'd heard that you had filed for divorce."

"I have," she said. "He dropped by unexpectedly last night."

"Is there anything I can do to help?"

"Help? Yes, you can tell him to stay away from me."

"What's wrong?"

"Everything is wrong. He's not the same person since he won that damn award. He's drinking more, too. He's unbearable to be around."

"How are the kids taking it?"

"To be honest, they feel the same way."

"Is there anything else?"

"Yes, there's something else," she said. Chase could hear her begin to sob.

"Another woman?"

"I don't know who it is but there is somebody else."

"Sheila, I'll tell you now that I've never seen him with another woman. I've never heard any rumors around the newsroom and you know how reporters love to gossip."

"He hasn't touched me in months."

Chase paused for a few seconds, not sure how much he should inquire about their intimate relationship.

"Are you still there?" Sheila asked.

"I'm sorry, I was just thinking for a moment," Chase said, trying to gather his thoughts.

"I apologize for telling you all this," she said. "It's not your problem."

"We've been friends for a long time, Sheila. I'll do whatever I can to help you."

"I appreciate that, Chase. I've always thought the world of you. You've been a friend to Taylor and me. I hate to drag you in on this."

"Don't worry about that," he said assuredly. "Please feel free to call on me anytime you need to."

"Thanks again, Chase," she said. "Good bye."

"Good bye," Chase said as he hung up the phone and smiled.

"Another one of your interviews?" asked Riggins, who was standing next to Chase's desk.

"The last one," Chase said with a knowing grin. "It's time to start writing."

~ * ~

"There's something funny about this article written by Riggins," Slone said to Bennett in the office.

"Funny? What do you mean by funny?"

"I've tried to make contact with everyone mentioned in the article but have been able to reach only about half of them," she said. "I've tried like crazy to trace some of these people but it's been practically impossible."

"You'd think that some of the people would have records."

"That's what I thought but their names aren't popping up anywhere on any crime checks."

"Have you called Riggins to find out why?"

"Not yet," she said. "I was hoping that I could find someone who would talk."

"Of those people you reached, what did they have to say about the article?" Bennett asked.

"They all seemed to like the article. They thought he was very deserving for the award he received because he apparently dug up some things that had never been written about before."

"What did you think about the article?"

"I must admit that I thought it was very good. He got some very good interviews with some drug users and dealers."

"Do you think he could have changed names to protect them?"

"I suppose that's entirely possible but it never mentioned in the article that names had been changed."

"It does make you wonder why Johnson called him bogus."

"That came to mind as well."

"That the story was bogus?"

"Perhaps."

"Isn't that kind of a stretch?"

"Probably so, I guess," she said with a shrug, "because I thought stories were scrutinized by editors and everyone."

"More calls to make?"

"I'm afraid so," she said. "Maybe I'll call one of the reporters."

"I've talked to Chase Elliott a few times. He seems to have been good friends with the deceased and Taylor Riggins."

"You think it would be safe to call him?"

"I think so."

"I don't want to tip off Riggins."

"That's why I mentioned him."

"I'll do it then."

Slone picked up the telephone and dialed the newspaper's main number and asked for Chase. He answered on the first ring.

"Hello, Mr. Elliott, I'm Marcia Slone of the detective unit. How are you today?"

"Fine, thank you."

"Would you mind if I ask you several questions."

"I don't mind."

"Is this a bad time to talk to you? Would you prefer meeting somewhere or some other time?"

"This is fine. What do you want to ask?"

"Are you familiar with Taylor Riggins's award-winning article?"

"Somewhat."

"Have you heard any comments about it from other reporters?"

"Some liked it," he said.

"And some didn't like it?"

"That's correct."

"Why didn't they like it?"

"Some of it could be attributed to professional jealousy."

"Anything else?"

"I really don't like to spread hearsay."

"It's between us."

"I've heard some people in the newsroom say it wasn't an honest effort."

"How so?"

"I'm really not sure," he said. "I would assume that they question some of the sources in the article but I'm not sure. You would have to ask them."

"I understand that you knew Mr. Johnson well."

"We were friends. He was a good, solid newspaperman."

"I've been told that you and Mr. Riggins are friends as well."

"We've known each other for several years."

"Do you hold him in high regard?"

"I suppose so, for the most part."

"I thank you for answering my questions, Mr. Elliott."

"I don't think I've been much help to you."

"You've been of some assistance. I may be calling you back at a later date."

"That's fine. You can reach me here or at home. I believe Detective Bennett has my home number."

"Thanks again, Mr. Elliott," Slone said and hung up the phone.

"Was he any help?" Bennett asked.

"Not much but he did say that some of the reporters have questioned Riggins's honesty with the story."

"That's something you can pursue then."

"Do you think it's time to see Riggins?"

"Not yet. You may even try his superiors such as the newspaper's editor, Jordan Means."

"How about the woman who is reporting on the story?'

"Who is that?" Bennett asked.

"Bernadette Robbins."

"Oh yeah. You may want to feed her some information and see what happens.

"I feel sorry for her because they won't allow her to talk to reporters."

"That doesn't make sense to me."

As they were talking, Bernie walked into the office. Her pant legs were drenched after being out in a driving rain.

"Please forgive my appearance," she said drearily. "It's raining cats and dogs out there."

"What can we do for you?" Bennett asked.

"I think you know," she said. "Any news on the Johnson case?"

"We've got a few more leads," Slone said. "Nothing much though."

"So what is it?" Bernie asked, her eyes a bit wider.

"It seems like Johnson may have had problems with another reporter so we're looking into that," Bennett said while glancing over at Slone.

"Anything more specific?" Bernie asked with an opened notebook in her hand.

"We can't divulge any names at this point," Bennett said.

"Anything else?"

"Not really," Slone said.

"How about the whisky on Johnson's clothing?"

"We should be getting something on that any day."

"You haven't heard anything from the neighbors?" Bernie asked.

"Not really," Slone said. "Nobody heard a thing that night."

"Should that mean something?" Bernie asked.

"Such as?" Bennett asked.

"That perhaps it wasn't a burglar but someone who may have known Johnson."

"We've considered that," Bennett said. "Do you know of anyone in the newsroom who may have paid a visit to his house?"

"Not really," Bernie said. "I really don't recall him socializing with anyone other than Chase Elliott. And there's Angela Cook, but somehow I can't imagine her being at his house, if you know what I mean."

"Just keep checking with us and we'll let you know if we come up with anything," Bennett said.

"Thanks," Bernie said with a grin. "You know I'll do that."

Twenty-three

Bernie left the police station and drove to Johnson's neighborhood. She parked her car a block from the Johnson's house, got out and walked to some of the adjacent streets. She tried to see if there was a way a person could enter the Johnson house without being seen but it appeared that every angle was unobstructed.

She knocked on some of the doors. No one answered at most of the houses, and of those that did, they had little or nothing to say about Johnson's death. Either they didn't know him very well or that nothing looked suspicious the night he died. Bernie knocked on Johnson's door. She heard footsteps inside and about thirty seconds later Victoria opened the door. She was still in her bathrobe and clung to the top of it with her slender hands.

"I apologize for dropping by without calling you first," Bernie said. "I'm still covering the story and I've run in to so many dead-ends, I mean, empty leads."

"Please come in, Bernie," Victoria said as she opened the door. "Forgive my appearance. I've been sorting through lots of Brett's things."

Victoria led her to the kitchen and offered her a cup of coffee. Bernie declined but Victoria poured herself a cup and they sat down at the kitchen table.

"Have you found anything interesting?" Bernie asked.

"Not really. He didn't keep much."

"Have you been down to the office and gone through his desk?"

"The police looked through his desk and someone from the newspaper dropped off his belongings last week. There wasn't much."

"I've talked to several of your neighbors."

"What did they have to say? We don't have many friends around here"

"Actually, they didn't offer much of anything."

"Can you believe we've lived here twelve years and know only about five people? Isn't that ridiculous? Brett wasn't one to get out and know people because he was always afraid that it would lead to some kind of conflict of interest. Other than Chase and a few people at the newspaper, we didn't have any close friends. It's kind of sad, isn't it?"

"You're probably right," Bernie said with a frown. "I must admit that my life is pretty much the same way."

"Well Bernie, you should change then because life is too short. You're only robbing yourself of a full life. I know that if I ever remarry, it won't be to a newspaperman."

Bernie smiled.

"Did Brett do anything unusual in the days leading up to his death?"

"I've gone over that in my mind many times and I can't come up with a thing," Victoria said. "He seemed a bit distracted but I thought that was because of that hussy he had been seeing."

"Angela Cook?"

"Yes, dear, that's the one. The only one. I don't think he ever realized so many people knew about it or suspected something going on."

"And he never mentioned anything about work?"

"Only that he thought Taylor Riggins was a fraud."

"Did he say why?"

"He never did. When his name ever came up, he would just laugh and shake his head."

"Did Mr. Riggins ever come over here?"

"Actually, he came over the other day," Victoria said. "He was offering his condolences. Would you believe that we used to socialize with Taylor and Sheila Riggins when we were younger? We kind of grew apart after we started having babies."

"Did Brett ever mention others?"

"Just the usual grumbling about stories he had to cover."

"He never said anything about sources?"

"He was always very close-mouthed about those things. I really never knew what he was working on until I saw something he'd been working on in the paper. For the most part, he left his work at the office."

"Except when it came to Riggins?"

"And I guess you could add Angela Cook," Victoria said sadly.

~ * ~

Chase dropped by Pappy's after work and noticed several reporters sitting in one of the booths. He ordered a draft beer and walked over to their table.

"How's it going, Chase?" James Hernandez asked. "Care to join us?"

"I'm doing well," Chase said as he sat next to Hernandez. Simpson and Richardson sat across from them, and they nodded and said "Hi."

"We're just jawing about work," Richardson said.

"Are you having problems?" Chase asked before taking a sip from the mug.

"Isn't everybody having problems there anymore?" Simpson said. "It's suffocating the way things have changed in the past month or so."

"I assume you're talking about Riggins," Chase said. "I've heard some complaints."

"I don't know a person at the paper that can stand the guy anymore," Hernandez said. "He wasn't exactly 'Mr. Personality' before he got the promotion and it has certainly gone to his head."

"I guess I don't deal with him that much," Chase said. "Or at least as much as the news desk."

"Maybe we should get transfers to sports," Richardson said with a laugh.

"That's not to say he hasn't said anything to the sports-writers," Chase said. "He's hammering the hard-edge stuff."

"That's his code word now," Richardson said. "You would think he invented investigative journalism. In all my years here, the drug story was the only big investigative piece he ever wrote."

"And there are some suspicions about that," Hernandez said.

"How so?" Chase asked, hoping to hear some other explanations.

"I guess it's a question on how reliable his sources were in the story," Simpson said. "Some people believe the article is part fiction."

"Of course you guys know that Bernie is working up a story on Brett's death," Chase said. "Can any of you give her some assistance? Riggins has told her she can't talk to any of the staff."

"I've heard that," Hernandez said. "That's really unbelievable. Isn't this supposed to be a free press?"

"Most people in the newsroom think it's a joke that Taylor put her on the story," Simpson said. "She doesn't have any background in that."

"Regardless of her background, she's been stonewalled at the office in digging up any information," Chase said. "I'd appreciate it if you could do something to help her."

"I'll see what I can do," Hernandez said. "The only problem would be if Riggins found out. He's made it clear to everyone on news side not to talk to her about the story."

"Does Jordan Means know what is going on?" Chase asked.

"He's been behind Riggins on every single decision," Simpson said. "It's the strangest situation I've seen. You'd think they were in bed together."

Chase hailed the barmaid and ordered a round of drinks for everyone.

"I thought you and Riggins were friends," Hernandez said to Chase.

"We used to be," Chase said. "We've gone in separate directions."

"Does he ever mess with you?" Richardson asked.

"To some extent," Chase said. "I don't believe anyone in the newsroom is immune to him."

"Unless it's Angela Cook," Richardson said. "She has a free rein to do about anything she wants to do."

"I wonder why?" Chase asked.

"Rumor had it she was fucking Johnson, now she's supposed to be screwing Means," Richardson said.

"Are you serious?" Chase asked. "I thought he was married, as if that makes any difference."

"I believe he and his wife have recently split," Hernandez said.

"Taylor and his wife are separated as well," Chase said.

"We know that," Simpson said. "We just can't figure out why."

"There's not another woman?" Chase asked.

"Nothing that we've seen or heard," Simpson said. "He spends most of his time at the newspaper. I don't think he has much of a social life. You might say that he's married to the job."

"Guys, I need to be going," Chase said as glanced at his watch and he took the last swallow from the mug.

"Same here," Hernandez said. "The wife is probably wondering where my sorry ass is at."

They laughed as they eased out of the booth. They left the bar together, and after chatting for a few minutes in the parking lot, went to their homes.

Chase arrived at his house twenty minutes later and was greeted by Hannah. She was sitting in her car in the driveway.

"How long have you been here?" Chase asked as he walked up to her.

"About ten minutes," she said. "Where have you been?"

"I stopped at the watering hole and had a few drinks with some of the reporters," he said as they walked to the front door.

"Did you have a good time?" she asked.

"It was okay," he said while unlocking the front door. "You should have called me on my cell phone." Chase opened the door and stepped aside to let her go inside before him."

Chase sat down next to her and put his arm around her and gave her a gentle squeeze. She looked at him and he kissed her softly on the mouth.

"Can we do something this weekend?" she asked quietly.

"Dinner and movie?"

"That would be nice," she said with a smile.

"I have a ballgame on Saturday but I should be able to go out Sunday night."

"That sounds great."

"Have you had dinner tonight?" he asked.

"Not yet."

"How about if I order a pizza?"

"I'd like that."

Chase picked up the phone and ordered a large pizza and breadsticks.

"It'll be forty-five minutes before they deliver it," he said as he sat down next to her again.

"I don't mind," she said. "It will give us some time together."

Chase pulled her closer to him and he held her in his arms and kissed her several times on the mouth. Before they realized it, the doorbell rang. Hannah tugged at her top and softly ran her hand through her hair.

Chase got up and answered the door, expecting to see the pizza-delivery person. Instead, Riggins stood unsmiling.

"I didn't expect to see you," Chase said with a bewildered look.

"Am I catching you at a bad time?" Riggins asked.

"Yes you are," he said. "I've got company."

"Who is it?"

"Well, it's Hannah, if you need to know," Chase said, a bit perturbed.

"I'll check back later," Riggins said. "Do you mind if I call?'

"That's fine. Ten or so?"

"I'll check back then," Riggins said as he turned around and went to his car.

"Who was that?" Hannah asked after Chase closed the door.

"Would you believe Taylor Riggins?"

"What did he want?"

"I have no idea. He's going to call later."

"Do you want me to leave?"

"No, darling. He shouldn't be coming back here anyway."

The doorbell rang again, and this time it was the pizza delivery. Hannah sat out some plates and poured soft drinks and brought it to the living room while Chase opened the container. He turned on the television and they watched a news program while eating.

At ten o'clock Chase waited for the phone to ring. Hannah left at ten-thirty and he still hadn't heard from Riggins.

Twenty-four

Λ steady drizzle began halfway through Chase's drive to work the next morning. Since he was getting to the newspaper earlier than most of the news staff, he was able to park close to the building. He made a quick dash to the entrance. Bernie was standing at the elevator talking to several female reporters. She glanced at Chase and smiled.

They all got on the elevator together and rode it up the newsroom floor. Chase stood quietly while the others talked about stories they were working on. They all knew what Bernie was doing and didn't bring up the topic of Johnson's death.

As they got off the elevator, Bernie stayed with Chase in the lobby.

"What are you doing here so early?" she asked.

"There was nothing to do at home so I decided to come on it and finish up on a few things."

"I wish I had known. We could have met for breakfast somewhere."

"I'll try to remember that next time," he said with a chuckle. "So what are you doing here so early?"

"I have a meeting with Taylor," she said with a shrug.

"Your daily report?"

"I suppose so."

"Has he been satisfied with your progress?"

"I believe so. He hasn't said much lately, one way or the other. He seems preoccupied with other things."

"What does he do when you meet with him?"

"Usually sits there, taking a few notes."

"That's interesting. When will you have a story?"

"I'm not sure. There may not even be a story if I don't come up with anything substantial."

The elevator opened and Riggins stepped out carrying a Styrofoam cup of coffee.

"Good morning," he said, nodding to both of them.

"Hi, Taylor," Chase said. "I waited for your call."

"We'll discuss that later," he said with a curt smile. "Bernie, I'll see you in my office in about fifteen minutes."

"I'll be there," she said.

Riggins turned without saying anything and walked to his office.

"What was that about?" Bernie asked.

"He dropped by my house but I had company. He said he'd call back but he didn't."

"Do you have any idea what he wanted?"

"You never know with him anymore."

"I better get to my desk and get my notes ready for him," Bernie said as she headed toward the newsroom. "I hope you have a great day."

"Same to you," Chase said with a wink. "Good luck."

"I think we both need it."

"Nice piece on the college programs," Green said as Chase entered the sports department. "We're going to run it on Sunday."

"Thanks, Cole," Chase said as he sat down at his desk.

"If we can just have someone doing some in-depth story each week, we'll keep you-know-who off our asses for awhile," Green said with a laugh. "It's as if we don't already have enough to do and being short-staffed."

"That's a newspaper for you. It'll chew you up and spit you out after it's all over with."

"I can't argue with that. I've seen it happen at too many places."

"But you know one thing?"

"What's that?"

"It goes in cycles," Chase said. "One of these days there'll be a change in management and the focus will shift to something else."

"I'm looking forward to that day," Green said with a grin. "I need to take care of some things before the news meeting. I'll see you later."

"Have a good one," Chase said as Green headed back to his office.

Chase got up and went to the mail area and picked up his several envelopes and faxes in his box. He took them back to his desk and sorted through them. He picked out one with a handwritten to him with no return address.

He opened it and there contained a short note:

Dear Mr. Elliott, Don't sit back and do nothing. You're a target.

As usual, it was unsigned. He glanced around the sports department to see if anyone was watching him read the note. Not a soul. His phone rang; it was Riggins.

"Can you come down to my office for a few minutes?" Riggins asked.

"I'll be right there," Chase said. He put down the receiver and walked briskly through the newsroom to Riggins's office. The door was open, but Chase knocked twice on the door frame and Riggins motioned for him to come in.

"Please close the door," Riggins said.

Chase closed the door and sat down on the chair across from Riggins's neat and organized desk.

"What do you need?"

"First of all, I'm sorry I didn't get back with you last night," Riggins said. "Something came up and time slipped away. I didn't want to call you past midnight."

"That's okay," Chase said with a ready smile. "I appreciate it. Not calling after midnight, that is."

"Have you been sticking your nose in the Johnson story?" Riggins asked coldly.

"What do you mean?"

"Exactly what I just asked."

"I wouldn't say I'm sticking my nose in it," Chase said defensively. "Brett was a good friend and I think it's only natural that I would have an interest in it. Don't you agree?"

"You have enough to worry about without helping others."

"I don't understand what you're talking about."

"It's gotten back to me that you're involved in the Johnson story. I want you to stick to sports. If I wanted your help on the story, I would have asked. Understand?"

Chase slowly shook his head. "I think I understand."

"That's all I want," Riggins said viciously. "I don't want to hear from anyone about your involvement."

"Anything else?"

"No," Riggins said while looking at some papers on his desk.

Chase hesitated for a moment, then got up and left the office without saying a word. On the way to his desk he passed Bernie sitting at her desk. She looked up at him with sad, watery eyes as he walked by. He glanced at her without saying a word. Several other reporters stared at him but there was silence. After he left the news side, he could hear faint chatter among the reporters. He knew they were talking about his meeting with Riggins.

When he got back to his desk, he picked up the note and reread it. He put it back in the envelope, folded it and put it in his shirt pocket. *So I'm a target.*

Twenty-five

"Mr. Riggins, I'd like to drop by and see you," Slone said on the telephone. "What time would be convenient for you?"

"I'll have to check my calendar," he said. "I also need to see what's going on at the news desk. Is there something in particular you want to speak to me about?"

"Some things as they pertain to the Johnson case," she said quickly.

"Oh really? What could that be?"

"I'd prefer to discuss it in person than on the telephone," she said. "Would you like me to come to your office or would you like to come down to the station? Or we could meet somewhere else."

"How about the coffee shop a few blocks east of the station? It wouldn't be a distraction as it would in the newsroom. I could be there in the morning at nine. Would that work for you?"

"That's fine," Slone said. "I'll see you at nine."

After putting down the phone, Riggins got up from his desk and went to the restroom. He went to the basin and washed his hands and splashed water on his face. Hernandez was sitting on the toilet in a stall against the wall.

Means came in as Riggins was drying off his face with a paper towel.

"Bad news?" Means asked as he stood at the urinal.

"Nah," Riggins said. "A little eye strain. Looking at computer screens for a prolonged period can dry out your eyes. At least they do mine."

Means walked over to the basin and washed his hands.

"So how's Bernadette coming along with the Johnson story?"

"She really hasn't made much progress. I did learn that she's been encouraged to talk to some of the reporters for background."

Hernandez slowly lifted his legs to where his feet couldn't be seen. He breathed lightly, almost to the point of holding his breath.

"Has she done it?" Means asked.

"Not to my knowledge. I think she knows better."

"Anything going on with the police?"

"Actually, I got a call from a detective a few minutes ago."

"What do they want?"

"I'm going to meet a detective tomorrow morning at nine."

"That's all you know?"

"She wouldn't say what it was about other than having to do with the Johnson case."

"Maybe you can come up with something that Bernie hasn't."

"That shouldn't be too difficult," Riggins said with a chuckle.

"Well, let me know what you hear."

A few seconds later, Riggins and Means left the restroom. Hernandez heard the door close and he slowly planted his feet back on the floor. He breathed a deep sigh of relief. He stood up and peeked out the stall door, making sure they had left. He walked over to the basin and washed his hands.

As he left the restroom, he noticed Means and Riggins standing about fifteen feet from him. Their backs were to him so he quickly returned to the restroom and to the stall where he had been. He sat there for five minutes, until he heard the door open. Looking over the top of the stall, he saw Richardson standing at one of the urinals. Hernandez opened the stall door and went to the basin.

"Hi, Allen," he said. "Did you see anyone outside the restroom when you came in?"

"I can't say that I did," Richardson said. "Waiting for someone?"

"Waiting for someone to leave."

"Who was that?"

"Means and Riggins."

"I didn't see them so I guess the coast is clear."

"Thanks."

"Why don't you want to see them?"

"Ah, nothing," Hernandez said. "I just like to avoid the powers-that-be."

"I can't say I don't blame you anymore," Richardson said as he washed his hands.

"I think we need to help Bernie with her story."

"And get our asses fired?"

"She has the decked stacked against her."

"How do you know?"

"Because I overheard a conversation."

"Between whom?"

"Means and Riggins."

"Are you kidding me?"

"They didn't come out and say it but it was the gist of their conversation."

"And why were you privy to their conversation?"

"Because I was sitting here in the privy while they were talking," Hernandez said with a laugh. "Right over there." He pointed to the stall.

"And they didn't see you?"

"I don't believe so."

"What should we do then?"

"I think we need to nose around the newsroom and other places and see what we can turn up about the case."

"Count me in," Richardson said. "We've just got to be very careful who we talk to. There are too many loose tongues in the newsroom."

"No shit, Sherlock."

~ * ~

Chase sat on the recliner in his living room, his eyes closed as he contemplated what was going on in his life. He almost wished he had told someone about Riggins's story when he first learned about it. He never thought that it would go to this extreme. He was suddenly jarred from his thoughts by the doorbell. It was Angela.

"Good evening," he said as he opened the storm door. "Please come in."

"I hope you don't mind me dropping by unexpectedly and uninvited again," she said inside the house.

"I guess that's okay," he said. "I didn't have any plans."

"Oh, that's good," she said brightly as she headed toward the couch.

"So why the pleasure of your company?"

"Seriously, I was in the neighborhood and saw the light on in your house and decided to stop. I don't have to be home for several hours. My husband is out of town at a conference and my mother has the kids."

"Can I get you anything to drink?"

"I'd love some wine."

"I believe I have some red wine," Chase said.

"Yes, that would be nice."

Chase went to the kitchen and poured a wine glass about three-quarters full and returned to the living room."

"Thank you," she said as he handed her the glass. "Aren't you having any?"

"I don't think so."

"Are you working on any big stories now?"

"I just finished one on funding for minor sports at the university."

"I'm working on one about alleged corruption in the police department."

"Now that's a difficult story. Did you come up with that on your own? I thought you covered the thoroughbred industry?"

"I do but Riggins thought I was the perfect person to do it," she said.

"Why does he think there is corruption with the police?"

"He says there's always corruption because of bad cops."

"I wish you luck with it."

"Thanks," she said after taking a sip of wine. "I'm looking forward to doing it."

"So really what brings you over here?" Chase asked.

"I think you're a nice guy and I just wanted to see you. Is that all right?"

"I guess so but you're a married woman."

She smiled. "Can't a married woman flirt?"

"I suppose so."

"And do you have a problem being friends with a married woman?"

"I have female friends who are married."

"So what's the problem?" she said, shrugging her shoulders and smiling.

"I guess there's not a problem then."

"What would you say if I told you that I found you sexy?"

"I guess I'd be flattered," he said. "But I don't give that stuff much thought."

Angela crossed her legs and looked directly in his eyes. She took the glass of wine and took a slow swallow and put the glass down on the coffee table.

"I can't believe you aren't married," she said. "Several women in the newsroom say the same thing."

"There is a woman I see on a regular basis," he said. "We'll probably end up getting married unless she gets tired of waiting."

"Has she given you a timetable?"

"Not that I know of."

"Are things going well with her?"

"I sure hope so," he said with a boyish grin. "I'd hate to lose her."

Angela picked up the glass and finished the wine. She slowly licked her lips as she put the glass on the table. Her hands dropped below her ample bosom and she heaved a big sigh, causing her breasts to rise and drop slowly. Chase couldn't help watching them. He glanced back up to her face and she smiled coyly.

"How are you and Taylor Riggins getting along?" she asked.

"My, you sure changed the subject quickly."

"I didn't feel I was making any progress. Should I continue?"

"You're a lovely woman but I'm committed to another woman, and please don't take offense, but I don't get involved with married women."

"I could sense that," she said. "That's a shame."

Chase laughed and shook his head.

"As for Riggins, I guess things are going well. Why do you ask?"

"I was just wondering. I know some people are having problems with him."

"Do you hear lots of complaints?"

"Quite a few. They find him very difficult to work with."

"And you don't?"

"I can't say that I do," she said.

"Why is that?"

"Probably because I have friends in high places and he knows that."

"I guess it's good to have those kinds of friends."

"He doesn't bother me at all."

"Does it bother you that he makes life difficult for others?"

"Not really," she said. "They're adults and they should be able to fend for themselves."

"But they don't have friends in high places."

"Don't you think they should then?" she said with a wink.

"Perhaps so but I've always been pretty much of a loner."

Angela stood up and ambled toward the front door. Chase followed her and stood next to her with his hand on the door knob. Before he could react, her mouth was against his and her arms were tightly grasping his shoulders. Her felt her wet tongue enter his mouth. Almost in a state of shock, he finally stepped back from her.

"I've wanted to do that for the longest time," she cooed softly. "I hope you enjoyed it."

Chase cleared his throat and opened the front door. He looked at her momentarily. "Really, you shouldn't have done that. You know how I have someone. And no, I didn't enjoy it."

"It was just a harmless kiss, honey," she said. "It didn't mean a thing."

Chase didn't say anything and opened the storm door. She smiled and stepped onto the porch.

"I'll see you at work," she said with a wink, and then turned and walked to her car.

Chase didn't wait to see her drive off. He closed the door and wiped the back of his hand over his mouth. He walked over to the phone and called Hannah.

"What are you doing tonight?" he asked after she answered.
"Nothing," she said. "Why?"
"How about catching a late movie?"
"I'm game. What's the occasion?"
"Only that I want to be with you."
"Come over any time. I should be dressed by the time you get here."
"You pick out the movie then."
"Are you sure?"
"Believe it or not, I am."
"Even a romance?"
"Especially a romance."

Twenty-six

"Is something the matter?" Hannah asked as they drove to the movie theater.

"I'm fine," he said, glancing at her and smiling. "I just wanted to be with you. "

"Are you sure?"

"Well, there is something."

"What is it, darling," Hannah said with a look of concern.

"Angela Cook kissed me."

"What? Angela Cook kissed you?" Hannah's perplexed look was momentarily frozen on her face. "You're teasing me!"

"She just reached up and kissed me," Chase said. "I don't know why."

"When did she kiss you?"

"At my house, just before I called you," he said. "It was out of the blue."

"And you didn't provoke her."

"Of course not, honey," Chase said a bit irritated by the comment. "I don't care about her. I love you."

Hannah reached over and placed her hand on his shoulder. "That's nice to hear. Thank you for telling me. So she gave no reason for doing it?"

"Other than she just wanted to," Chase said, slowly shaking his head. "That woman has some problems. I'm beginning to understand what Brett must have experienced with her."

"I suppose you'd better be careful when you open the door."

"You bet I will. That woman is nuts. Her moods bounce all over the place."

"Maybe we can have a secret knock," Hannah said with a laugh. "Two regular knocks and three quick knocks."

"That's funny," he said. "I don't think we need to go to that extreme. I can usually sense when you're in the vicinity."

"Really?"

"I feel my temperature rising," he said with a smile.

"Now you're being funny," Hannah said.

"So you've found us a good movie?" Chase said, ready to change the subject.

"It's a romantic comedy with Tom Hanks."

"Well, you can't go wrong with a Tom Hanks movie," Chase said with a nod.

"It starts in about twenty minutes so we've got time to make it there."

"How was your day?"

"It was rather ordinary. I'm thinking about looking for another job."

"Burned out?"

"I hate that phrase," she said with a frown. "Let's just say I want something new and challenging."

"That's fair enough. I get the same way at times."

"Even to the point of wanting to leave the newspaper business?"

"The only thing that keeps me going is the variety of things I get to cover. Other than that, I'd leave in a heartbeat if I could find the right job."

"I'm surprised to hear that. What kind of job would you like to have?"

"I'm really not sure," he said. "That's part of the problem. I don't know what I'm really qualified for."

"There are all kinds of jobs for people with your writing talent," Hannah said.

"And ninety-nine percent of those jobs are boring. If I leave, it will be something out of writing. Much like you, I'd like to have something new and challenging."

"Perhaps we could find something to do together."

"Honey, if you find it, let me know and we'll be partners."

Chase pulled into the parking lot and they sat in his car for several minutes before going to the ticket window. He purchased the tickets and they went inside the lobby. They decided on buttered popcorn and soft drinks and stood in line to buy them.

Coming out of the theater were Conner and Bernie. They noticed Chase and walked over to him.

"How was the movie?" Chase asked. "But don't tell me the ending."

"It was cute," Bernie said. "I think you'll enjoy it."

Chase introduced Hannah to Conner.

"So what have you got planned now?" Chase asked.

"We'll probably go get a pizza or something. Don't forget we have to work tomorrow."

"Don't remind me," Chase said as he moved to the counter and placed his order.

"I guess we need to be going," Bernie said. "Let me know what you think about the movie."

"It was nice meeting you, Hannah," Conner said politely.

"It was nice meeting you as well," she said with a smile.

Hannah carried the large bag of popcorn while Chase held the soft drinks as they walked to the auditorium. He followed her inside and sat down next to her near the middle row of seats.

"You know, Conner really looks familiar," Hannah said as they waited for the movie to start.

"Well, he does get around town a lot since he's a photographer. And he's a big guy so he'd be difficult not to notice."

"Maybe that's the reason."

"He's one of the best shooters on the staff."

The movie started and Chase put his arm around her and she moved closer to him. She dozed off to sleep midway through the movie and was awakened by the closing credits.

"How did you like the movie?" Chase asked with a chuckle. "I mean, what you saw of it."

"Oh, be quiet!" she said with a grin. "I was tired."

"It wasn't a bad movie. You'll have to catch it on DVD some day."

"I'll never hear the end of this, will I?" she said shaking her head.

"I'm just teasing. I've fallen asleep at places."

"So what are we going to do now?"

"We can stop and get a pizza or I can take you home."

"How about if we call in a pizza and take it to my house?"

"Sounds like a plan," Chase said.

Hannah took the cell phone from her purse and called a pizza restaurant she had in her directory. They said they would have the pizza ready by the time they got there.

"I've been thinking more about Conner," she said.

"Did you remember where you saw him?"

"I think it was him."

"Where?"

"Several days ago some of the girls and I went to that new Italian place for lunch and that's where I saw him."

"I guess he didn't see or notice you."

"Probably not," Hannah said. "We were sitting in the corner and he was near the other end with Taylor Riggins."

"Taylor Riggins?"

"Yes, why?"

"No reason," Chase said with furrowed eyebrows. "I'm just surprised to hear that he was with Riggins."

"They're not friends?"

"Not to my knowledge."

"Maybe it was just a business lunch."

"I sure hope it wasn't social," Chase said as he pulled into the pizza place. He left the car running as he went in to pick it up. He came back out carrying a large veggie pizza and handed it to Hannah.

"Are you having problems at work?" Hannah asked as he drove toward her house.

"No," he said. "Why do you ask?"

"You just seem a bit distracted, like something is bothering you. Are you feeling all right?"

"I'm probably a little run down but I'm fine," he said, giving her a tender smile.

"Please take care of yourself," she said.

"Don't worry. I will. I plan to take it easy this weekend."

A few minutes later, Chase pulled into her driveway. He took the pizza and carried it up the walk as she went ahead and unlocked the front door. He placed the pizza on the kitchen table as she took out two soft drinks from the refrigerator and sat down with him.

After they finished eating, he looked at the clock on the stove and saw that it was twelve-ten.

"I should be going," he said. "I didn't realize it was this late."

"Do you have to leave?"

"We both have to work in the morning."

"Can't you go in a little later than usual?"

"Is this an invitation to spend the night?"

"What do you think?" she said seductively.

"I think I can sleep in."

Chase stood up and put the remaining pizza slices in the box and set it in the refrigerator. Hannah cleared off the table and took his hand and led him to the bedroom.

In the faint light filtering through the curtains, they undressed each other, one piece of clothing at a time. Chase pulled her close to him and they kissed long and passionately.

Hannah took several steps to the side of the bed and pulled back the cover and sheets. She lay down and Chase slid in next to her as she cuddled up close to him. Their hands explored each other's bodies. She moaned with delight as they made tender love until they fell asleep in each other's arms.

~ * ~

"I appreciate you taking the time to meet me this morning," Slone said while she and Riggins waited for their coffee to be served.

"To be honest, I felt I didn't have a choice," he said with a nervous laugh.

"You're right but we still like people to be cooperative during an investigation."

The waitress brought over their coffees. She took hers black while he put one packet of sugar in his.

"So how is the investigation coming along?" Riggins asked while stirring his coffee. "I hope you're making good progress."

"It could be going better but we're getting there," she said with a smile before tasting her coffee.

"So what can I do to help you?"

"We've been going over some of the stories you wrote."

"My stories?" he asked in amazement.

"Yes sir, Mr. Riggins," she said. "We looked over the prize-winning stories."

"Were you hoping to find a clue in them?"

"That was the idea."

"Did you find anything?"

"That's why we're here."

Riggins grew silent for a moment and took a slow sip from his cup. He glanced around the café and then looked at her.

"Am I a suspect?"

"Not necessarily"

"Then what did you find?"

"We checked on the people you quoted in your story."

"Was there a problem?"

"We couldn't locate about half the names in it."

"So?"

"Do they exist?"

"Of course they do," he said. "They wouldn't have been in the story if they hadn't been real."

"Could you help us in locating them?"

"I think not," he said, straightening up in the chair.

"It would help us tremendously if you would cooperate with the investigation of one of your reporters."

"You're asking me to be forthcoming with everything when you guys are seldom the same with us."

"It's a little bit different matter, Mr. Riggins."

"Yes it is," he said, his tone growing stronger and firmer. "We're talking about freedom of the press."

"Let's not get carried away, Mr. Riggins. This is a possible murder investigation and we're trying to get all the information we can to solve it. We'd think you'd want to cooperate since the victim worked with you."

"There are limits as to what I can and will do."

"Could we have your notes from the stories?"

"Are you serious? What have we just been talking about?"

"If we have to we'll get a court order to seize them."

"You do what you have to do but I don't believe a court will allow you to infringe on my rights to report the news. There would be a breech of confidentiality I have with the people I interviewed. Don't you understand the ramifications?"

"I'm sorry you feel this way, Mr. Riggins."

"Is there anything else?" he asked as his eyes narrowed to tiny slits.

"No, sir," she said. "But you'll probably be hearing from us."

"I would suggest that next time you get in touch with the newspaper's attorney."

"If that's the case, we will."

Riggins scooted his chair away from the table and looked directly into her eyes.

"I'm indignant about this. You and the police department are going to regret ever messing with me and the newspaper."

Riggins paused for a moment and stormed out of the café. Slone picked up the check and shook her head in disbelief.

Bernie was in the department casually talking to three detectives when Slone returned to her desk.

"Any good news for me today?" Bernie asked with a smile.

"I may have some news," Slone said.

"That would be great. What is it?"

"I just had coffee with one of your people."

"From the newspaper?"

"Yes, Mr. Riggins."

"Oh, shit," Bernie said with a frown. "Pardon my French."

"What's the matter?"

"Oh, nothing," Bernie said. "He's the person I'm reporting to at the paper."

"Really?"

"I have to let him know everything I do in the case."

"I bet that's interesting."

"Yeah, especially since I'm not supposed to talk to people at the paper."

"Are you?"

"Well, I am trying to get some help from them."

"What have you learned?"

"Hey, aren't I supposed to be asking the questions?"

"Aren't we doing the same thing?"

"In a way, I suppose."

"So have you learned anything from the reporters?"

"Nothing yet," Bernie said. "Most of them are afraid of getting caught by Riggins and getting fired."

"Oh really?"

"It's kind of bad working down there now."

"So he controls what is going on?"

"Pretty much so."

"Has anyone looked at the stories he wrote for the award?"

"I've heard some mention the past few weeks. Several reporters have claimed that it's not what it appears to be?"

"What do they mean?"

"They think he fabricated some parts of the story."

"Do they have any proof?"

"I don't believe so although I think a few reporters are really looking into it."

"Does Riggins know about that?"

"Not to my knowledge. He hasn't said anything to me about it, not that he would."

"You don't get along with him?"

"Probably about as well as anyone on the staff, which isn't saying much," Bernie said. "Now what are you going to tell me?"

"This is still preliminary so I ask that you don't write about it."

"Okay, what is it?"

"We've been doing our own investigation into Riggins's stories and have found similar problems with sources."

"Really?" Bernie asked wide-eyed.

"As I said, we're still not sure what we have or if it is even relevant to the Johnson case so please keep that in mind."

"I don't know if I should tell Riggins about our conversation."

"Do what you want but I think I'd keep it under wraps for a few days."

"I think I'll do that. Maybe our reporters will come up with something as well."

"I'd like to know if they find out anything."

"I'll see what I can do," Bernie said. "This investigative stuff is all new to me."

"We want to work with you on it," Slone said with a smile.

Twenty-seven

Chase drove to Victoria Johnson's house in a drizzling rain. A "For Sale" sign was posted in the front yard. The house had a barren look with no flowers decorating the front yard and the lawn in need of a mowing. Marcy answered the doorbell.

"Hi, Mr. Elliott," she said with a smile that revealed two missing upper front teeth. "Mommy is downstairs washing clothes. She'll be back in a minute."

"Thank you, Marcy," Chase said with a grin. "How are you doing?"

"Did you know we're going to move?"

"No. Where are you moving to?"

Victoria walked into the living room, fluffing her hair with her hands and trying to get it back in place. She shooed Marcy to her bedroom. "Good bye, Mr. Elliott," Marcy said as she smiled and waved while leaving.

"So how are you doing, Vicki?" Chase asked.

"We're hanging in there," she said. "Please sit down, Chase."

Chase followed her to the couch and sat down on one end and she sat down at the other.

"I see that you're moving," Chase said.

"The sign out front went up two days ago. We haven't had any callers yet but that's fine with me because I need to get the house presentable."

"Are you moving out of town?"

"We're going back to Ohio and live closer to my family."

"I hope everything goes well for you. How is everything else?"

"As far as Brett's case is concerned, everything is about the same," she said with a sigh. "I almost wish that it's determined he had an accident so I could put all of this behind me. I need some closure."

"But do you really believe it was an accident?"

"No," she said wearily. "Not anymore."

"Then you wouldn't be able to go on with your life. It would always stay on your mind."

"I know but I just wish they would make some progress."

"Somehow, I think there's more the police know than what they're letting on."

"I hope you're right. It seems to have been dragging on forever."

"How is the newspaper treating you?"

"Okay, I guess. I received a check the other day for Brett's unused vacation time, which I didn't expect. I've had a few people come over and check on us so I really can't complain."

"That's good to hear."

"I wish I could help Bernadette more on her story but there's not much I know."

"I know she's working hard at trying to find out what happened."

"I know she is," Victoria said with a tired smile. "I don't believe she's getting much help or making much progress. She seems like such a nice person."

"Have you thought any more about that night, about what possibly could have happened or something Brett may have said in the days leading up to his death."

"Chase, I think about those things all the time," she said. "I really can't think of anything that connects to what happened. Other than that affair he had, nothing was really unusual."

"He didn't say or do anything?"

"He was just angry with Taylor," she said. "That's all I remember. He kept calling him a bogus reporter."

"Did he ever say anything about Angela Cook?"

"He just asked me to forgive him and that it was a stupid fling that he regretted."

"How did you feel about that?"

"Chase, he hurt me deeply," she said, wiping away several tears. "I thought we had a good, strong marriage and then he did that. I was shattered. Even though he is gone, I don't feel like I will ever be able to totally forgive him."

"I think I understand," he said. "Do you see anything connection between the affair and his death?"

"I wish I could but I can't," she said. "I would love to see Ms. Cook tied to it but I don't see how. She seemed to go on her way."

"How are the children?" Chase asked, quickly changing the subject.

"They seem to be adjusting," she said. "Marcy stays around the house a lot while Jody plays with the neighborhood boys. He hopes to play baseball again this summer."

"Is there anything I can do to help you?" Chase asked.

"You've been a good friend for a long time," she said with a soft smile. "I appreciate your concern about me and the children. That means a lot to me."

"If there is anything I can do, you know where to reach me," he said while standing up. She walked with him to the front door and he turned around and hugged her.

Chase drove away, trying to think of something she might have said that would give some clue or reason for Brett's death.

The rain let up but the sky was still overcast. He drove to the newspaper. It was mid-afternoon and reporters had begun to file in to work on stories and make phone calls. There was a slight buzz through the newsroom.

"Anything going on?" Chase asked Dakota Young, a sports copyeditor, as they stood by the water fountain.

"I believe there's been some more reshuffling in the newsroom," he said. "Riggins is taking on a few more responsibilities. The assistant city editor and state editor are reporters again, if they want to be."

"What do you mean?

"Either stay or leave."

"Any reason?"

"Not really other than not sharing the same focus as the other editors."

"Other editors?"

"Well, you know what I mean. Riggins's focus."

"That surprises me because they've been here for several years."

"The word is that they crossed him a week or so ago at a news meeting. Apparently they disagreed with him over something and expressed their opinion. He didn't take too kindly to it."

"I guess we'd better watch out what we say or do around here."

"No shit," Young said with a laugh "You won't hear me spouting off about anything."

"That's probably a wise thing to do for the time being."

~ * ~

"You're certainly not going to report that," Riggins said.

"I'm just telling you what the police told me," Bernie said timidly. "Isn't that what you want me to do?"

"It's pure bullshit and they're trying to discredit me," he said, leaning forward in his swivel chair. "I don't know where they came up with that crap. They're not reporters. That department has bungled so many cases that it's funny they would question something I did. It's pure jealousy."

"I'm sure it is," Bernie said, forcing a smile.

"Do you have anything else?"

"Not really."

"So it's looking more like an accidental death?"

"At this point."

"I'd like for you to work up some kind of story about it."

"It won't be much."

"That's fine," he said. "You only report what you know."

"If you say so."

"I say so. You can leave now."

Bernie got up and walked out of his office, holding back tears until her back was to him. She went to the women's restroom to get composed. While standing in front of the mirror, she heard a flush and seconds later a stall door open and Angela stepped out.

"Any problems?" Angela asked curtly.

"No," Bernie said. "I've just got a headache."

"I've got some aspirin if you want one."

"No thanks. I'll be all right."

"So you're still working on that Johnson story?"

"Yes," Bernie said while wiping her eyes with a tissue.

"You're not going to get anywhere with that."

"I'm beginning to believe it."

"Don't you know why?"

"Not really."

"You are so naïve," Angela said, shaking her head. "It's because it wasn't an accident."

"How do you know that?"

"I've got my sources."

"Will they talk to me?"

"Hardly."

"So why are you telling me this?"

"Because I don't want you to give up."

"What would you suggest I do?"

"Talk to the police some more. Ask them where some of their suspects were that night."

"But they don't have any suspects."

"That's what they're telling you. They have some people in mind. You just need to hit them a little harder."

"Does it involve someone here at the paper?"

"I'm not saying. And furthermore, you didn't hear any of this from me. I'm just trying to give you something to work on."

"Thanks," Bernie said.

Angela smiled and walked out of the restroom. Bernie looked at herself in the mirror, making sure her makeup and hair was in place. She tucked in her blouse and returned to her desk.

"Hey lady," Conner said as he approached her. "What have you been up to? I haven't seen you in awhile."

"I'm still working on the story."

"Are you making any progress?"

"Not really but I have a few more leads," she said.

"What are they?" he asked while sitting down next to her desk.

"Well, I was told to question the police about where some of their suspects where the evening Brett died."

"That's interesting. So it may not have been an accident?"

"Apparently."

"Anything else?'

"I'd rather not say."

"It's safe with me," Conner said.

"I met with Taylor this morning," she said. "I told him that the police had questioned his stories."

"How come they're doing that?"

"It seems like they think he made up some things."

"I bet he wasn't too happy to hear that."

"He told me not to report it. He said it was lies."

"I really don't envy you," Conner said. "You're really caught between that proverbial rock and a hard place."

"You're just now figuring that out?" she said with a light laugh.

"I have an assignment to shoot so I'd better take off," Conner said, tapping her desk. "Good luck with everything."

"I need it," she said looking up at him with a smile.

After he left the newsroom, Bernie picked up the telephone and called Slone at the police station.

"I need to ask you something," Bernie said. "Do you have any suspects?"

"What do you mean?"

"Do you have a list of names of people you think may have killed Brett Johnson if it wasn't an accident?"

"I wouldn't go that far," Slone said. "But yes, some names are more suspicious than others as it relates to his death. But at this point, it's still an accident. We're still gathering information and any kind of evidence to see if it was otherwise."

"Would it be fair if I reported that you have some names?"

"Don't quote me directly but you can use it as background."

"And there is still no timetable?"

"It's an ongoing investigation. If we get to the point where we are satisfied that it was an accident, then it will be considered such and we'll close the book."

"I probably shouldn't tell you this but Riggins said the investigation of his stories is just lies."

"Oh, he did," Slone said with a laugh. "Why did he say that?'

"He said it was jealousy."

"We'll have to wait and see about that."

"Some reporters here have even questioned those stories."

"That's even more interesting. I may have to talk to them."

"You didn't hear it from me."

"Of course not, Bernie. We've got to keep some things to ourselves."

Twenty-eight

Chase met Hernandez and Richardson in a nearly empty Pappy's bar after work. They ordered two pitchers of beer and a pizza that had apparently came from a freezer and spent too much time in an oven.

"I've checked and cross-checked twelve names in his drug story and I can't locate the people," Hernandez said. "I think they're fictitious."

"I've gone over the names with folks in the social agencies and only two were identifiable," Richardson said. "I tend to agree with you now."

"So what do we do?" Hernandez asked, glancing at Chase and Richardson.

"I think we need to compile whatever we have and approach Jordan Means with it," Richardson said.

"I don't think that would be a good idea," Chase said.

"How come?" Richardson asked.

"Because Means has been such an adamant supporter of Riggins since the award," Chase said. "I don't feel it would be a smart thing to do right now."

"So what do you suggest?" Hernandez asked.

"I think we should hold off for a little while and see what Bernie and the police come up with," Chase said. "I understand the police have made some inquiries about his stories. They believe there could be some connection to Brett's death."

"Wouldn't that be a hoot?" Richardson said with a chuckle.

"I believe that might be a stretch," Hernandez said with raised eyebrows. "But you never know. Maybe Brett knew something."

"That's what the police seem to think," Chase said.

"So we're just going to sit on things now?" Richardson asked.

"That's the best thing to do," Chase said. "I'm going to snoop around some more and see if I can come up with anything. I know Brett's widow is bitter. I'd like to talk to Taylor's wife but that's been kind of difficult. I think Angela Cook can provide us with some information as well."

"That sneaky bitch?" Richardson asked. "I wouldn't trust her as far as I could throw her."

"I don't trust her either but she does have some connections with Riggins and Means," Chase said. "I sense that she's not very fond of Taylor."

"She turned out not to be fond of Brett and look what happened to him," Hernandez said.

"I believe it was the other way around," Chase said. "It was Brett's decision to end the relationship."

"Do you think she could have done him in?" Richardson asked.

"I guess we'll have to find out."

They finished the beer and half of the pizza and decided to leave as the bar was becoming more crowded. Several other reporters drifted in, but sat at other tables. Conner came in as they were getting up from the table.

"Are you guys taking off?" he asked. "It's still early."

"We've been here for an hour or so," Richardson said. "It's time to go home. My wife probably has dinner on the table."

"I've got some errands to run," Hernandez said.

"How about you, Chase?" Conner asked. "Can't you stay for a little while, at least until I drink a beer."

Chase looked at the clock on the wall. It was nearly seven o'clock.

"I can only stay another twenty minutes or so," he said.

"Great," Conner said as he sat down at the table.

Hernandez and Richardson nodded good bye and left as Chase sat down.

"What were you guys bullshitting about?" Conner asked.

"Just office stuff."

"There is a lot of crap going on there," Conner said as the waitress brought him a pitcher of beer.

"I couldn't agree more."

"I talked with Bernie and she seems to be making a little headway on her story."

"That's good to hear."

"She told Riggins that the police have problems with his drug story. He wasn't too happy to hear that."

"That doesn't surprise me," Chase said. "I'd be upset as well."

"Do you think he fabricated any of it?"

"There are people who have their doubts about it."

"But how about you?"

"I'd rather not say," Chase said. "I'd rather wait until I see and hear everything."

"Always playing it safe," Conner said with a wink.

"What do you think about it?" Chase asked.

"I guess I'm like you," Conner said as he refilled his mug. "I'd like to think Taylor's story will hold up. He's been a good reporter for too many years to do something that stupid. And I think he's a good man."

"You haven't had any problems with him?"

"He doesn't bother the photography department that much. He's been okay with us."

"You should feel fortunate then."

"Has he been on your ass?"

"Not much, but some," Chase said. "We go back a ways so I suppose that helps."

"I thought you and him were good friends."

"I wouldn't go that far but we've gotten along well. We arrived at the paper about the same time."

"I guess you know that Taylor and his wife are splitting?"

"I've heard that," Chase said. "Any reason?"

"I think it's work-related," Conner said. "Some women just can't stick by their man."

"Huh?"

"I mean, she should be happy that Taylor has done so well instead of turning her back on him."

"Where did you hear that?"

"Just rumor."

Chase looked at the clock and noticed it was nearing seven-thirty.

"I really need to be going," he said.

"No need to rush off," Conner said. "You don't have a woman at home waiting for you."

"But I still have some things to do."

"Okay then," Conner said. "I'll catch you later."

Chase worked his way through the crowd and out the bar. The sun was already down as he walked to his car. A vehicle pulled up beside him as he was about to open the door.

"Good evening, Mr. Elliott."

Chase was startled for a moment and stared at the car, unable to make out who was talking to him.

"Yes?" Chase asked.

"Gene Bennett of the detective bureau."

"Oh, how are you doing?" Chase asked. "I didn't recognize you for a moment."

"Are you getting ready to leave?"

"Yes," Chase said. "I met a few friends here."

"I was thinking about stopping but it looks too crowded."

"It is," Chase said. "That's one reason I'm going home."

"Anything interesting going on at the newspaper?"

"Not much," Chase said with a grin. "How about at the police department?"

"We're working on a few leads right now."

"Can't tell me now?"

"I'd better wait. You'll find out soon enough. Maybe tomorrow."

Ten minutes after Chase got home, he telephoned Bernie. She didn't answer and he left a message on her answering machine to call him. He put a frozen dinner into the microwave oven and sat down at the kitchen table and flipped through the pages of a magazine while waiting for the meal to be finished. Moments later, the doorbell rang and he got up and went to the front door. Squinting through the peep hole, he saw Hannah and quickly opened the door.

"Hi," he said cheerfully. "You're a pleasant surprise."

"I'm not catching you at a bad time, am I?"

"I've got a microwave dinner heating up. That's about it. Have you eaten?"

"I grabbed a bite to eat after work," she said as she followed him into the kitchen. "But I will take something to drink."

Chase put ice in glasses and poured sodas for them and sat them on the table. The buzzer on the microwave sounded and he removed the meal.

"I hope you don't mind me eating in front of you," he said.

"I got the weirdest phone call this afternoon."

"An angry customer?"

"Would you believe Taylor Riggins?"

"What in the world did he want?"

"I'm not really sure," she said before taking a sip of soft drink. "It really wasn't anything in particular. It was more chit-chat stuff."

"Such as?"

"Like how I was doing and what I've been up to lately and things like that."

"Did he mention me?"

"Well, he did ask if we were still seeing each other."

"And?"

"I told him we were and he didn't pursue it."

"I wonder what he was up to. What time did he call?"

"It was mid-afternoon," she said. "To be honest, he sounded as if he had been drinking. He wasn't slurring any words but they were coming out very smooth. Too smooth."

"Did he say he would call again?"

"No," she said. "We talked for about ten minutes or so and that was it. Like I said, it was rather strange."

"It sure sounds that way," said Chase, who was holding his fork but hadn't taken a bite of his dinner. "I want you to be careful."

"I don't think there's anything to worry about but I will," she said.

"Maybe he was lonesome. You know that he's split with Sheila."

"Really?" she said. "Why?"

"I've heard it's work-related."

"That doesn't surprise me."

"Let me know if he calls again," Chase said.

"Are you jealous?" she asked with a wink.

"Hardly," Chase said. "He's just not the same person you knew. He's really changed."

"Maybe people really never knew him to begin with."

"That could be the case."

"You've heard that power corrupts."

"I think with him the corruption came before the power."

"Why do you say that?"

"I've got my reasons," Chase said. "I'll tell you one of these days." She smiled and nodded.

Chase finished eating dinner as Hannah talked about her day at work. They got up and sat on the couch in the living room, with her head resting on his shoulder.

"I went over to the bar after work and when I was leaving I ran into one of the detectives working the Johnson case. He said there could be some kind of announcement in the morning."

"Do you have any idea what it could be?

"Not really," Chase said. "It could be anything."

"Call me when you hear something," Hannah said as she rose from the couch. "I'll be in the office most of the day."

Chase picked up his dinner container, placed it in the trash can, and walked over to Hannah. He put his arms on her waist.

"I'll do that," Chase said before kissing her tenderly on the mouth.

"I really need to be going," Hannah said after the long kiss. "I've got some things I need to take care of before work tomorrow."

Chase walked her to her car in the driveway, giving her a quick kiss before she got in her car and left.

When she arrived home, there was a car parked out front. She eased her car in to the garage after the automatic garage-door opened. After getting in the house, she peered through the living-room curtain at the car. She noticed a man in the car. A few seconds later it drove off.

Hannah went back to her bedroom and put on lounging pajamas. She gathered the papers from the office and went to her study. After sitting down for a few minutes, she heard loud knocking on her front door. She went to the living room and pulled back a corner of the curtain and noticed the same car was out front, but this time it was empty. She couldn't see who was at the door. There were a few more knocks. She decided not to answer.

After another minute, she could see a figure walk away from the door. It was Taylor Riggins. She saw his head turn toward her and she quickly closed the curtain and held her breath. Moments later, she heard the car start and leave.

Twenty-nine

Startled by the ringing of the telephone, Chase reached over and turned on the light next to his bed, then picked up the receiver.

"Chase?" Hannah said excitedly.

"What is it Hannah?"

"I'm frightened."

"What's the matter?"

"Taylor Riggins has been at my house."

"What are you talking about?"

"When I got home this evening, he was parked outside my house. Then he came up to my front door."

"What did you do?"

"I didn't answer it. He left after a minute."

"Do you want me to come over?"

"Would you mind? I'm afraid to be alone in my house."

"I'll get dressed and be there in less than thirty minutes."

After hanging up the phone, Chase quickly put on some khaki pants and polo shirt and left his house. She was waiting at the door for him when he arrived. She wrapped her arms around him as he stepped into the house and he hugged her securely.

"Everything is going to be all right," he said reassuringly.

"Thank you for coming over," she said as she rested her head on his shoulder. "I just don't feel safe tonight."

"Are you sure it was Taylor?"

"Yes," she said with a trembling in her voice. "I saw him through the front-window curtains."

"I wonder what he wanted?"

"I didn't want to find out at this time of the night. He has never come over here before."

They sat down on the couch in the den for several minutes as she calmed down. They hardly said anything as he put his arm around her and held her tightly. He kissed her tenderly several times on her forehead.

"Are you ready to go to bed?" he asked quietly.

"I think so," she said while slowly getting up from the couch. He followed her to the bedroom and waited for her to get under the sheets before turning off the lights, taking off his clothes and sliding in beside her. She snuggled next to him and within minutes was sound asleep. He lay quietly listening to her soft breathing and waiting to hear if there was any noise around the house. Before long, he was asleep, his arm around her as they shared an oversized pillow.

Chase was awakened in the morning by the aroma of freshly-brewed coffee. The clock radio read five-thirty. He rose in bed and noticed the light was on in the bathroom. He heard the shower come on. After a few seconds, he slipped off his boxers and went to the bathroom. Hannah was standing under the gentle flow of the water, her back to Chase. He stepped into the stall with her and gently touched her shoulders. She turned around and smiled, pressing her breasts against him as they stood under the steady stream of water.

They kissed several times while their hands slowly explored the other's wet body. Chase lifted her from the waist as she put her arms around his neck and spread her legs around his waist. They kissed even more passionately until their bodies reached a satisfying oneness.

Chase kissed her softly across the face as she lowered her feet to the floor. Their mouths connected again in a long wet kiss.

"That was nice," she cooed. "You need to be here every morning with me."

"I may take you up on that," he said with a smile.

Hannah lathered a large sponge with shower gel and began rubbing it across Chase's chest. She slowly ran it over his neck and shoulders and down to his belly. He turned around and she gently scrubbed his back, down his buttocks and legs.

Chase took the sponge from her and squeezed out the soap and put it under the water. He put on more shower gel and moved it gently over her body. When he was finished, he took the shampoo from the shower tray and washed her hair, slowly massaging her scalp. After he finished, he quickly washed his hair and they turned off the water. The bathroom was steamy. She stepped out and handed him a beach-size towel, which he quickly enveloped her body as he patted her dry. They kissed again before she wrapped the towel around her and went to the bedroom. Chase took another towel and dried himself off.

When he entered the bedroom, she was wearing a pink chiffon robe and brushing her hair in front of the vanity mirror. He walked over and squeezed her shoulders tenderly several times and kissed her on the cheek.

"Are you ready for breakfast?" she asked.

"I already had breakfast," he said with a smile. "But I guess I could use a cup of coffee."

They walked to the kitchen and he sat down at the table while she prepared their coffee.

"Are you sure you don't want some eggs or cereal or toast?" she asked.

"Coffee is fine."

"I think I'll eat some cereal," she said.

She opened the cabinet and took down a bowl. She put wheat flakes into it and took milk out of the refrigerator. Chase watched her graceful moves. She sat down at the small table across from him and poured the milk over the cereal.

"So are you going to be all right?" Chase asked. "Would you like for me to come over tonight?"

"I think I'll be fine," she said.

"You know you can come over to my place."

"I appreciate that."

"I'm going to say something to Taylor this morning."

"I hope you don't get in trouble with him."

"I'm not concerned about that. I want to know why he called you and came over here."

"I'd like to know as well."

Chase arrived at the newspaper office shortly after nine o'clock. He stopped by the cafeteria to get a cup of coffee and noticed Hernandez sitting by himself at a table. The room was nearly empty.

"Mind if I join you for a minute?" Chase asked as he approach Hernandez's table.

"Oh, good morning, Chase," Hernandez said. "I didn't see you come in. Have a seat."

Chase sat down and stirred his coffee for a moment. Hernandez was drinking coffee and eating a pastry.

"It appears relatively safe here," Chase said, glancing around the room and making sure no one was within earshot.

"I think so," Hernandez said. "I was upstairs a little earlier and some of the editors were getting ready for a meeting with Riggins."

"He loves those meetings."

"I would say so," Hernandez said. "He seems to be in meetings most of the day."

"I haven't told you or anyone this but I've received several anonymous notes from someone the past few months."

"About Johnson?"

"Yes."

"Well, don't keep me in suspense," Hernandez said with a light chuckle.

"They really don't say much but I thought it might be something to compare to your notes on his story."

"That would be great. Why are you telling me now?"

"Because I didn't know what they meant and didn't want to jump to any conclusions."

"I can understand that."

"Have the others turned up anything?

"Not much," Hernandez said. "They've been too damn busy on some of Taylor's projects."

Riggins and Means along with several sub-editors came into the cafeteria and stood in line for something to drink. Riggins looked around and noticed Chase and Hernandez. He didn't smile. He stared for a few seconds and then turned around and began talking to an editor.

"I wonder what he's thinking?" Hernandez asked.

"He gave us an evil eye," Chase said.

"Sometimes I think he's so paranoid that he suspects everyone is talking about him."

"To be honest, I would think just about everyone in the newsroom has talked about him so you could be right on the mark with that."

"I think I'm going to head back upstairs," Hernandez said. "I've got a few calls to make."

"I think I'll stay here a few more minute just so Mr. Riggins doesn't get too suspicious," Chase said with a grin.

Chase picked up a newspaper on the next table and skimmed over the headlines to familiarize himself with the day's events. He finished his coffee and took his empty cup to the trash receptacle and tossed it in. He could feel someone's eyes on him and looked over to his side. Riggins was glaring at him. Chase nodded but Riggins didn't acknowledge him.

Chase turned around and walked out of the cafeteria to the elevator. He rode it up by himself, his thoughts on Riggins and what he was going to have to do about his visit to Hannah's house. He knew it wasn't going to be easy or pretty.

Twenty-nine

Hernandez saw Chase enter the sports department and walked over to his desk.

"Can I see the notes?" he asked.

Chase opened a side drawer and took out the messages. He removed them from an envelope and handed them to Hernandez, who looked at them for several seconds. Hernandez took a reporter's notebook out of his back pocket and wrote down some notes and handed them back to Chase.

"This is very interesting," Hernandez said. "Are you going to share it with the police?"

"Not right now," Chase said. "As much as I want the Brett's case to be solved, I figure they can do their own investigation."

"How about Bernie?"

"I guess I could show them to her."

Chase put the notes back into the drawer and closed it. A moment later Riggins and two of the editors walked into the newsroom. Riggins glanced at Chase and Hernandez.

"Oh shit," Hernandez said. "I forgot about him coming back. I wonder what he thinks now."

"Don't sweat it."

"I work on his end of the floor," Hernandez said. "I may end up talking to him after this."

"Just tell him you were asking me something about sports."

"That's a good idea. I don't want to get on his shit list," Hernandez said as he nodded and returned to his desk.

Chase checked e-mail and sorted through mail, throwing most of it away.

"You're here early this morning," Green said. "Anything going on that I should know?"

"I just wanted to get a head start on a few things before the day got away."

"Any ideas on your next hard-edge story?"

"I may do something on the disparity of salaries in athletic departments. These coaches and athletic directors and getting paid big bucks and bonuses while the support people barely earn enough to make a living."

"I'm sure that story will make you a popular figure with the powers that be on the campuses."

"So be it," Chase said with a shrug of his shoulders."I suppose the main thing is to be popular with the powers that be in this building."

Green chuckled. "I've got a news meeting coming up in a few minutes. I'll see you around later."

At the other end of the floor, Hernandez's phone rang and he answered on the first ring.

"James Hernandez speaking. Can I help you?" he asked politely.

"Can you come to my office for a few minutes?" Riggins asked without identifying himself. "I need to ask you something."

"Sure," Hernandez said, cringing at hearing Riggins's voice. "I'll be right there."

Hernandez put down the receiver and went to Riggins's office. The door was open and he took a step inside.

"Need me for something?" he asked.

"Come on in."

Hernandez sat down in a chair facing Riggins. After a few seconds of shuffling through some papers, Riggins put them aside and looked at Hernandez.

"Are you working with Chase Elliott on any story?"

"No, sir," Hernandez said softly.

"I've seen you with him and was wondering if there's something I need to know."

"Not really," Hernandez said, raising his eyebrows while smiling. "Just some sports stuff. I was asking him about some baseball games coming up in Cincinnati that I was thinking about attending with my family."

"So how's everything going on with you?" Riggins asked, apparently satisfied with Hernandez's answer. "Are you working on any hard-edge stories?"

"I've got one really big one but it's in the preliminary stages."

"Do you care to share?"

"If you don't mind, I'd rather wait and see if it pans out," Hernandez said. "It may be nothing."

"I can understand that," Riggins said in a patronizing tone. "I had many of those kinds of leads when I was an investigative reporter. Sometimes you come across some really good nuggets of information, or at least you think so, and they turn out to be fool's gold."

"That's exactly what I'm learning here, sir. You just have to be persistent and persevere if you're going to come up with some good, hard-hitting stories."

"You know my door is always open if you need any advice or assistance," Riggins said with a big smile.

"I really appreciate that, sir," Hernandez said. "I'm glad that we have someone of your stature here that we can go to on stories."

"Well James, I have a budget meeting about to start in one minute so I'd better be going. Good luck on your story."

Hernandez rose from his chair, smiled with pursed lips, and walked out of the office. After he returned to his desk, he picked up the phone and called Chase.

"Guess who I had a meeting with?"

"You've got to be kidding."

"I told him I was asking you about upcoming ball games."

"Anything else come up?"

"He just gave me some advice on covering stories," Hernandez said. "You know, he's really not a bad guy."

"Are you serious?"

"Just kidding, friend," Hernandez said with a quiet snicker.

"Very funny," Chase said, smiling and shaking his head. "You just be careful."

"I will. I know him too well. I'll talk to you later."

After putting down the receiver, Hernandez felt a pat on his shoulder as someone walked by his desk. He looked up and saw Riggins walking toward the conference room.

Hernandez opened his notebook and compared the initials to the names he was checking up. They all corresponded.

"I think I may have a story, Mr. Riggins," he said quietly to himself.

~ * ~

"Good morning, Bernadette," Bennett said as she entered the detective unit.

"Why don't you just call me Bernie?" she said with a grin. "That's what everybody calls me."

"If that's what you like but Bernadette is such a nice-sounding name."

"You think so?"

"Very much," Bennett said. "Very soft and feminine."

"Hmm, I may prefer Bernadette now," she said with a soft laugh.

"I think we have something new for you," Bennett said, taking out a forensics report in a folder on his desk.

"Great," she said. "I could use some good news."

"I don't know if this is good news or not but it's something."

"Well, go ahead and tell me," she said anxiously.

"As you know, we only found trace amounts of alcohol in Mr. Johnson's body," Bennett said. "The lab found that the liquor on his clothing was Lucky Star bourbon. It's our suspicion that someone poured it on him to give the impression that he was drunk and passed out."

"So you're saying that he was murdered?"

"That's the indication we have now."

"How did you find out the brand of whiskey?"

"That took a while because they had to break down several whiskeys to see if there was a match. Every whiskey has a little different composition of grains and such, along with the aging that gives each brand its distinctive taste."

"And they were able to find out that it was Lucky Star on his clothing. That's very interesting."

"Considering that Mr. Johnson didn't drink bourbon, and that only trace amounts of alcohol were found in his blood, it points to a perpetrator doing something to him."

"Does that make it any easier in solving the crime?"

"I don't know if it's that much easier but it does narrow our investigation by taking out the accident component."

"I appreciate you sharing this with me," Bernie said. "Where's Marcia?"

"She's at the library doing some research."

"What kind of research?"

"Just some preliminary research that goes with every investigation."

"I need to be going," Bernie said. "I have something to report now."

"Do me a favor?"

"What's that?"

"Please don't mention the brand of whiskey. Just say that we've determined it was whiskey. We don't want to tip off anybody."

"I can understand that."

"Thanks, Bernadette," Bennett said with a wink.

Bernie left the police station and drove directly to the newspaper building. She went to the newsroom and walked to Riggins's office. His door was closed.

"He's out of town for three days," the secretary said, briefly stopping her typing to acknowledge Bernie.

"That's a shame. I had something to tell him."

"He's at a meeting and won't be back until Friday afternoon. In fact, he may not return to the office until Monday."

"Thanks," Bernie said as she shrugged, turned away and went to her desk.

"Hey there, Bernie," Hernandez said several desks away.

"Hi, James," she said. "How are you?"

"We need to talk soon."

"Really? About what?"

"You know what."

"How about down at the cafeteria?"

"Okay," Hernandez said as he got up from his desk and approached her. She stood up and they walked to the elevator at the end of the floor.

"I heard some good news from the police today," she said as they waited for the elevator.

"What was that?"

"It seems that Brett may have been murdered and that whiskey was poured on his body to make it appear that he was drunk."

"Have you told anyone?"

"I was hoping to tell Riggins but he's out of town until Friday."

They stepped into the elevator. Three other people were already inside.

"So what's the weather like this morning?" Hernandez asked with a smile. "I've been inside all morning."

"Oh, bright and sunshiny," Bernie said.

"It sure looked overcast when I came in," a man said.

"I was only referring to my outlook," Bernie said with a giggle.

"Oh," the man said, raising his eyebrows and smiling. "I understand."

The elevator door opened and Bernie and Hernandez were the only ones to get off. They went to the cafeteria. Hernandez bought their coffee and brought it to a table in the rear where Bernie had sat down.

"That's really interesting about the whiskey," Hernandez said.

"They even know the brand," she said.

"What kind?"

"They asked me not to tell anyone."

"Don't you think it might be safe with me?"

Bernie grinned. "Lucky Star."

"Thank God it's not my favorite," Hernandez said with a laugh. "Plus it's too expensive for my budget."

"So what did you want to tell me?"

"Chase said that I should let you know that I've been doing some investigative work on the side."

"Have you come up with anything?"

"I'm not sure but we thought you should know."

"What is it?"

"It seems that some of the people mentioned in Riggins's story were fictitious."

"Oh, my God!"

"I've been told the police are working on the same thing."

"Detective Bennett told me that another detective was at the library doing some research. He didn't say what it was about but I'm thinking it was this same thing."

"Anyway, I'm doing some work on that end. I thought you'd want to know."

"Does Riggins know you are doing that?"

"Of course not," Hernandez said, shaking his head in disbelief. "Only a few people know."

"It's safe with me."

"I'll keep you posted on anything else that turns up."

"I'll do the same with you."

Thirty

"I don't know what to do with this stuff," Bernie said after telling Chase on the telephone about the whiskey. "I met with James Hernandez this morning. I'm really afraid to pass any information on to Riggins."

"Of course, you can't say anything to him about James because you're not supposed to be talking to reporters," Chase said. "Furthermore, it could get James in a lot of trouble."

"What should I do then?"

"Just pass along the information about the whiskey to him. That information could lead to a lot more."

"I wonder if I should talk to Jordan Means?"

"I believe I would hold off on that. Anyway, he's too close to Taylor. He might not like hearing anything negative about him."

"But wouldn't you want to know if one of your editors was involved in something he shouldn't be?"

"I think I would but that doesn't necessarily mean that Jordan would."

"I see," she said. "Are you coming into the office today?"

"I'm working at home this afternoon. There's a lot more peace and quiet here to make calls and write."

"I wish I could get by with that," she said with a laugh. "I'll let you get back to work then."

"Thanks for calling. I'll talk to you later."

After putting down the receiver, Chase went to the kitchen and poured a glass of water and sat down at the table. He sipped on the water while thinking about the circumstances of Brett's death. It wasn't an accident. He wondered who had sent him the notes. He figured it had to be someone in the newsroom but who was it? An editor? A reporter? A secretary? A photographer?

Chase got up from the table and went to his study. He looked over some notes he had taken on a story he was working on but couldn't concentrate. He picked up the telephone and called Victoria Johnson.

"How are you, Vicki?" he asked when she answered the phone.

"I'm doing well, Chase. How are you?"

"I was just thinking about you and the kids and decided to call."

"The children haven't caused any problems. They seem to be adjusting to life without their dad."

"I know it has to be difficult for them."

"The grandparents and other relatives and friends have been good to them so it really hasn't been too bad for them."

"How about for you?"

"I just wish the police would finish their investigation. They're nice and polite but they don't seem to be making a lot of progress."

"Did they tell you about the whiskey?"

"What about it?"

"They identified the brand and have determined that it must have been poured on Brett, apparently to make it appear that he was drunk and had stumbled."

"I could have told them that," she said. "Brett was not a heavy drinker. In fact, he didn't drink very much at all, and when he did, it was beer."

"Vicki, have you given any more thought as to who may have killed Brett?"

"I think about it every day," she said. "About the only person that comes to mind would be Taylor Riggins but I can't see why he would want to do that."

"Even though Brett considered him a so-called bogus reporter?"

"I don't know if Brett ever said that to his face. You know he was kind of soft-spoken and didn't speak out about things he didn't like or agree with. He took a lot of grief from editors without saying anything. That used to upset me because he would bring that anger home with him and it would simmer inside him until he exploded."

"What happened then?"

"He would just yell at me and the children. It wouldn't last long, and after it was over, he would apologize and everything would be normal for several months."

"And you can't think of anyone else who may have carried a grudge against him?"

"You would probably know more than me because you're at the newspaper. Did you ever see him have run-ins with others?"

"Truly, I can't say that I did," Chase said. "He kind of moved with the flow. He was well-liked to my knowledge."

"I guess the only other person would be Angela Cook but why would she want to do anything to him?"

"I don't know why either."

"It's all a puzzle to me."

"I'll keep on looking around and see if I come up with anything," Chase said. "Please let me know if anything comes to mind."

"I'll do that, Chase," she said. "I appreciate you calling."

"Perhaps I can take you and kids out for hamburgers some evening."

"That would be nice," she said. "They always thought a lot of you."

Chase put down the receiver and leaned back in his chair and closed his eyes. He knew he had to get in touch with Angela. Chase took the company directory out of the side drawer of his desk and looked up her number. He got her voice mail. He hesitated a few seconds, and then left his name and number. He decided to stay at home until he heard from her.

Several hours later a rapping on the front door startled Chase from a quick nap after dozing off in his chair. He wiped his eyes and went to the door and opened it. Angela stood there, a bright smile showing her perfect teeth, and a short skirt displaying shapely legs, and a form-fitting top to amplify her curvy body.

"Hi, Chase," she said. "I got your message and decided to drop by. I hope you don't mind."

"That's fine," he said as he opened the door. "But you could have called instead of making the long trip over here."

Angela sat down on the couch and Chase eased into his recliner.

"So what did you want?" she asked.

"You seem to be plugged in to what is going on at the paper."

"I know a few things but not everything," she said, grinning "What do you want to know?"

"I'd like for this to be in confidence."

"Of course, Chase," she said. "I don't run my mouth like some people do over there."

"I'd like to get straight to the point."

"Go ahead."

"What do you know about Brett Johnson's death?"

"What do you mean?'

"Do you know anything about it?"

"You do go straight to the point," she said, nervously.

"You seem to be connected to the right people at the newspaper. I thought perhaps you've heard something."

"I know that some people are concerned about Brett's death. They were hoping it would be found accidental."

"Why?"

"I'm not sure but I believe because they know it wasn't."

"Who are these people?"

"I'd rather not say," she said, looking away from him.

"Why are you protecting them?"

"It's not that I'm protecting them. A lot of it is hearsay and I don't like to repeat those things. I shouldn't even say anything to you."

"Have you heard anything about Taylor Riggins's award-winning story?"

"Only what you've probably heard, that he made up some things and quotes," she said. "I think that has been floating around the newsroom for some time now."

"What do you think about it?"

"I wouldn't be surprised if he did," she said. "He's such a deceitful bastard."

"Why do you say that?"

"Because you can't trust him. You couldn't trust him as a reporter and now it's worst now that he's an editor because he's trying to cover up past mistakes."

"Past mistakes?"

"The drug story isn't the only one that he's fictionalized. He had some minor stories in the past that a few people questioned."

"Why didn't anything happen?"

"Because they were either fired or moved on to other papers."

"I never heard any of this."

"Because you work in sports and no one in sports has a clue about what goes on in rest of the newsroom."

"Oh," Chase said, unable to keep a smile from crossing his face.

"You know it's the truth."

"Probably."

"Anyway, Taylor has made a close friend with the right person to protect him."

"Who is it?"

"You guess."

"Jordan Means?"

"Good guess," she said with a smile.

"Aren't you plugged in with him as well?"

"We're good friends."

"Nothing more?"

"That's about it. And no, I'm not sleeping with him."

"Would you talk to the police again?"

"I don't have anything to say to them. All I really know is hearsay, much like the rest of the newsroom."

"Angela, the police work on hearsay and weed things out," Chase said. "It wouldn't hurt to talk to them off the record."

"I'll think about it."

Angela crossed her legs and smiled. Chase couldn't help looking at her, and slightly blushed when their eyes met.

"Would you care for something to drink?"

"I really need to be going," she said. "I have to go pick up the children soon."

"I appreciate you stopping by."

"I must confess that I was hoping it wouldn't be about this."

"Brett was a friend of mine and I'm trying to find out what happened. I hope you understand."

"Just be careful who you talk to."

"Anyone in particular?"

"Jordan Means."

Thirty-one

Bernie had just finished eating dinner with Conner and was sitting on the couch listening to country music when the phone rang.

"How are you tonight?" Chase asked.

"I'm sitting back and listening to George Strait." She knew every song by heart but never seemed to grow tire of them. "Why are you calling so late?"

"Is it that late?"

"Well, anytime past eight is late if you're calling me."

"Oh, funny."

"I couldn't resist. So what do you want to tell me?"

"I met with Angela Cook late this afternoon. She came over to the house."

"Is she trying to start something up with you?" Bernie said, giggling.

"Hardly," Chase said. "I called her and she came over instead of calling me back."

"Likely story," Bernie said, unable to suppress the giggles.

"Okay, okay, enough of that. Do you want to know what she said?"

"If it's not too personal."

"I'm being serious."

"I'm only teasing, Chase. Chill out."

"She said the person to watch out for is Jordan Means and to be careful what you say around him."

"How come?"

"She wouldn't say. I wanted to talk to her about Brett. She suspects foul play as well."

Conner read a magazine, occasionally glancing at Bernie when she would laugh or her voice would change. She looked at him and smiled.

"I haven't made a lot of headway since the bourbon discovery and Riggins is out of town until Friday or maybe even Monday."

"Just be careful who you tell," he said. "We don't want any leaks around the newsroom. And you know how reporters talk."

"I know Chase. Mum is the word now."

"I'll let you know if I hear anything else."

"Thanks, Chase. Maybe I'll see you at work tomorrow."

After putting down the receiver, Bernie sat down next to Conner. He took the remote and put the volume control on mute.

"What was that all about?" he asked.

"Chase said I'd better be careful who I talk to about Brett Johnson. He said that includes Jordan Means."

"Really? That's interesting."

"Yeah, he met with Angela Cook today and she said to be careful around Means. He really doesn't know why."

"That's very interesting," Conner said, arching his brows. "I'd like to know why she would say something like that."

"Me, too. I guess I'll have to find out why."

"Be careful."

Conner opened the magazine and went back to reading. Bernie looked at him for a second, then went to the kitchen and put the dirty dishes in the dishwasher and wiped off the table.

She returned to the living room and sat down next to Conner, who had turned off the stereo and turned on the television.

"Anything good on TV tonight?" she asked.

"Nah," he said. "Just a bunch of reality shows. I think I'll be going pretty soon."

"So early?"

"I have an assignment early in the morning and I need to take care of a few things."

"What do you have to do?"

"Tonight or tomorrow?"

"Both."

"I have to get my equipment together that I'll be taking with me."

"And tomorrow?"

"I'm not sure what it will be. I'm going out with one of the reporters."

"Who?"

"I'm not sure," he said. "I'll find out in the morning."

"Oh."

"Well, I need to go," he said, standing up. "Thanks for dinner. It was delicious, as usual."

Bernie remained seated as he walked to the door. He looked at her for a few seconds, and then opened the door, smiled and left. Tears trickled down Bernie's cheeks.

~ * ~

Chase arrived at the newspaper early Friday morning. He stopped by the cafeteria and bought a large coffee to take to his desk. When the door to the elevator opened, Hernandez stood next to several employees.

"Good morning, James," Chase said. "Are you getting an early start on a story?"

"I'm trying to finish one," Hernandez said with a half-wink.

The elevator door opened and they stepped into the newsroom lobby and waited for the others to scatter to their offices.

"Have you got a minute?" Chase asked while looking around to make sure no one was around to hear him.

"Sure. What's up?'

"I met with Angela yesterday and she told me to be careful around Means. I thought you should know."

"I've been careful around him for a long time," Hernandez said. "I'm to the point that I hardly trust anyone in the newsroom except for you and Bernie."

"How about Fred Simpson and Allen Richardson?"

"They're okay but they're worried too much about covering their asses than uncovering anything. Some people are simply afraid of their own shadow."

"I know what you mean but I want you to be extra cautious. I don't want you and or anyone else getting into trouble until we have the goods. That's how we'll cover our butts."

"Don't worry."

"Have you seen Means lately?"

"He went to some editors' meeting. I think he's supposed to be back today."

"The same one that Riggins went to?"

"That would be my guess."

The elevator opened and Conner stepped out by himself.

"Hey guys," Conner said. "How are things going?"

"Staying busy," Hernandez said.

"You know what I'm talking about," Conner said.

Chase and Hernandez looked at each other briefly and shrugged their shoulders in unison.

"What are you talking about?" Chase asked.

"The Brett Johnson story," Conner said.

"That's what Bernie is working on," Chase said. "You know that. You'd have to ask her."

"Okay, if you want to play that game," Conner said with a knowing grin. "I can play along with you."

"I need to get to my desk and make some calls," Hernandez said as he began to walk away. "I'll see you guys later."

Chase stood next to Conner for a few seconds and said, "So how are things going with you?"

"I'm staying busy," he said. "I don't have anything going on this morning so I thought I'd take care of a few things in the department."

"Well, I've got to finish a column for the Sunday edition," Chase said.

"Just be careful what you say and do," Conner said, flicking his eyebrows.

"I will," Chase said as he took a few steps toward the sports department. "You do the same."

After Chase cleared the corner, Conner walked to Means's office at the corner of the lobby. Only his secretary was there.

"Mr. Means probably won't be back until late today," she told Conner.

"Could you have him give me a call when he gets back?" Conner said. "There's something I need to discuss with him."

"Will you be in the photography department?"

"Just have him call me on my cell phone," Conner said. "He can reach me any time."

"Can I tell him what you want?"

"It's personal," Conner said with pursed lips as he turned and left the office.

As he walked toward the photography department, he saw Bernie talking to another reporter in the middle of the newsroom. He quickly turned around and headed to the library where he stayed for several minutes, thumbing through magazines before coming out and looking across the newsroom. She was busy on the telephone with her back to him.

Conner went to the elevator, took it down to the first floor, and hurried to his car.

Thirty-two

"Can you come over tonight?" Hannah asked Chase on the telephone.

"I don't see any problem," Chase said. "I have to finish a column I'm writing for the Sunday paper. Can I stop and pick up anything?"

"Thanks but I'll prepare something. Give me until seven. Okay?"

"I'll be happy to take you out to dinner."

"Are you saying you don't like my cooking?" she asked with a laugh.

"You know better than that. I just hate to see you go to all that trouble."

"I enjoy cooking for you so it's not any trouble at all."

"I'll see you at seven."

~ * ~

Bernie noticed Chase at his desk and headed toward him. She ran into one of the photographers halfway down the newsroom.

"Hey, Bob," she said. "Do you have any idea when Conner will be back from his assignment this morning?"

"What assignment?" he replied with a perplexed expression.

"He told me last night that he was going out with one of the reporters this morning."

"That's news to me," he said. "I saw him earlier but he wasn't on any assignment. I think he was filing some photos."

"Hmm," she said. "Maybe I misunderstood him."

"I'll tell him you asked about him."

"No. I'll talk to him later."

Bernie shook her head slightly and went to Chase's desk. He looked up and saw her when she was about ten feet away.

"Good morning," he said. "Any news?"

"Not really," she said.

"It looks like something is on your mind."

"Oh, it's nothing. Just a misunderstanding with someone."

"Are you up for lunch a little later?"

"I should be. What time?"

"How about eleven-thirty?"

"Great. That gives me about an hour to do a few things," she said. "Do you want to come down and get me?"

"I'll do it," he said.

~ * ~

Chase finished his column and perused it before putting it in the Sunday file for the copyeditors. He picked up his day calendar and thumbed through it for a moment, stopping on the date when Brett Johnson was killed. It was circled in red ink. He remembered that Riggins was working that weekend. He wondered what Means was doing at that time.

Chase got up from his desk and strolled over to Means's office. His secretary was on the telephone and nodded to him that it would only be a minute. He eased over to table that had several magazines and picked one up.

"Yes, Mr. Means," she said. "I'll take care of that for you before you come in on Monday. I hope you have a nice weekend. Oh, by the way, Conner Rhodes wanted you to call him on his cell phone. I don't think it was anything urgent."

After a short pause, she said, "Have a safe trip home. I'll see you Monday. Bye."

Chase stood over to the side, giving the impression that he wasn't eavesdropping while looking at a journalism magazine. *Call Conner on his cell phone?*

"Hi, Chase," she said cordially. "What can I do for you?"

"I was hoping Jordan would be here," he said, smiling. "I needed to ask him about something."

"Oh, he's still out of town at the editors' conference and won't be back in the office until Monday. Maybe there is something I can help you with?"

"Maybe you can," he said. "It's really something minor. I was going over some expense reports and I remembered that we attended a meeting together."

"What day was it?"

"I believe it was March 21."

"Let me see," she said and began flipping through the calendar on her desk. "It looks like he was in Louisville that day."

"That must have been it," Chase said. "Would he have come back that night?"

"Oh, I'm sure," she said. "It was a noon meeting."

"I wasn't sure if it was something during the day or an overnight thing," Chase said.

"He came back because he met Mr. Pembroke and Mr. Riggins for dinner."

"You've been a big help," Chase said with a friendly smile.

Chase returned to his desk, glad that he was able to find out Means's whereabouts that day but troubled by Conner's message for Means. He noticed that it was almost eleven-thirty on his computer clock and walked over to Bernie's desk.

"Are you ready for lunch?" he asked.

"Let's go," she said, standing up quickly. "I need a break."

"Any preferences?"

"Your place?" she said with a wink.

"Yeah, right," he said smiling and shaking his head.

"Just kidding, Chase," she said. "How about that little café a few blocks from here."

"That's fine with me. The weather seems to be cooperating since the sun is out."

They left the newspaper building and strolled leisurely to the café.

"Have you ever considered Jordan Means in your story?" Chase asked.

"Jordan Means? You've got to be joking."

"I was curious."

"Now you are more than that. What did you ask?"

"Because he and Taylor have been rather close for several months. I thought there might be a connection," Chase said.

"I never thought about that. And with Angela saying that we should be careful around him, that kind of sent up a red flag."

"It's certainly worth looking in to."

"I wonder if the cops have checked into it."

"I could ask Gene or Marcia."

"Isn't that stepping over the line?"

"I don't think so," she said. "The newspaper has tied my hands on my story. Furthermore, it's only a question. They may have already done something and cleared him."

They found a table near the front of the café and sat down. She ordered a diet cola and he asked for unsweetened tea as they looked over the menu. The waitress returned and took their orders for large garden salads.

"How is Hannah?" Bernie asked. "You haven't mentioned her in awhile."

"She's doing fine. I'm having dinner at her place tonight."

"That's nice. I had Conner over at my place last night."

"Really?"

"Yes, really," she said with a laugh. "What's the big deal?'

"Oh, nothing. Was he there when I called?"

"Yes," she said. "Are you jealous?"

"Terribly," he said, rolling his eyes.

"Okay smarty," she said. "Why do you ask?"

"Does he have much interest in your story?"

"Yeah, he's really interested," she said between taking a bite from her salad. "He wants to know everything."

"That's interesting."

"Well, Mr. Elliott, if you hadn't noticed, Conner and I have been dating the past couple of months."

"I don't keep up with your busy social life."

"I'm a regular social butterfly," she said with a laugh.

"Does he ask many questions about what you're doing?"

"I guess so," she said. "Like I said, he's interested in what I do. Why are you asking me this?"

"Oh, I'm just trying to figure out who knows what is going on," Chase said. "It's not a big deal."

They went back to eating their salads as the conversation drifted over to stories they'd read in the newspaper. After they finished, they returned to the newspaper.

"I enjoyed lunch," Bernie said as they went up the elevator.

"We'll do it again soon since the weather is nice," he said.

"Promise?"

"Yes, I promise," he said with a chuckle.

"I hope you and Hannah have a nice time tonight."

"Do you have any plans?"

"I have a free night," she said. "Did you want to come over a little later?" She gave him a playful wink.

"You never give up," he said.

"Not when it comes to you."

~ * ~

After lunch they returned to the newspaper office. Chase talked with several sportswriters while Bernie went back to her desk and picked up the telephone and called Slone.

"I got a question I need to ask but I ask that you please keep it between us," Bernie said.

"I don't know if I can do that but I won't tell anyone where I heard it from."

Bernie paused for a moment. "I guess that's fair enough."

"So what is it?"

"I was wondering if you've considered our editor in your investigation?"

"Taylor Riggins?"

"No, Jordan Means. Riggins is the managing editor. Means is his boss. The editor."

"Other than some preliminary questioning about Brett Johnson, we haven't done much with him. Why do you ask?"

"Someone here at the newspaper said we should be very cautious about what we say about the investigation to Means. It made me wonder if there is something that he wants to hide."

"That's interesting. We'll go back over our notes and see if there's anything suspicious."

"Remember that you didn't hear it from me. I could lose my job."

"Don't worry, Bernie. Everything you say is safe with me."

"So how's Gene?"

"He's doing all right," Slone said. "Do you want me to have him call you?"

"No, that's okay. Just tell him I said, 'Hi.'"

Bernie looked up after putting down the receiver and Conner was standing next to her desk.

"Hi, Bernie," he said.

"What happened to your assignment?" she asked.

"What assignment?"

"The one you talked about last night."

"Oh, it was cancelled," he said with a smile. "The reporter got sick."

"Really?" Bernie said with furrowed brows.

"Who were you talking to on the phone?"

"I was making my daily call to the police station."

"Any breaking news?"

"Not really," she said. "Same oh, same oh."

"Are you busy?"

"Actually, I have some more calls to make," she said. "I hope you don't mind."

"Don't let me get in the way," he said. "I just wanted to stop by for a second. Are you busy this weekend?"

"I'm not sure yet," she said.

Her telephone rang and she picked it up quickly. Conner looked away but remained standing next to her desk.

"Oh, hi, Detective Bennett," she said. "I'm doing well."

Bernie glanced up at Conner and caught his eye. He grinned and walked to the photography department.

"I understand you just talked to Marcia," Bennett said. "I was wondering if you had anything else to contribute about Means?"

"Not really," Bernie said. "It was just an anonymous tip, so to speak."

"We'll look into it."

"I hope you let me know what you find."

"We will," he said. "Can I ask you another question?"

"Sure."

"This one is personal."

"Uh, I guess so," she said.

"Are you married or seeing somebody?"

"I'm single," she said. "There's one guy I've seen off and on but nothing serious."

"So you date others?"

"I suppose so," she said. "Why do you ask?"

"I know someone who would like to ask you out."

"Who is it?"

"I'll let you know after we get finished with this investigation."

"Do I know this person?"

"Yes, but not very well."

"Well, I'll keep my date book open," Bernie said with a laugh.

"I need to get back to work," Bennett said. "It was nice talking to you. Have a great day."

Bernie put down the receiver and walked to the women's room. Angela was inside, applying a dark red lipstick. She made eye contact through the mirror.

"Hi, Angela," Bernie said. "Are you having a busy day?"

"It's not too bad," she said. "I hope to get out of here early today."

"Do you have big weekend plans?"

"I'm really not sure," she said as she put the lipstick back in her purse. "It's just been a long week and I'm ready to relax."

"I know what you mean," Bernie said.

"How is your story coming along? I haven't seen anything in print yet."

"It's coming along very slowly. I'm trying to put all the pieces together."

"I know it must be difficult. They haven't given you an easy assignment."

"No kidding," Bernie said. "I shouldn't even be talking to you about it."

"Anyway, good luck with it," Angela said as she walked toward the door.

"Thanks," Bernie said. "I hope you have a nice weekend."

Thirty-three

Chase arrived at his house shortly after five p.m. A light rain that fell for several hours had just ended, leaving a glistening sheen over the lawns. After pouring a soft drink, Chase sat down on the recliner and turned on the television. He flipped through several channels, finally stopping on CNN to get a quick review of the news. Before long, he was dozing as night began to fall over the city. He was awakened by a knocking on the door. He pulled up from the chair and answered the door.

Riggins stood on the porch, steely-eyed and erect.

"May I come in?"

Chase opened the storm door and Riggins went directly to the couch and sat down. Chase closed the door and returned to the recliner.

"What's going on?" Riggins asked.

"What are you talking about?"

"You know what in the hell I'm talking about. I don't appreciate what you've been doing."

"Can you be more specific?"

"I've known you for a long time and I considered you a friend," Riggins said, leaning forward and clasping his hands. "I confided some things with you. I've trusted you for a long time. I don't know what to think now."

"I haven't told a soul about what you told me," Chase said, addressing him firmly. "Not that I haven't wanted to tell the world. I wish you had never told me what you did. That was going over the line with a friendship. All you were doing was unloading your deceitfulness on me."

"I've been told that you're somewhat of a ringleader in some things at the newspaper."

"I don't know where you would hear things like that."

"I've got my sources, too," Riggins said. "I've heard that you've had people questioning the sources on my story and that you've even hinted that I may be involved in Brett's death."

"As you know, you can't always trust sources. Sometimes they make up things."

"I don't see the humor in that remark."

"It's not supposed to be funny."

"I'd suggest you back out of everything you've insinuated about me or face the consequences."

"What is that suppose to mean?"

"You'll find out if you persist in what you're doing."

"While you're here, I'd like to ask you something. What were you doing at Hannah's house earlier this week?"

"You don't really want to know."

"If I didn't want to know, I wouldn't be asking."

"You know Sheila and I have separated."

"I know."

"I was lonely and wanted to see if Hannah wanted to go out."

"Even though you know she's been with me for quite some time?"

"That doesn't make any difference," Riggins said. "You interfere in my life and I have the right to interfere in yours."

"You frightened her."

"I can't believe that."

"Well, you did."

"There are some things you don't know."

"What are you talking about?" Chase asked angrily.

"I've known Hannah for a long time."

"And?"

"We had a fling before you knew her."

"Bullshit."

"Ask her."

"She's never mentioned anything about you."

"This was back when I first started working at the paper."

"Why are you telling me this?"

"Does it bother you to know that I've fucked your woman?"

"Get the hell out of my house!" Chase rose quickly with clenched fists.

Riggins got up slowly from the couch, a smirk across his face, and walked to the front door.

"Like I told you," Riggins said. "You're messing with the wrong person. Keep it up and you'll suffer the consequences. And that includes Hannah."

"Don't threaten me," Chase said. "Don't think I won't blow the whistle on you. I should have done it months ago."

Chase moved toward him but Riggins opened the door and slipped away quickly. Chase went to the door and watched him get in his car. Riggins gave him a snide look as he was backing out of the driveway.

Chase closed the door and returned to the recliner. He wanted to pick up the telephone and call Hannah but was too upset. Emptiness came over him as he thought about Hannah with Riggins, no matter that it may have happened years ago.

After sitting in silence for a few minutes, Chase went to the refrigerator and took out a can of beer. He opened it and sat down at the kitchen table, slowing taking sips while he tried to take in what Riggins had told him. It nearly made him sick in his stomach the more he thought of the two of them together, even though it was years ago and before he met her. Even the thought that Riggins was cheating on his wife back then was something that Chase couldn't understand. He wondered how deceitful Riggins had been in other things and if the false newspaper story was only the tip of the iceberg.

After finishing the beer, Chase put on a pot of decaf coffee and sat down at the kitchen table. He picked up the newspaper and skimmed through the pages, nothing catching his eye to spend any time reading. When the coffee was ready, he poured a large cup and went to the living room and sat down in the recliner and turned on the television. He mindlessly flipped through the channels, unable to stay on one for more than a few seconds. He finally turned it off and picked up a news magazine but found that he couldn't keep his mind on the content. All he could think about was Riggins and Hannah. His mood changed from anger to depression.

The doorbell rang. Chase sat in his chair, unsure if he wanted to see who was visiting him at nine-thirty at night. It rang again. A few seconds later, he heard, "Answer the door, Chase," Bernie said. Chase got up and opened the door.

Standing at the front door with the coffee in his hand, Chase looked dejectedly at Bernie. She took the initiative of opening the storm door and stepped inside the house as Chase moved aside.

"What's the matter?" she asked. "You look as if you lost your best friend."

"I'm fine," he said, forcing a half smile. "I dozed off on the recliner."

"I apologize for coming here so late," she said. "I didn't think you'd be asleep this early."

Chase followed her to the couch. She sat down at one end and he at the other.

"Do you mind if I have a cup of coffee?" she asked.

"Go ahead," he said. "It's decaf."

"Great," she said as she got back up and went into the kitchen and prepared a cup. She returned and sat back down.

"So what brings you here tonight?" Chase asked as she took a sip from the cup.

"Taylor and Jordan are back in town," she said. "I saw Jordan come into the newsroom around five or so, just as I was leaving."

"Did you talk to him?"

"Hell no," she said with a laugh. "But there was something I thought was odd."

"What was that?"

"As I was leaving, I could have swore I saw Conner go into Jordan's office."

"Perhaps he's doing something for Means."

"He would have told me," Bernie said. "He tells me everything."

"You think so?"

"I thought so. Why do you say that?"

"When I was at Means' office the other day, the secretary took a call from Conner."

"Why haven't you told me?"

"Because I didn't know what to make of it."

"I wonder what he wanted to tell Jordan?"

"You'd have to ask Conner."

"He has been acting a bit strangely lately."

"In what ways?"

"The other night after I talked to you, he left right after that. He said he had an early shoot but I was at the paper the next morning and he didn't have anything. And come to think of it, he's been a little too nosy about what I'm doing."

"Could he be a spy?"

"More like a snitch," she said, irately.

"Now don't jump to any conclusions. You don't have any facts yet."

"I know, but it still angers me to know that he could be doing something."

"I may as well tell you something else."

"What is that?"

Chase put his cup on the end table and turned his body toward her, with a leg underneath him.

"Taylor dropped by here this evening," he said.

"Are you serious? What did he want?"

"He accused me of being a so-called ringleader in gathering information about him."

"Now where would he hear that from?"

"Your guess is as good as mine."

"Who do you think it could be?"

"There's only a handful of people who know what's going on," Chase said. "Hernandez, Simpson, and Richardson are the only reporters. Maybe Angela Cook knows something. And then there's Conner."

"How about the cops?"

"I can't imagine Bennett or Slone saying anything. How about Riggins's wife?"

"I guess that would be a possibility since I talked to her but I seriously doubt it."

"Did Taylor say anything else to you?"

"Uh, not really," Chase said, reaching to pick up the cup and avoid any eye contact.

"That really takes a lot of nerve for him to come over here and make that accusation," Bernie said. "Who does he think he is?"

"Are you working this weekend?" Chase asked.

"No, but I may have to do some snooping around before I go back to the office Monday."

"Same here," Chase said. "I'm sure Taylor will be waiting to see you Monday morning."

"Do you think he may call me this weekend?"

"I really wouldn't be surprised," Chase said.

Five minutes after Bernie left, the phone rang.

"I thought you were coming over tonight," Hannah said.

"Oh damn!" Chase said. "I'm sorry. Things got crazy today. Can I get a rain check?"

"Of course you can. Is anything the matter?"

"No." Chase paused a moment. "I just got caught up in some things and time slipped away from me."

"That's okay, honey," she said. "We all have those days."

"Unfortunately."

Thirty-four

Chase slept poorly during the night, tossing and turning and waking up every hour or so. He finally got out of bed at four forty-five and went to the kitchen and put on a pot of coffee. He looked out the front door but the newspaper hadn't arrived. There was hardly any activity in the neighborhood but it would gradually pick up later in the morning since it was Saturday and children were out of school.

While the coffee brewed, he shaved, took a shower and got dressed. Thirty minutes later he was sitting at the kitchen table drinking coffee and eating toast. He heard the flop of the newspaper hitting on his front porch and stepped outside to pick it up. He glanced down both sides of the street and noticed a parked car with someone in it. After he stepped back inside the house, he heard the car drive by slowly.

Chase returned to the kitchen table and took his time reading the paper. He poured a second cup of coffee. Moments later, he heard something in the backyard. He went softly to the kitchen window and peeked but didn't see any movement. He stood there for a minute before deciding it must have been an animal and returned quietly to the table but he couldn't concentrate on the newspaper. His thoughts were on other matters, mostly about Riggins's remarks about Hannah.

Finding himself yawning at six, he sat down in the recliner and turned on the television. Before long, he dozed off to sleep. The storm door creaked open and Chase opened his eyes and got out of the chair. He looked at the clock on the wall. Six-forty-five. The floor creaked slightly as he moved slowly to the front door. As he was about to look through the peep hole, three loud knocks on the door caused him to jump backward.

"Chase Elliot?"

He recognized Bennett's voice. Chase opened the door and let him in the house.

"You scared the hell out of me," Chase said, shaking his head.

"I didn't mean to do that," Bennett said.

"Would you care for some coffee?"

"Sure," Bennett said.

Bennett followed Chase to the kitchen and sat down at the table while Chase poured two cups of coffee. Bennett took his black.

"So what brings you here on a Saturday morning?" Chase asked as he sat down across from Bennett.

"I received a call from Bernadette Robbins last night and she told me that you had an encounter with Taylor Riggins."

"That's right," Chase said, "but I didn't give it that much thought. You know I'm trying to help her with her story about Brett Johnson?"

"I'm aware of that."

"Riggins seems to think that I'm the ringleader," Chase said with a laugh. "I'm only trying to help her."

"Have you heard anything else from him?"

"No," Chase said. "I don't imagine I'll see or hear from him until Monday."

"Why were you up so early today?"

"I couldn't sleep last night."

"Were there any disturbances around your house?"

"I'm not sure," Chase said. "I did hear something outside but it could have been a dog or cat. How did you know?"

"We thought we saw some unusual activity," Bennett said. "I had a patrol car drive by here before six. The officer thought he saw some kind of movement in your backyard. By the time he could check it out, things appeared to be quiet."

"A prowler in the neighborhood?"

"We're not sure," Bennett said. "But I'd suggest you be careful. Make sure your windows are locked."

"I keep them locked," Chase said. "Thanks for the alert."

~ * ~

"Hernandez, what in the hell is going on?" Riggins said Saturday in his office.

"What do you mean?"

"You know damn well what I'm talking about."

"I'm sorry, sir, but I don't."

"You're not checking into my award-winning story?"

"Well, uh, there have been some inquiries about it," Hernandez said meekly.

"And what have you found?"

"Nothing," Hernandez said.

"I believe I'm going to put you on a one-month suspension without pay."

"Sir, that's not fair."

"It's not fair for you to spy on me behind my back."

"I have bills to pay and I can't afford not to get paid."

"You should have thought about that before you started prying into my story."

"But we haven't found anything."

"We?"

"I'm speaking in general terms," Hernandez said. "Bernie is working on the story but she's not doing the newspaper angle."

"Bernie is working on the Brett Johnson story," Riggins said. "She's not working on a story about me. Or is she?"

"No sir, I didn't mean it that way," Hernandez said nervously.

"I don't believe you're being straight with me."

Hernandez sat silently, looking away from Riggins and staring into the distance outside the window.

"Is there anything else?" Riggins asked.

"No."

"Then get of my office. You have fifteen minutes to leave the newsroom or I'm calling security."

"I don't believe this is fair," Hernandez said, his voice shaky as he stood, almost at military attention.

"You don't know what fair is."

Hernandez walked out of the office and to his desk. There were hardly any reporters in the newsroom since it was a weekend and early in the afternoon. He quickly went through his belongings, making sure he had his file on Riggins, and left.

As he reached the far end of the newsroom, Riggins stepped out of his office.

"What are you taking with you?" Riggins shouted. Several copyeditors were startled by the outburst and looked at him. Hernandez ignored him and hurried to the vacant elevator and took it to the first floor. Riggins called the security desk, but Hernandez had already left the building and was heading toward his vehicle. By the time Riggins got the message to the security officer, Hernandez had pulled out of the parking lot.

~ * ~

Hernandez stopped at a coffee shop and sat at the counter. After his order of coffee and Danish roll arrived, he opened the file on Riggins and smiled. "I'm going to get you, you son of a bitch," he said quietly to himself.

He glanced over his notes, then closed the folder and slowly sipped on his coffee. The waitress came over and warmed his coffee. He felt a tap on his shoulder and turned around and Conner was standing behind him.

"Hi, Conner," Hernandez said.

"What are you doing here this time of day?" Conner asked.

"Grabbing a late breakfast," Hernandez said with a chuckle. "What about you?"

"I thought I'd get an early lunch. Mind if I join you?"

"There's a stool," Hernandez said, nodding at the one next to his.

Conner sat down and placed an order for hamburger, fries and soft drink.

"Are you working today?" Conner asked.

"I was."

"Early day then?"

"Not really," Hernandez said, then taking another sip of coffee. "I'm on a thirty-day vacation."

"What are you talking about?"

"I just got suspended by Riggins."

"You're shittin' me."

"I wouldn't do that," Hernandez said. "He found out that I was doing a little investigative work on his investigative work."

"I wonder how he found out?"

"I have no idea."

"So what are you going to do?"

"I guess I'll get in to touch with someone at the newspaper on Monday and see what I can do."

"Who?"

"I don't know," Hernandez said. "Perhaps Means. Maybe Mr. Pembroke. I'll probably call human resources."

"This really sucks," Conner said. The waitress placed his food on the counter and he smothered the fries with ketchup and took a big bite of the hamburger.

"At least I still have the goods."

"What are you talking about?"

Hernandez held the folder up and smiled. "These are my notes on Riggins," he said. "I was able to leave the newsroom with them before Riggins could do anything."

"Interesting," Conner said. "What are you going to do with them?"

"I need to go talk to Bernie and Chase," he said. "I need to find a place for safekeeping."

"I'll hold them for you if you want me to. They'll be safe with me."

Hernandez paused a moment and finished his coffee. "I appreciate the offer but I need to go over them with Chase and Bernie. Maybe I'll let you have them after I've talked to them."

"Just call me at work or home," Conner said. "I'll do anything I can to help."

"I need to be going," Hernandez said. "I hope you have a nice weekend."

"I'm working," Conner said. "I'm going to the newspaper after I finish eating."

"Let me know if you hear anything."

"You'll know it."

Thirty-five

"Got a few minutes?" Conner asked Riggins outside his office.

"Sure, Conner," Riggins said. "What's up?"

Conner walked into the office and sat in the chair facing Riggins's desk.

"I saw Hernandez a little while ago," Conner said. "He told me that you've suspended him."

"So?" Riggins shrugged his shoulders.

"He had a file on you and said he plans to talk to Bernie and Chase. I thought you would like to know that."

"That little fuckin' conspiracy. I don't know what they think they can do."

"They probably want to keep things stirred up."

"They're succeeding at that," Riggins said, bitterly. "I wonder if they're feeding anything to the cops?"

"I'm really not sure. I can find out."

"I'd appreciate it if you would do that," Riggins said.

"I'll get back with you when I hear something," Conner said as he got up from the chair. "I'll sweet talk Bernie."

"Thanks," Riggins said with a grim smile. "Keep a close eye on them. Do whatever you think is necessary."

As Conner walked out the door, Bernie turned the corner after getting off the elevator. He turned red-faced. She looked puzzled.

"Oh hi," Conner said as he followed her into the newsroom. "What are you doing here this afternoon? I thought you were off this weekend."

"I was in the neighborhood and decided to come in and pick up something."

"What's that?"

"Oh, nothing important," she said. "Just some notes. What are you doing here?"

"I had to pick up a camera and a lens."

"I need to be going," she said after picking up a notebook.

"Are you doing anything tonight?"

"I'm not sure," she said with a smile on her way to the elevator. "I need to run. Bye."

"See ya," Conner said, remaining at her desk.

Bernie reached the elevator, took it down to first floor and hurried to the parking lot. She practically ran to her car, parked near the building, and drove away. As she pulled out of the parking lot, Conner walked out of the building and watched her drive down the street.

~ * ~

A few minutes later, Bernie arrived at Chase's house. His car was in the driveway and she parked behind it. She banged on the front door three times.

Chase cracked open the door and let her in.

"What brings you here so early?" he asked as she went to the living room and sat down.

"I was just at the newspaper," she said. "I had to pick up a notebook."

"So?"

"As I got off the elevator, I saw Conner walking out of Riggins's office," she said. "Then he followed me to my desk."

"Did he say anything?"

"He wanted to know what I was doing there."

"What did you tell him?"

"Nothing," she said. "Do you expect me to tell him that I was there to pick up a notebook containing stuff about Taylor?"

"I'm sorry," Chase said. "I didn't mean it that way."

"That's okay," she said. "I'm a little upset right now. I sure wish this was over. Sometimes I feel like an innocent bystander in all of it."

"I know what you mean."

"And I wish the damn police would find something or do something. This has dragged on too long."

"I hope we're making some progress now."

~ * ~

As they sat in the living room, Conner drove slowly past Chase's house. He went to the end of the block and turned around and parked his car two blocks away. After sitting there for twenty minutes, he was startled by a knock on the passenger side window.

"Please roll down your window," said the man on the outside. He took out a badge and identification. It was Gene Bennett.

"Yes sir," Conner said. "Anything the matter?"

"May I ask why you're parked here?"

"I work for the newspaper and pulled over to think about a feature shot I need to get for tomorrow's newspaper."

"Can I see some identification?"

"Is it really necessary officer? Can't you see the equipment in my backseat?"

"Identification please?" Bennett said forcefully.

Conner took his billfold out of his back pocket and showed Bennett his driver's license and police-issued press I.D.

"Okay, Mr. Conner," Bennett said. "I would suggest that you find another place to contemplate. We've had some burglaries in the neighborhood and we have the area under surveillance."

"I apologize, officer," Conner said as he turned on the ignition. "I hope you find your burglar."

Conner slowly pulled out into the street and drove past Chase's house again. When he looked at the house, Chase and Bernie were standing on the front porch looking at his car. He tapped on the accelerator and speeded away.

~ * ~

"Can you believe it?" Chase asked.

"That S.O.B. followed me here," she said. "This is unreal."

A minute later, Bennett parked his unmarked car in front of Chase's house.

"How are you folks doing?" Bennett asked.

"We were just watching one of our co-workers drive by."

"Conner Rhodes?"

"Yes," Bernie said. "He's been acting suspicious lately."

"I just questioned him a few minutes ago," Bennett said. "He was parked a couple of blocks down the street."

"He must have followed me here," Bernie said. "I saw him at the newspaper a little while ago."

"Why would he follow you here?" Bennett asked. "He said he was looking for some kind of feature shot, whatever that means."

"Maybe I shouldn't say this but I saw him in Taylor Riggins's office and then he followed me here."

"Do you have any idea why he was in Mr. Riggins's office?" Bennett asked.

"To be honest, I have no clue," Bernie said. "He just had a funny look on his face when he saw me. And now for him to be here, it makes me wonder."

"Wonder what?" Bennett asked.

"I'm not sure," she said.

"You're not sure?"

"Well," Chase interjected, "we think Conner might be a spy."

"A spy?"

"He might be feeding information to Mr. Riggins and Mr. Means," Bernie said with a frown. "But we're not one hundred percent positive yet."

"You folks had better be careful," Bennett said.

"We will," Bernie said. "I need to be going."

"I'll follow you out of the neighborhood, just in case Mr. Rhodes is still around," Bennett said.

"I appreciate that," Bernie said. She turned to Chase. "I'll talk to you later. Bye."

"Don't do anything foolish," Chase said. "I'll see you."

Chase went inside and poured another cup of coffee. He was reading the newspaper in the recliner when the telephone rang. He eased himself up and answered the phone on the fifth ring.

"Hi, Chase," Hannah said. "Were you busy?"

"I was reading the paper," he said, dryly.

"How are you doing?"

"Just staying busy with work."

"Anything interesting?"

"Not really," he said. "Same old stuff."

"Oh," she said. "Are you sure I'm not interrupting something? You sound preoccupied."

"As I said, I was reading. That's about it."

"Do you want to do something today?"

"I'm not really up to it. I'd like to get some rest today. It's been a busy week. I'm sorta drained."

"Okay," she said with a tone of concern. "Call me when you get a chance."

Before Chase could reply, she hung up the phone. He really didn't care. After Taylor's revelations, he wasn't sure he wanted to be with her again. He felt somewhat foolish holding something against her that happened years ago but with the problems he had encountered at work, he wanted to be left alone to gather his thoughts.

He went to the bathroom, took off his clothes and got under the shower. The water streamed off his skin as he closed his eyes and tried to relax. He spent fifteen minutes under the beating water before stepping out into the steam-filled room. He opened the door and turned on the ceiling exhaust to clear the air, then dried off with an over-sized towel before wrapping it around his waist and walking to the bedroom. While deciding what to put on, he heard the doorbell ring. Through the peephole he saw Hannah waiting on the porch.

Chase opened the front door and she stepped inside the house.

"I guess I should have called again and told you I was coming over," Hannah said.

"No problem," he said. "I was about to get dressed."

"Do you have any coffee?" she asked.

"I think there's a cup or two left in the pot."

"I'll fix myself a cup while you get dressed," she said as she turned and walked to the kitchen. Chase went to the bedroom, took out a pair of khaki slacks and a yellow polo shirt from the closet. He brushed back his hair, splashed on after-shower cologne and returned to the living room. Hannah was sitting on the couch.

"You look very nice," she said. "Feeling better?"

"Yes, thanks," he said. "I needed a shower to wake up."

"Can we talk?"

"Sure," he said. "Anything in particular?"

"What's wrong?"

"What do you mean?"

"You were cold and aloof on the phone. I want to know if there is a problem. I can sense when things aren't right between us."

"Just a lot of things happening right now."

"We've always discussed things in the past. Can't we do it now?"

"I suppose so," he said.

"Well?"

"The police were over this morning. They believe there was a prowler at the house."

"And they didn't catch the person?"

"No," he said with a shrug. "Just told me to make sure things are locked up. And Bernie came over a little later and told me that she saw Conner in Riggins's office. She was upset about that."

"How come?"

"He may be a snitch."

"Conner? That's hard to believe."

"Maybe for you but he's been acting somewhat suspicious lately. Remember when you saw him at the restaurant with Taylor a few weeks ago? He was even parked a couple blocks down the street this morning after Bernie came here. Apparently he had followed her."

"Oh my goodness. Did anything happen?"

"The police questioned him and sent him on his way."

"Oh Chase," Hannah said. "I'm beginning to worry about you and the others."

"We'll be all right."

"It makes me wonder about Brett Johnson."

"I know but there's still not enough evidence to tie anyone to his death."

"Is there anything else you want to discuss?"

"Not really."

"What is it, Chase? You're not telling me everything."

"Do you really want to know?"

"Yes, I want everything out in the open. Wouldn't you want the same with me?"

"Perhaps."

"Then tell me."

Chase paused for a moment, then cleared his throat. "Were you ever involved with Taylor Riggins?"

Hannah sat quietly on the couch. She lifted up the cup and took a slow sip of coffee. Tears filled her eyes. She took a deep breath.

"A long time ago, Taylor and I had an affair that lasted a very short time," she said. "It happened right after I moved here. We met at some function and he asked me out. We dated a few times."

"And you slept with him?"

"Yes," she said. "But only once."

"Only one time?"

"I found out that he was married and immediately broke it off with him."

"Why didn't you tell me this before?"

"Because I didn't think it was important," she said. "It happened several years before I met you."

"He told me about it," Chase said. "I was shocked."

"Did he tell you everything?"

"I guess he didn't. He didn't tell me that he had deceived you. I guess I shouldn't be surprised."

"I try to be open with you about everything," Hannah said. "Is there anything else you want to know?"

"I suppose not."

"I've always considered that the people we dated before we met to be of no consequence," she said. "I've never wanted to know who you went out with."

"Were you close to Taylor?"

"Looking back, I don't think I was," Hannah said. "I was new in town and lonely so he was nice to be with. But when I found out that he was married, and had only been married for a couple of years, it made me sick. I met his wife several years later and found her to be a delightful person, despite being married to him."

"I hope you forgive me for acting so insecure."

"I'd probably feel the same way."

Chase rose from the recliner and sat down next to her. He put his arm around her and kissed her softly on the mouth. She moved closely to him and rested her head under his chin. He held her hand as they sat quietly with their eyes closed.

Thirty-six

"Can you tell me what in the hell is going on around here?" Means asked Riggins.

"I only know what you know, Jordan," Riggins said, sitting across from Means's expansive cherry desk. "I really don't think it's that serious."

"Why do you say that?"

"Because we control whether or not the story sees print."

"Only in our paper. Have you thought about TV, wire services, other newspapers?"

"I guess not," Riggins said, lowering his head. "But I still don't think they have much."

"Damnit, Taylor, anything they say would be damaging to the newspaper. Don't you realize that?"

"I'll see what I can do."

"You'd better do it damn fast."

Riggins rose and exited quickly from Means's office. As he made his way through the newsroom, several copyeditors and reporters kept their eyes on him until he was in his office. He closed the door, picked up the phone and dialed Conner's cell phone. A few seconds later Conner answered.

"Have you found out anything?" Riggins asked.

"She went to Chase's house after leaving the newspaper."

"That's not surprising."

"I've got bad news though."

"What in the hell is it this time?"

"I was parked a couple blocks from Chase's house and a cop questioned me."

"Damn!"

"I told him I was on assignment for a feature picture for Sunday's paper and pulled over to think about what I was going to do. He seemed to buy it."

"I sure as hell hope so."

"He saw my equipment in the backseat and seemed satisfied."

"So where are you now?"

"I'm a few blocks from Bernie's place."

"She hasn't returned from Chase's?"

"Nope."

"Maybe she went to Hernandez's apartment."

"I never thought of that. Do you want me to go over there?"

"Go ahead. Just don't get your ass caught again."

"Will you be in the office much longer?"

"Call me on my cell if you see or hear anything. I'm leaving the office in five minutes."

~ * ~

Conner headed to the Hernandez's apartment on the south side of town, about a fifteen-minute drive if the traffic wasn't too bad. About a mile from his destination, he ran into a heavy congestion from an accident. It took him twice as long to get there. He didn't see Bernie's Ford Escort or Hernandez's Chevrolet Cavalier in the in the parking lot.

To make sure they weren't inside, he got out of his car and walked up to Hernandez's apartment and knocked on the door. A few seconds later, a small boy answered.

"Hi," Conner said. "Is your daddy at home?"

"No, sir," the child said. "He went to see friends."

"May I help you?" an attractive woman asked as she approached the door. "My name is Susana. I'm James's wife."

"Hello, my name is Conner Rhodes. I'm a photographer at the newspaper. I was wondering if James is around."

"I'm sorry, but he left a few minutes ago to see some friends downtown."

"Oh my goodness," Conner said as he tried to turn on the country charm with an aw shucks grin. "Do you know where that would be?"

"I wish I could help but I don't know," she said, shrugging her shoulders and smiling.

"Did he say who he was planning to see?"

"Actually, they were some people from the church we attend."

"Oh," Conner said. "When do you expect him back?"

"Probably not for a few hours. They do Bible study and then go out to get a bite to eat."

"Well, thank you ma'am," Conner said. "It was nice meetin' ya. I'll just get back with him on Monday."

"I'll tell him you dropped by."

"That's all right," Conner said. "You don't need to. It was really nothin' important. I was just in the neighborhood and thought I'd drop by. You take care now."

After Conner left, Susana went to the telephone and called Hernandez on his cell phone.

"A photographer from the newspaper just left," she said. "His name was Conner."

Hernandez put his hand over the mouthpiece and said to Chase and Bernie, "Conner was just at my place."

"Did he say what he wanted?" Hernandez asked his wife.

"No," she said. "He said it wasn't important and that he'd call you on Monday."

"Okay, honey. Thanks for calling me. I'll be home a little later. Be sure and lock the doors."

Hernandez, Bernie and Chase sat in a small Mexican café tucked away in a shopping strip, drinking Coronas and eating tortilla chips and salsa during happy hour. The place was nearly empty.

"So what are we going to do?" Bernie asked.

"I believe we should go ahead and call Bennett," Chase said. "This is getting a bit too serious. We may be getting in over our heads."

"Yeah, I agree," Hernandez said. "I'm not sure if any of us is safe."

"Why don't we meet at my place tomorrow and you two see what kind of story you can come up with," Chase said. "I'll have Bennett come over and fill us in on what they've found."

"Can I ask a favor?" Bernie asked wide-eyed.

"What is it?" Hernandez said.

"I'm afraid to go to my place tonight. Could I spend the night with one of you?"

Chase and Hernandez looked at each other and lifted their shoulders in unison.

"We have a spare bed," Hernandez said. "You're welcome to stay at my place."

"Same here," Chase said. "I don't mind if you stay over."

"Are you sure it wouldn't be a problem?" she said, looking at Chase.

"Just as long as you don't snore so loud that it keeps me awake," Chase said with a laugh.

"I'll need to run over to my place and grab a few things but that shouldn't take long," she said.

"If you stay at our place, I'm sure Susana has something for you to sleep in," Hernandez said.

"If it's okay, I think I'll stay at Chase's," Bernie said. "I appreciate the offer but I don't want to be too disruptive on your family."

"It wouldn't be a problem, but I understand."

"I'm going to go now," Bernie said. "Chase, I'll be over at your house in about an hour or so."

"Call me if you have any problems," Chase said. "And let me know if you see Conner."

"I will," Bernie said as she pushed back her chair and stood. "I'll see you later."

~ * ~

Daylight was fading when Bernie arrived at her house. She went to the bedroom and removed a small overnight suitcase from the top of the closet. As she started packing sleepwear and a jeans and T-shirt to wear the next day, the doorbell rang.

As she entered the living room to answer the door, Conner was standing inside the doorway. Bernie stopped in her tracks, holding her hands to her chest.

"You scared the living daylights out of me, Conner," she said. "What are you doing here?"

"I'm sorry, Bernie" Conner said as he walked toward her. "The front door was open and your car is in the driveway so I figured it would be safe to come on in."

"Don't ever do it again," she said as her hands trembled. "I could have had a heart attack."

"Hey, we're friends," Conner said, grinning. "What are you getting so excited about?"

"I'm just tired," she said. "This has been a busy week for me."

"Why did you leave so quickly at the paper this morning?" Conner asked as she sat down on the couch. "That's not like you to rush off so quickly without saying anything."

"I was meeting a friend."

"What friend?"

"That's none of your business, Conner," she said derisively.

"Any plans tonight?"

"I'm going out in a few minutes and plan to stay overnight with a friend."

"Who?"

"Gee, Conner. You are sure nosey. It's not any of your business."

"I think it is," he said. "Haven't we been dating?"

"Yes, but so what? That doesn't mean I can't do other things and see other people."

"So it shouldn't be a big deal about telling me where you're going."

"It is a big deal because it's none of your business. Just like it's none of my business what you do."

"Touché," he said. "Be that way. I thought we had something between us but I guess I was wrong."

"I've got to be going in a few minutes," she said impatiently. "Is there anything else you want?"

"Were you at Chase's house today?"

"Were you spying on me?"

"I just asked you a simple question."

"Yes, I visited Chase today. We've been friends for a long time. You know that."

"Is that where you are spending the night?"

"You need to go now," she said angrily. "I've got things to do. Now leave!"

Conner rose from the couch and walked to her. He grabbed her arm tightly.

He twisted Bernie's arm slightly as she backed away. "Let go, Conner. You're hurting me."

Conner eased his grip. He looked sternly into her eyes.

"I don't like what you've been up to lately," he said. "Just because you haven't been able to get much on Brett Johnson doesn't mean you have to dig up dirt on other people."

"I'm just doing my job. You know that."

"Have you thought about those you could hurt?"

"Just leave, Conner. You're talking stupid."

Conner released her from his grip and took a step back. He pointed his index finger at her. "You'd better watch out," he shouted. "I would hate to see you get hurt, too."

"What are you talking about?" she asked.

"You just be careful," he said, pointing his forefinger at her.

Conner turned around and walked briskly out of the house. A few seconds later, he was in his car, screeching the tires as he backed out of the driveway. Bernie shut the door and locked it. She picked up the telephone and called Chase.

"Guess who visited me?" she asked, her voice trembling.

"Conner?"

"Good guess," she said.

"What did he want?"

"He wanted to know who I was going to see," she said. "He also warned me to back out of what I was doing. He said I could hurt someone or get hurt. It was scary. I've never seen him this way."

"You need to get out of the house and get over here as quickly as possible."

"I'm about packed. I'll be out of here in five minutes."

"Well hurry. He may return."

After putting down the receiver, Bernie went back to her bedroom and finished packing. She was out of the house in four minutes as she scrambled to her car.

As she drove on New Circle Road to Chase's house, she looked in her rear-view mirror and saw Conner's car in the distance. As she turned off Harrodsburg Road, Conner followed her. When she reached Chase's subdivision, Conner's car was nowhere to be seen. She parked behind Chase's car in the driveway and nearly sprinted to the front door. Chase let her in.

"He followed me most of the way here," Bernie said, nearly out of breath.

"I believe Bennett is going to have someone tail him," Chase said. "I called him after I talked to you. I think our Mr. Rhodes has suddenly become a suspect."

"Oh, thank God," Bernie said. "He was really acting strangely at my place. He was upset that I was spending the night with someone."

"Did you tell him where you were going?"

"No, but I'm sure he's figured that out by now."

"At least you'll be safe here."

Thirty-seven

Chase led Bernie to the sparsely furnished guest bedroom. She left her travel case on the four-drawer dresser and followed Chase into the living room.

"I appreciate you letting me spend the night," Bernie said as she sat down on the couch. "I hope James is safe."

"I'm sure James is doing okay," Chase said. "He'll be coming over tomorrow so we can go over notes and prepare some kind of story to give to the paper."

"Do you smell something?" Bernie asked, squinting her nose and eyes. "Like smoke?"

Chase sat still for a few seconds trying to pick up some kind of scent. "I don't smell anything."

"I guess it must be me," she said. "Maybe it's something you cooked today."

"I haven't cooked anything but that's not to say there isn't some kind of odor from the kitchen," Chase said with a laugh. "I probably need to clean the oven."

Suddenly there was banging on the front door and Chase opened it. A next-door neighbor stood wide-eyed on the porch. "There's a fire in the rear of your house! I've called the fire department. You'd better get out."

Bernie jumped from the couch and ran outside while Chase darted to a rear bedroom. Flames were shooting up outside the window and smoke was seeping into the house. He raced behind the house and turned on the faucet and began spraying the fire as Bernie and several neighbors stood and watched. They heard a siren in the distance. A few minutes later, a fire truck parked in the front of the house. It was only a matter of seconds before the firemen were dousing the fire with two heavy streams of water. After the flames were extinguished, several of the firemen went through the house to see if there was anything that had the potential of catching fire.

"Mister, this sure looks like arson to me," a fireman said to Chase. "I don't see any electrical connections or anything around here that would cause the fire. And for it to be confined to the exterior makes it appear more likely to be arson. But we won't know for certain until we have an investigation."

Chase stood silently and stared at the charred section of his house. Bernie came to him and put her arm around his waist.

"I wonder who did this?" Chase asked as if he already knew the answer.

"I can't believe someone would do this to you," Bernie said. "They have to be crazy."

"At least we caught it in time. There's not a lot of damage."

"Do you want to stay at my place tonight?" Bernie asked.

"We may have to unless we go to a motel. Let's go inside and get our things together and decide what we're going to do."

Bernie followed Chase inside the house. The power was turned off but a fireman gave Chase a flashlight to gather his overnight belongings. Bernie picked up her suitcase and waited in the driveway.

~ * ~

As the firemen were putting away equipment, Bennett pulled into the driveway.

"I just heard about this," he said to Bernie. "Was anyone hurt?"

"No," she said. "Chase is inside getting some things together. I guess we'll be staying at my place tonight."

"I may be giving you a call a little bit later to make sure everything is all right," Bennett said. "You have my number if you need me."

Bennett got into his unmarked car and drove away as Chase was walking out of the house.

"I guess we should take separate cars to your place," Chase said. "I'll follow you."

As they drove to Bernie's house, they could see smoke in the distance. When they got to her neighborhood, she realized the fire was in the vicinity of her home. As they turned on her street, there were three fire trucks parked in front of her house. Her home was ablaze as the firemen tried to keep it from spreading to neighboring home. Bernie stopped her car two houses from her home and ran to the front yard. Chase got out of his car and quickly followed her. She stood in front of the house motionless. Chase came up behind her and put his hands on her shoulders. She turned and put her head on his shoulder and sobbed.

After questioning from a fireman, Bernie learned that the fire probably started in the rear of the house. Since the fire was out of control when they arrived, they didn't speculate about the cause.

"Who did this?" Bernie asked, shaking her head as tears welled in her eyes. "I don't understand."

"I don't either," Chase said as he held her hand.

Chase quickly took out his cell phone and called Hernandez. He told him about the fires and cautioned him to be on the lookout at his apartment

Bernie called Bennett and told him what had happened.

"Have you seen anyone from the newspaper tonight?" Bennett asked.

"I saw Conner earlier, before I went to Chase's house. That's about it."

"You and Chase need to be extra careful," Bennett said. "Do you have a place to stay tonight?"

"I guess we'll find a motel now," she said while looking at the smoldering remains of her house. She began to sob again.

"Are you going to be okay?"

"I will," she said. "I just can't believe this happened. I've lost everything."

"I'll check back with you tomorrow."

~ * ~

After they finished talking, Bennett drove to Conner's house. It was dark outside and Conner's car wasn't in the driveway. Bennett drove a block down the street, turned around and parked his car. He decided to wait for Conner to return home. Just before midnight, Conner arrived in the quiet darkness.

Bennett watched as Conner got out of his car and ambled slowly to the house. A few seconds later, several lights flicked on. Bennett got out of his car and walked to the front of the house. He could see the light from a television and noticed Conner move about in the living room, finally sitting down.

Bennett went to the front door and knocked twice. Conner was quick to open the door and turn on a front-porch light.

"I'm Detective Bennett. May I ask you several questions?"

Conner stepped out onto the porch, holding a bourbon and water in a slender tea glass.

"What is it detective?" Conner asked. "Haven't I seen you at the newspaper?"

"Yes. I've been investigating the Johnson case. And I talked to you earlier today."

"Oh, I remember," Conner stammered. "Well, what can I do for you? It's awfully late. Nothing serious, I hope."

"Where have you been tonight?"

"I went out to eat with a friend and then I took in a movie. I just got home a few minutes ago."

"Who were you with tonight?"

"I had dinner with my boss."

"And who is that?"

"Umm, Taylor Riggins. He's the managing editor at the newspaper."

"I know. What time did you finish eating?"

"I'd say it was around nine-thirty or so. After that I went to over to the discount movie theater and watched part of a movie. I got bored with it and decided to come on home."

"Were you alone at the movie?"

"Yes sir. Is there anything else?"

"Not right now," Bennett said. "I may be getting back with you tomorrow or Monday."

"Anytime, detective," Conner said as Bennett returned to his car. "Anything I can do to help. By the way, what's this all about? Has anything happened to anyone?"

"Read about it in the newspaper," Bennett said as he walked away.

~ * ~

Conner watched as Bennett got into his car, turned on the lights and slowly drove away. He picked up his cell phone and dialed Riggins.

"Why are you calling at this hour of the night?" an indignant Riggins asked after being awakened. "It's past midnight."

"The police came around tonight."

"Are you kidding me? For what reason?"

"He wanted to know my whereabouts this evening."

"So?"

"I told him I had dinner with you," Conner said.

"You what?"

"Your name popped into my head. If he calls you, tell him we had dinner until around nine-thirty."

"Why was he concerned about where you had been?"

"I don't know," Conner said. "I'll let you know if I find out."

"Good night," Riggins said abruptly and hung up the phone.

"Don'tcha wanna know where we ate?" Conner said to a silent cell phone.

~ * ~

"Hannah?"

"Who's this?" Hannah asked sleepily. She glanced at the clock radio on the nightstand. Twelve-eighteen a.m. She reached over and turned on the lamp.

"It's me. Chase."

"Oh, I didn't recognize your voice. Is anything wrong?"

"I was wondering if I could spend the night."

"You know you can."

"I'm bringing along a friend."

"Who?"

"Bernie."

"What's the matter, Chase?" Hannah asked as she sat up on the side of the bed. "Something's wrong."

"I'll explain when I get there," he said. "We had a little fire."

"A fire?"

"Don't worry. I'll be at your place in about ten minutes."

After disconnecting the cell phone, Chase looked over at Bernie in the passenger side of his car. She was asleep, her head sideways on the headrest. He drove slowly through the night streets. As he pulled into Hannah's subdivision, he reached over and tapped Bernie on the shoulder. She stirred for a moment and opened her eyes.

"Where are we?" she asked.

"A few blocks from Hannah's house," Chase said. "We're spending the night with her."

"This entire evening seems like a nightmare," she said as she sat up in the seat and ran her fingers through her hair. "I can't believe any of this. Tell me it's a nightmare. Tell me I didn't lose my house and everything in a fire."

"I wish it weren't so," Chase said as he pulled in front of Hannah's house. They picked up their suitcases from the trunk and walked up to her house. The porch light was on, and Hannah opened the door when they were a few steps from the house. She was clutching a pink robe around her neck and reached out and took Bernie's suitcase as they entered the house. Chase kissed Hannah on the cheek.

"Do you want some coffee or anything to eat or drink"? Hannah asked.

"I'll take a soda," Bernie said. "I need to wind down."

"Same here," Chase said.

Chase and Bernie followed her into the kitchen and sat down at the table as Hannah prepared their drinks in glasses. Chase told her about the events of the evening. By one-thirty Bernie said she was ready for bed and Hannah took her to a spare bedroom and returned to the kitchen with Chase.

"Oh, honey," she said. "Do you have any idea who may have done it?"

"I've got my suspicions but I'd rather not say."

"Is it someone you know?"

"I believe it's someone at the paper. I'll tell you when I'm sure."

"Are you ready to go to bed?"

"I thought you'd never ask," Chase said. "I'm drained and exhausted."

They went to her bedroom and within seconds Chase had taken off his clothes down to his boxers and was in bed. Hannah turned off the lamp and snuggled up next to him. Within minutes, he was snoring lightly.

~ * ~

Hannah had pancakes and coffee on the table when Chase and Bernie woke up the next morning. They rehashed the events of the previous night while eating.

"I need to call James and see how he's doing," Chase said.

"Be sure and set up a time when we can meet today," Bernie said.

Chase picked up the receiver on the wall phone and dialed James's number. It rang several times before an answering machine came on. Chase left a message for Hernandez to call Hannah's house.

"I wonder where he could be on a Sunday morning?" Chase said.

"Some families go to church," Hannah said.

"I never thought about that," Chase said with a grin.

Bernie excused herself and took a shower while Hannah poured another cup of coffee for Chase.

"I'm really worried," she said. "You know you and Bernie can stay here for as long as you like."

"I appreciate that," Chase said. "But I feel that this thing is coming to a head. I believe we're going to find out who is behind this stuff very soon. To set our homes on fire shows that someone is desperate."

"I just don't want them to be so desperate that they try something else."

"We'll be careful. And the police are on this now."

Thirty-eight

Chase and Bernie got into his car and drove to Hernandez's apartment. They knocked on the door five times before he answered.

"Man, are we glad to see you," Bernie said. "After last night, we weren't sure if we'd see you or not.'

"We didn't take any chances," Hernandez said as he stepped aside to let them enter his living room. "We have some friends a mile or so from here so we spent the night with them. My wife and child are still over there. The police also kept the apartment under surveillance overnight. I'm sure my neighbors appreciated that."

"I thought we could compare notes and see if we have a story," Bernie said.

"Let me get my folder out and we'll get to work," Hernandez said.

"I think I'll leave you guys for awhile and take care of a few things," Chase said. "You have my cell phone number if you need to reach me."

"Just be careful," Bernie said.

"I will," Chase said. "I'll check back in a few hours."

Chase left the apartment and drove to Victoria Johnson's house. She was in the front yard, pulling weeds from a flower bed next to the house. The children were in the back yard playing on a swing set.

"Hi, Chase," Victoria said as she removed work gloves while walking toward him. Chase gave her a hug and kissed her on the cheek.

"I was wondering if anything has come up regarding Brett's death?"

"I haven't heard anything from the police," she said. "Occasionally I'll hear from Bernadette or Conner."

"Conner?"

"Oh yes," Victoria said with a smile. "He's been very sweet."

"What does he want?"

"He usually just asks about the kids and if he can do anything for us. He was here the other night and brought them some ice cream."

"Has he asked much about Brett's death?"

"Just the regular things that I hear from most people."

"Has he ever asked to look for things in the house?"

"Of course not," Victoria said. "He's offered to help me move things but he hasn't been snoopy. He's even offered to watch the house if I decide to visit my parents. Why are you concerned about Conner?"

"I was just curious," Chase said. "No reason. I'm glad folks at the paper are assisting you. You know you can always call on me."

"I appreciate that, Chase."

"I would like to tell you something but I don't want you to be alarmed."

"What is it?"

"Someone set fires at mine and Bernie's houses last night."

"Oh my goodness! Was anyone hurt?"

"We discovered the fire at my house soon enough to minimize the damage but Bernie lost everything."

"That's awful," Victoria said, her eyes welling with tears. "Why would anyone do something like that?"

"I'm not sure if it's connected with Brett's death but I just wanted to let you know. There's a nut out there and who knows what could happen next."

"Do the police know?"

"Detective Bennett has been notified."

"I sure hope everything turns out all right for you and Bernie."

"Thanks, Vicki," he said as he stood. "I need to be going. Please don't hesitate to get in touch with me if you need anything."

Victoria rose from her chair and hugged Chase. He kissed her again on the cheek before leaving. After backing out and driving a block down the street, Chase saw Conner heading toward her house in his car. Chase made eye contact with him, but Conner didn't acknowledge him. Conner parked in the Johnson's driveway. Chase was tempted to turn around but decided to go on to his house.

He found Bennett walking around the perimeter of his property with another man.

"Chase, this is Peter Thompson of the fire department's arson unit," Bennett said. "We're going over to Bernadette's after we're finished here."

"Find anything?" Chase asked.

"It appears to be gasoline," Thompson said. "I think whoever did it doused the side of your house, lit it and ran."

"I haven't found anything," Bennett said. "There were neighbors here after the fire so they may have inadvertently tampered with evidence or trampled over it."

"I'll look around as well and see if anything looks out of place," Chase said.

Thompson excused himself and returned to the side of the house while Chase and Bennett remained near the rear of the yard.

"Where's Bernadette?'" Bennett asked.

"She's with another reporter. They're going over some notes to see if they have enough for a story."

"I'm glad she's all right," Bennett said. "I'll try to call her a little later."

Chase wrote down Hernandez's phone number and handed it to Bennett. "You can reach her at this number. She should be there for most of the day. I'm sure she would appreciate a call after all she's been through."

"Thanks," Bennett said, tucking the paper in his shirt pocket.

"I was over at Victoria Johnson's house earlier."

"How is she?" Bennett said.

"She seems to be doing well. As I left, I saw Conner Rhodes heading to her house."

"Oh, really?" Bennett arched his eyebrows.

"He's been checking on her as well."

"Perhaps I'd better make a call on Mrs. Johnson."

"It probably wouldn't hurt."

"What other plans do you have today?"

"I may drop by the newspaper a little later."

"Is it open on Sunday?"

"The newsroom is always open," Chase said.

"Chase, I think you know that you should be careful. Don't take any unnecessary chances. Call me if you run across anything suspicious. Whoever set these fires means business. These aren't warnings."

"I'm aware of that," Chase said. "I just want to get to the bottom of this."

"We're going to have something very soon. I just don't want you or anyone to jeopardize our investigation. Let us do our job."

"So you have some likely suspects?"

"Chase, we've had some strong suspects from the beginning. We're just waiting for the wrong move or the right piece of evidence."

~ * ~

Bernie and Hernandez took out their folders and began comparing notes on the kitchen table.

Bernie picked up the news clippings from Riggins's award-winning story and looked over the highlighted names that may have been fictitious. She glanced at the photographs.

"It's a shame that story may have been total bullshit," Hernandez said.

"Well, at least partial bullshit. Some of the names aren't highlighted," Bernie said with a laugh.

As silence prevailed for a few seconds, Bernie continued to look over the story.

"Oh my God!" she exclaimed.

"What is it?" Hernandez said as he looked at the newspaper.

"Did you notice the photos?"

"I guess," he said. "What's the big deal?"

"Did you see who took most of them?"

Hernandez squinted at the credits on the photos. "Hmm. Conner Rhodes. I had never noticed that before."

"Me neither," Bernie said. "No wonder he's been so interested in what we've been doing."

"Yeah, I see a connection now," Hernandez said, "and I don't like what I see.'

"I'm going to call Chase and let him know."

"The phone is over there," Hernandez said, nodding toward the wall between the kitchen and living room.

Bernie picked up the phone and dialed Chase's number.

"What is it?" Chase asked.

"Have you ever noticed some of the photo credits on Riggins's story?"

"I must admit that I haven't. Who is it? Wait, let me guess. Conner?"

"Yep," Bernie said.

"Why don't you call Bennett?" Chase said as he drove through an intersection about five blocks from the newspaper building. "I'll be at the office in a few minutes. I'll let you know if I see or hear anything there."

"Talk to you later," Bernie said before hanging up the receiver.

"What did Chase say?" Hernandez asked.

"He guessed correctly on who took the photos. He told me to call Bennett."

"Good idea."

Bernie called Bennett's cell phone and he answered on the second ring.

"I hope I'm not calling you at a bad time?" Bernie said.

"Anytime hearing from you is fine with me, Bernadette," Bennett said. "What's going on?"

"James Hernandez and I were looking over Riggins's newspaper clips and noticed that Conner took most of the photographs. We weren't sure if you noticed it."

"I'd have to check with Marcia but I don't believe so," he said. "Thanks for the tip."

"I don't know if it's much but we thought you ought to know."

"I find it interesting," he said. "Call me again if you see anything else."

~ * ~

Chase walked into the newspaper building. The newsroom was nearly empty except for two clerks compiling stories off the wire. He went to his desk and thumbed through his daybook.

"What brings you in here today?" Conner asked as he approached him from the rear.

"Probably the same reason as you," Chase said coldly.

"I'm here to do some work."

"Same here."

"I heard about the fire at your place."

"I was fortunate the fire was extinguished quickly."

"Yeah, a lot more fortunate than Bernie. That was so tragic."

"I agree," Chase said, leaning back in his chair. "Oh, I heard some interesting news."

Conner looked perplexed. "What was that?"

"I never knew you took photographs for Riggins's story."

Conner looked at him for a moment. "Oh, I thought everyone knew that. But again, most people don't pay any attention to photo credits. We kind of work in anonymity. You know what I mean?"

"Did you win any awards for your photos? They're awfully good."

"They've been entered in some contests. I would think they'd win something since they illustrated a prize-winning story."

"I wish you the best," Chase said with a forced smile.

"Have you seen Bernie today?" Conner asked.

"No."

"I thought you were with her last night?"

"Where did you hear that?"

"Just scuttlebutt, I guess."

"I'm not sure where she's at."

"If you hear from her, tell her I asked about her."

"I'll do that. One other thing."

"What's that?"

"Didn't I see you over a Victoria Johnson's house today?"

"I stopped by for a few minutes," he said. "You got a problem with that?"

"No," Chase said. "Just curious."

Conner turned and slowly walked away without saying another word. Chase watched Conner head toward the photo department and disappear behind a closed door. Chase picked up the phone and called Hernandez and told them about his conversation with Conner.

"I'm going to stay here a little bit longer and see if anything happens," Chase told Hernandez. "How are things coming for you and Bernie?"

"I think we may have something for publication."

After hanging up, Chase went to the break room and bought a soft drink. He sat down at one of the small tables. A few minutes later Means came in and poured two cups of coffee.

"Hi, Chase," he said. "How are you today?"

"I'm fine, Jordan. How about you?

"Nothing to complain about. What brings you here?"

"I was in the neighborhood and stopped by to check my daybook. I have some things coming up this week and I need to let Cole know what's going on."

"About the same for me. I was out this past week at a conference and had a few things to check up on here."

"Anything interesting at the conference?"

"You know how those things are," Means said. "There were lots of committee meetings and talks on efficiency and cutting costs. We can't get much leaner than we already are."

"I hope it doesn't impact the newspaper too much," Chase said.

"I don't believe it will unless advertising takes a tumble. We seem to have been steady despite the sluggish economy."

"That's good to hear."

"I need to get back to my office and finish up," Means said as he walked toward the door. "Don't stay too long."

"You have a good day as well," Chase said.

Chase left the room two minutes after Means and returned to his desk. He noticed an envelope taped to the top of his telephone. It had the familiar penmanship of the previous unsigned notes. He looked around the newsroom before he opened it: *You are getting hot on your leads. Stay focused and you'll put out part of the fire.*

Chase put the note back in the envelope and placed it inside his pocket. He surveyed the newsroom again and didn't notice anyone watching him. He got up and went to the elevator and left the building.

When he reached his car, he sat there for awhile and to see if anyone left the building. After about thirty minutes, the weekend janitorial staff exited and several copy editors entered the building. Means walked out and went to his car, parked in a reserved space next to the building. About thirty seconds later, Angela came out and went to her car.

Thirty-nine

Chase watched Angela back out of the parking space and drive to the exit. He turned the ignition in his car and followed her when she pulled into the street, staying a block behind her as she made her way to the north side of town.

He wondered where she could be going since she lived on the east side in one of the newer upscale neighborhoods. He couldn't think of any places she would be shopping, especially on a Sunday afternoon. There were plenty of places to go where she lived.

Angela didn't appear to be in any hurry to wherever she was going, Chase thought. He had no trouble keeping her car in his sight as he remained a safe distance behind her. She ended up at a motel right off the interstate highway, parking near the entrance. Chase stopped his car about fifty yards away and watched as she got out of her car and went inside.

A few minutes later, Means showed up and parked his car about thirty feet from Chase's. Chase ducked when he saw Means and waited until he thought the area was clear. He peeked over the dashboard and saw Means walking toward the registration area. Moments later,

Riggins drove by in front of him and Chase dropped his head on the passenger seat. "Damn!" Chase said.

Again, he waited a few seconds before lifting his head and peeking over the dashboard. Riggins parked five spaces away. He got out and walked quickly to the front entrance of the motel.

Chase wondered what he should do. He knew he couldn't barge in on them. So he waited. After nearly an hour, Angela came out of the motel by herself. She glanced in Chase's direction and smiled. He wanted to hide but knew it was too late. Angela walked on to her car and waved as she drove away. Chase followed her, this time not worrying about her seeing him. Angela pulled off in the parking lot of a department store and Chase parked beside her.

"What's going on?" he asked, standing by her door.

"Do you like following people?" she asked.

"I don't make a habit of it."

"Did you find it interesting?"

"I don't know what to think. Do you want to fill me in?"

"Oh, I think you can do it all right."

"Have you been the person leaving me notes?"

"What notes?" she asked coyly.

"So what is going on at the motel? A meeting of some sort?"

"I guess you could say that."

"Should I go back and see?"

"That may not be necessary. Maybe it's another clue."

"Damn."

"What's the matter, sweetie?"

"Why are you playing these games with me?" Chase asked.

Angela winked and started her car. "You'll see," she said as she slowly eased out of the parking lot.

Chase stood watching her. He then returned to his car and called Hernandez.

"How are things going?" he asked.

"We're about finished," Hernandez said. "Will you be back soon?"

"I'll be right over. It's been a weird afternoon."

"What's happened?"

"I was just at a motel on the north side of town."

"What were you doing there?"

"I watched Taylor and Jordan go in."

"What?"

"I know what you mean. I still don't know why."

"Maybe we should call Bennett."

"That wouldn't be a bad idea."

"I'll do that when we get off."

"I also received a note at work."

"What did it say?"

Chase took the note out of his pocket and read it to him.

"What do you think?" Chase asked.

"That's so damn obvious."

"Huh?"

"The note is telling you that Conner set the fires."

Chase read the note to himself again.

"Gee, I'm stupid," he said. "I can't believe I didn't see that."

"I'm going to tell Bennett about it," Hernandez said.

"Go ahead and call and I'll head over to Conner's house."

"Do you think that would be wise?"

"I don't want him getting away before Bennett arrives."

"Be careful and don't take any chances."

After disconnecting the phone, Chase headed to Conner's house. He lived about fifteen minutes away.

~ * ~

Hernandez told Bennett about the note.

"Why in the world is Chase going over there?" Bennett said. "Call him back and tell him to keep his ass away from Conner."

"I'll try," Hernandez said.

Hernandez called Chase's cell phone but all he got was an answering service. Chase had turned off his cell phone because the battery needed to be recharged.

"Christ!" Hernandez exclaimed.

"What's the matter?" Bernie asked.

"Chase is on his way to Conner's place and I can't reach him."

"Then call Bennett and let him know."

"Let's go ourselves," Hernandez said.

Bernie rose quickly from her chair. "I'm ready."

They quickly left the apartment and headed to Conner's home in Hernandez's car. When they arrived at Conner's house, Chase was already parked in the driveway. Chase got out of his car and walked over to them.

"He's not at home," Chase said, standing next to the passenger side.

A minute later, Bennett arrived in his unmarked car and walked over to them.

"You should know better than to come over here," Bennett said. "All of you!"

"He's not at home," Chase said, shrugging his shoulders. "I guess it doesn't matter."

"It does matter," Bennett said. "I know you're trying to help but don't get yourself killed doing it. And you're interfering with our investigation."

Bennett received a call from his car and went to answer it. He came back less than a minute later.

"There's been a fire in your apartment complex," Bennett said, looking at Hernandez.

"Shit!" Hernandez said. "My wife and kid."

"Everyone's been evacuated," Bennett said. "I think the fire's been contained."

"I'm going back," Hernandez said. Bernie got out of the car and stood next to Chase.

"Be careful," Chase said to Hernandez. "We'll be there shortly."

Hernandez backed his car out of the driveway and headed to his house.

"Why don't you leave now?" Bennett said to Chase. "I'm going to stakeout the place for Rhodes."

"Okay," Chase said. "We're going over to my girlfriend's place. You know how to reach me."

Chase and Bernie got into his car and left for Hannah's house. Chase tried to use his cell phone to call her but the battery was dead. He stopped at service station and called from a pay phone.

"Hi, honey," Chase said. "Bernie and I are coming over."

"Oh."

"Is there a problem?"

"Yes."

"What is it?"

"The package didn't arrive."

"What are you talking about?"

"I need to go."

"Is someone there?"

"Yes."

"Conner?"

"Yes. I need to go. Good bye."

Chase reached into his pocket for some more change to call Bennett but only had a few pennies and a nickel.

"Damn!" he said as he returned to his car.

"What's the matter?" Bernie asked.

"Conner is at Hannah's house."

"Oh my god!"

"I need to get over there. Would you mind calling Bennett and let him know what's going on?"

Bernie got out the car without saying a word and ran to the pay phone. When she turned around, Chase was speeding away toward Hannah's house.

~ * ~

"I really don't understand why Chase feels like he has to stick his nose into any of this," Conner said to Hannah. "It's really none of his business. It's nobody's business."

Conner held a small handgun as he sat on the end of the coffee table. He was wide-eyed as perspiration trickled down his cheeks and neck.

"Maybe he feels like he's doing the right thing," Hannah said while sitting on the couch. Her hands trembled slightly.

"Taylor Riggins is a good man. He's given his life to the newspaper and brought all kinds of recognition to us with his story. I don't understand why Chase wants to tear it all apart. It doesn't make a damn bit of sense to me."

"Have you discussed it with Chase?"

"There's no reason to. He's already made up his mind."

"But Chase has known Taylor longer than you have. They both started working at the newspaper at the same time. Don't you think he knows Taylor better than you do?"

"Not any more. I've really gotten to know Taylor in the past year, ever since I worked with him on the big story. Did you know that I took most of the photographs?"

"I wasn't aware of that," Hannah said. "They're very good."

"They've been entered in a national contest. It will bring more recognition to the newspaper."

"I'm sure it will."

"But if Chase and Bernie and James and the others discredit Taylor, then my photos won't stand a chance. They may as well toss them in the trash."

"Why don't you just wait and see what is going to happen? Have you ever thought that they may clear any suspicions about Taylor's story?"

"You know better than that, Hannah. Whenever a newspaper starts something, it doesn't end until they come up with something negative. That's always the case. That even happened to Taylor. He felt like he had to come up with something bad so he did what he had to do."

"Do you think that's right?" Hannah asked.

"I think it's right because he was forced into coming up with something. And he still wrote about truth. It was the essence of truth. That's what really matters."

The doorbell rang and Conner jumped to his feet. He walked quietly to the door and looked through the peephole. Bennett was standing on the porch. The doorbell rang again.

Hannah was about to get up from the couch but Conner motioned with his hand for her to remain seated.

"This is Detective Bennett. Please open the door."

"Go away!" Conner yelled.

"I need to talk to you, Conner."

"I don't have anything to say. I told you to leave."

Hannah dashed to her bedroom, and slammed and latched the door. She locked it before Conner could get to her. Bennett heard the commotion inside and pushed against the front door. Conner rushed back to the front door. Hannah opened a window and shouted, "Help! Somebody help me!"

Bennett sprinted to the rear of the house and pulled off the window screen. He grabbed Hannah's hand and pulled her out of the house as

Conner knocked down the door and bolted into the bedroom. Conner charged toward the window, holding the handgun in the air. Bennett took his gun out of his shoulder strap and fired at Conner, striking him in the chest. Conner immediately dropped to the floor. Hannah screamed and held her hands over her face as Bennett stood by the window. Conner lay in a pool of blood.

Bennett called for medical assistance on his cell phone. He put his arm around Hannah and walked with her into the house. She sat down on the couch while he went to the bedroom. Conner was still alive, but his pulse was faint and his breathing was shallow. A siren could be heard in the distance, getting louder as it approached the house.

Bennett looked up and saw Hannah standing at the doorway.

"Is he still alive?" she asked.

"Yes. The paramedics should be here soon."

"Can I do anything?"

"You can stand out front and make sure they stop here."

Hannah went to the front yard and waited for the EMT vehicle to arrive. Chase drove up and parked his car in the street. He got out of the car and ran to her. He embraced her as she rested her head on his chest.

"Are you okay?" Chase asked.

"Yes," she said while sobbing. "Conner was shot by a police officer."

The EMT truck pulled into the driveway and two men and a woman got out. The men carried a gurney and the woman had a medical bag as they followed Hannah and Chase into the house. Bennett was with Conner.

"He's lost a lot of blood," Bennett said to the one of the techs. "He took a shot in the upper torso."

Bennett moved aside as the techs opened Conner's shirt and began wiping away blood. They slowed the bleeding and put him on the gurney and rolled him out of the house. Moments later, they were on the way to the hospital.

"What happened?" Chase asked Hannah as they went to the living room.

"He was upset about people questioning Riggins's story. He didn't think it was fair."

"Did he say anything about the fires?" Bennett asked.

"Not a word," she said. "He just rambled on about Riggins."

"Did he threaten you?" Bennett asked.

"He held a gun but never pointed it at me."

Bennett went back to the bedroom, put on plastic gloves, picked up Conner's gun off the floor and put it in a plastic wrapper. He returned to the living room.

"What's the matter?" Chase asked.

"He never fired a shot," Bennett said with a perplexed look on his face. "All the cartridges were still in the chamber."

"I wonder why?"

"Well, my guess is that he was waiting for you," Bennett said, looking at Chase. "He was probably hoping that you would show up. You were his target."

Forty

Chase went out to the front porch of Hannah's house and picked up the morning paper. Below the fold on the local section was the story about Conner. It gave very few details, other than him being at a Hannah's house and being shot by a police officer. The story didn't carry a byline and no comments from anybody at the paper.

Hannah was asleep in the guest bedroom, tucked under powder blue comforter. It was six-fifteen and the neighborhood was relatively quiet. Chase put on a pot of coffee and sat at the kitchen table. He thought about the previous day and Conner's crazy attack that bordered on suicide. No person in their right mind would charge a police officer with an unloaded gun. Hannah walked softly into the kitchen, stood behind Chase and put her arms softly around him and squeezed. He turned his head and kissed her gently on the cheek.

"Did you sleep well last night?" he asked. He moved his legs around in the chair and she sat on his lap.

"Considering everything that happened, I guess I did," she said. "It all seems so surreal to me. I can't believe it happened."

"I know exactly what you mean," Chase said, patting her gently on the knee. "The fires and then the shooting. What's next?"

"Do you think Conner killed Brett?" Hannah asked.

"He may have. I need to talk to Detective Bennett and see what he thinks."

Hannah got up and prepared two cups of coffee and brought them to the table. Chase handed her the section about Conner. She read it quietly.

"I wonder what Bernie thinks about all of this?" she asked. "They seemed to be getting close."

"Damn! I forgot all about her," Chase said. "I wonder where she stayed last night?"

"Who can you call?"

"I really don't have any idea."

"Maybe she'll show up at the newspaper office this morning."

"I'll give James a call."

Hannah handed Chase a telephone and he dialed Hernandez's number. He answered on the fourth ring.

"This is Chase. I apologize for calling so early. Have you seen or heard from Bernie?"

"She went to a next-door neighbor's house," Hernandez said. "I checked with her last night and she was doing fine. That was a wild scene with Conner that you had."

"Can you believe it? I never thought Conner could be capable of what he did."

"It just shows you never really know someone."

"No doubt about that."

"So what did you find out about Riggins and Means?"

"I really don't know. I left them at the motel when I got the call from Hannah."

"So you have no idea why they were there?"

"Not a clue," he said. "I need to get back with Angela. She knows a lot more than she is letting on. Were you and Bernie able to come up with anything?"

"Bernie and I finished our combined story last night," Hernandez said. "I think it's pretty good. I'd like for you to see it before we give it to the newspaper."

"I'll be over a little later this morning and check over it," Chase said.

"Who in the world are we going to give it to?" Hernandez asked. "Riggins and Means?"

"We'll decide on that later. I may have to get in touch with my attorney and get his advice."

"I'm going to shower and get dressed so come over when you can," Hernandez said.

"I'll see you in about two hours."

After hanging up the phone, Chase finished drinking his coffee and eating a piece of wheat toast and honey. Hannah had taken a shower while he was talking to Hernandez. She returned wearing a light robe and brushing her hair.

"I'm going to run by my house and get some fresh clothes and then go over to James's apartment," Chase said. "Is there anything I can do for you?"

"I need to stay around here for awhile in case the police need to investigate some more," she said.

"Do you want me to stay here until they arrive?"

"You can go ahead," she said, pouring herself another cup of coffee. "I'll be all right."

"You have my cell phone if you need to reach me," he said, getting up from the table. "It should be recharged now. I'll call back a little later and check on you."

Hannah walked Chase to the front door, where they kissed before he left.

~ * ~

Chase wasn't gone five minutes when the doorbell rang. She was still in her robe and her hair wet when she opened the door. Riggins stood in front of her.

"May I come in?" he asked.

"What do you want?"

"I want to talk to you for a few minutes. One of my photographers was shot here last night and I'd like to see where it happened. We may have to bring charges against the police department."

"Charges against the police?" she asked, bewildered. "Are you serious? He attacked me!"

"I understand Conner didn't fire a shot."

"Taylor, you need to get in touch with the newspaper's lawyer," she said. "I'm not going to let you in here."

"I don't know why you're acting this way," he said smoothly. "We've known each other for a long time and you should be able to trust me."

"I'll never trust you again, Taylor. You've said and done things that don't make any sense. Now leave!"

"Be that way," he said. "You're going to regret everything you've ever said and done. Let that be a warning. Understand?"

Hannah slammed the door and locked it. She looked through the peep hole and saw Riggins looking at her with an evil grin and shaking his head. A few seconds later he turned around and walked slowly to his car.

Hannah, her hands trembling, went to the phone and called Chase. He was about halfway to his home.

"Taylor was just here," she said, tearfully.

"You've got to be kidding me?" he said. "Are you all right?"

"I wouldn't let him in the house. He wanted to look over the area where Conner was shot."

"You did the right thing," Chase said. "Do you want me to come back?"

"I'll be fine," she said. "I don't think he'll return. I'm going to get dressed now."

"I'll call Bennett and see if he can come over."

"You don't have to do that, Chase. I'll just wait around until I hear something from them."

"You just let me know if anything else happens."

"I will."

"I love you."

"I love you, too," she said.

~ * ~

After showering and changing his clothes at his house, Chase drove to Hernandez's apartment. Hernandez and his wife were sitting in the living room when he arrived. She watched television as they went to the kitchen and sat at the table while Chase read the draft of the story.

"This looks very good," Chase said. "I've been thinking about what to do with it and I thought perhaps we should set up a meeting with Dalton Pembroke."

"That's going to the top," Hernandez said. "Do you know him very well?"

"Only casually. We've chatted at ball games and on a few occasions at work. I don't see another alternative at this point."

"Not even talk to the Louisville newspaper or local media?"

"I think we need to exhaust our options at the paper. It seems like the right thing to do. It's our story."

"I hope you're right."

"Have you talked to Bernie yet?"

"She called about fifteen minutes before you got here. She plans to come over here in about an hour."

"I forgot to tell you that Hannah had a visitor this morning."

"The police?"

"Riggins dropped by."

"What did that sleazebag want?"

"He allegedly wanted to look at the crime scene."

"What did she do?"

"She wouldn't let him in," Chase said.

"Good for her."

"I need to get in touch with Angela Cook this morning."

"I wish I understood her connection in all of this."

"All I know is that she seems to have some kind of relationship with Taylor and Jordan," Chase said.

"Yeah, and no relationship with anyone else at the newspaper except you."

"Maybe she can help us in some way."

"Good luck," Hernandez said, arching his eyebrows and slowly shaking his head.

Chase's cell phone rang.

"An officer from the police department just left," Hannah said. "They asked some more questions and looked around the house."

"What are you going to do now?"

"I'm going to work," she said. "I don't want to hang around here any longer than I have to."

"Will you call me later on when you get the chance?"

"I will," she said. "Are you staying with me again tonight?"

"Most certainly," he said. "We'll go out to dinner so don't you prepare anything."

"I'll talk to you later," she said.

"Is everything okay with Hannah?" Hernandez asked.

"The police just left her house and now she's off to work. She's fine."

The door buzzer sounded, startling both Hernandez and Chase.

"That must be Bernie," Hernandez said as he went to answer the door. He quickly opened the door and Riggins stood facing him.

"What do you want?" Hernandez asked tersely.

"Got a minute?"

Hernandez moved to the side and Riggins stepped into the doorway. He looked toward the living room and smiled at an unsmiling Susana. He turned toward the kitchen and saw Chase.

"I should have expected to see you here," he said with a smirk.

"Probably so," Chase said. "Can I help you with anything?"

"I came to see James. I guess I picked the wrong time."

"Is there something you want?" Hernandez asked.

"I wanted to talk to you about your suspension," Riggins said with a forced smile. "I thought maybe we could sit down and discuss it."

"There's really nothing to discuss at this point," Hernandez said. "You made a decision and I can live with it."

"So be it, James. I was willing to wipe your slate clean but if you feel you're doing the right thing, then that's your decision."

"I appreciate your concern," Hernandez said sarcastically.

"One other thing," Riggins said.

"And what is that?"

"I'd be careful who I associated with. You may be getting the wrong advice on what you should be doing."

"Are you referring to me?" Chase asked.

"I think you know who I'm talking about," Riggins said. "This mission you're on is getting out of control and some people are going to get hurt."

"Such as Conner?"

"Conner was on his own but you get the picture."

Bernie came up quietly behind Riggins and stood, listening to the conversation without him realizing she was there.

"You've created the situation," Chase said.

"I haven't done any such thing," Riggins said angrily. "You're the ringleader behind this. You've gotten one reporter suspended and have another one way in over her head."

"Are you talking about me?" Bernie asked.

Riggins turned around and glowered at her.

"I knew I should have put a competent reporter on the story," he said.

"You did," she said defiantly. "And now that reporter has the goods on you."

Riggins looked at each of them without saying a word. He turned around and stormed out of the apartment.

"Don't let the door hit you in the ass," Hernandez said softly with a chuckle.

Forty-one

Chase left Bernie and Hernandez to work on their story and went to the newspaper building. It was nearly eleven o'clock when he walked into the sports department. The morning news meeting was still in progress. Chase could see Means and Riggins sitting at the head of the table in the conference room through the large wall window. He made brief eye contact with Riggins as he headed to his desk.

He glanced around and noticed several other reporters and copyeditors looking at them. He flipped through the mail on his desk and took a quick scroll through e-mail.

"Good morning, Chase."

Chase looked up as Bennett and Slone approached his desk.

"Good morning," Chase said. "What brings you here?"

"We have to meet someone."

"Who?"

"Taylor Riggins."

"He's at a meeting in the conference room right now," Chase said, nodding toward the room. "I believe it will be adjourning soon."

"I guess we can wait," Bennett said, glancing at Slone. "No sense in interrupting."

"Care for some coffee?" Chase asked.

"No thanks," Bennett said. Slone nodded in agreement.

"Well, have a seat then," Chase said as he got up and moved two chairs next to his desk. They sat down, both crossing their legs, and stared toward the conference room. Within two minutes, the meeting adjourned and editors began filing out. Bennett and Slone stood up and watched the door. They began to move slowly toward the conference room. As they reached the room, Riggins and Means walked out.

"May I ask what you are doing here?" Riggins said. "Haven't I asked you to call beforehand when you want to talk to reporters?"

"We're not here to talk to reporters," Bennett said.

"Then why are you here?" Means asked.

"We're here to make an arrest," Bennett said. "Mr. Riggins, you are under arrest for the murder of Brett Johnson."

"What?" Riggins said, incredulously.

Slone took out handcuffs and moved toward Riggins while Bennett read him his Miranda rights.

Riggins took a couple of steps backward. "I can't believe this. You don't know what you're doing. You can't do this."

Slone quickly moved behind Riggins and fastened the handcuffs so quickly on his wrists that he hardly realized they were on him. He squirmed a moment and then his arms fell limp behind him. Slone took a firm grip of his forearm and led him toward the elevator.

"Can you tell me what this is based on?' Means asked indignantly.

"Mr. Rhodes kept a journal that we discovered in his house," Bennett said. "He detailed how Mr. Riggins had gone to Johnson's house. Apparently Johnson knew that a story written by Mr. Riggins contained falsehoods."

"Are you serious?"

"Mr. Rhodes also was upset because he had taken a number of photos that were used in the story. He thought he would be discredited as well."

"This is unbelievable," Means said. "I'm really at a loss for words."

"The investigation isn't over," Bennett said.

"What do you mean?"

"There were some other entries in the diary that we have to investigate."

"You will have our full cooperation," Means said after clearing his throat. He glanced at Riggins and lightly put forefinger on his mouth.

"Thank you," Bennett said. "I'll be getting back with you soon."

"You're behind this," Riggins growled at Chase.

Chase stood quietly.

"I know you are," Riggins continued. "You've been out to get me from the beginning. I thought I could trust you."

Chase remained passive,

Bennett smiled and walked through the quiet newsroom toward the elevator with Riggins in tow. He glanced at Chase and grinned.

"What was that all about?" Green asked Chase.

"I don't know," Chase said. "I guess you'll have to ask Riggins."

~ * ~

"Do you think we should celebrate?" Hernandez asked Chase late in the afternoon as they sat in the break room.

"Perhaps we should get Bernie and a few others and go out for drinks," Chase said. "I can give Hannah a call to meet us."

"That sounds like a plan. Where do you want to go?"

"No reason to get fancy. Let's go to Pappy's."

"I'll get in touch with several folks and meet you over there at six."

Chase returned to his desk and called Hannah at her office. He got her voice mail and left a message for her to call him or meet him after work for drinks. He stayed at his desk until five forty-five, finishing his column and replying to e-mails. One e-mail was from Angela:

> *"Dear Chase... Why don't you take your girlfriend to Romano's tonight for dinner. Be there around seven-thirty. Wait at the bar for your table... Angela."*

Chase reread it and closed the screen. *So it was Angela all along sending the notes.*

When he arrived at Pappy's, Hernandez, Bernie and several others were huddled in the corner, chatting loudly over two pitchers of beer. They had a frosty mug ready for Chase.

"I guess we deserve this," Bernie said. "It takes a lot of pressure off us."

"You mean Taylor's arrest takes a lot of pressure off you," Chase said with a laugh.

"You don't know how much. The past few weeks have been a nightmare."

"I wonder what else is going to happen with the investi-gation?" Hernandez asked. "Bennett said he wasn't finished."

"I wonder if Taylor has anything to tell them?" Bernie asked. "I bet he could say a lot."

"I would guess that he's keeping mum about the whole thing," Chase said. "By the way, what's up with the story you wrote?"

"I still have it," Hernandez said. "After Taylor was arrested, I thought I might hold on to it for a bit longer."

"That's a good idea since the story apparently isn't over."

"You don't think we should let Jordan have it?" Bernie asked. "He seemed relieved after Taylor's arrest. I think he would be interested in reading what we came up with."

"I'm sure he would be," Chase said, "but I would hold off a little longer and see what else develops."

"I'll take your advice," Hernandez said before taking a big swallow of beer from his mug.

Chase looked over and saw Hannah walk through the front entrance. Her light breezy dress caught the eyes of several of the patrons but her eyes were focused directly on Chase. They pecked lightly on the mouth as she sat down in Chase's seat.

"I'm sorry I'm late," she said. "I had a meeting late in the afternoon."

"Would you like a beer or something to drink?"

"I'll take a soft drink," she said.

Chase waved to the waitress who came over and took his order for a soft drink and another pitcher of beer.

"So what was it like in the newsroom today?" Hannah asked no one in particular.

"It was electrifying," Chase said. "No one expected it and to see Taylor taken out in handcuffs was simply unreal."

"So it's over with?" she asked. "Finally?"

"Bennett said the investigation is ongoing so we'll see," Hernandez said.

"At least the creep is behind bars," Bernie said.

"When is his arraignment?" Chase asked.

"It's tomorrow," Hernandez said. "I don't think he'll be seeing the light of day for a while. I've heard bail may be set at one million dollars."

"The newspaper won't help him?" Hannah asked.

"I wouldn't think so," Hernandez said. "Taylor has already tarnished the newspaper enough. It may take years for it to recover."

Chase looked at the clock on the wall and saw that it was seven-ten. He smiled at Hannah.

"I think we'd better be going," he said.

"Rushing off so soon?" Bernie asked with a frown.

"I've got a dinner engagement tonight," Chase said.

"You do?" Hannah said with a puzzled look.

"Yes, I'm taking you over to Romano's."

"Oh really," she said with a smile.

"You look so lovely tonight that I want to take you to a very nice place."

Chase got up and Hannah slid out of her chair and stood next to him.

"Don't you guys celebrate too hard," Chase said. "And be sure to have a designated driver."

"We'll do that," Hernandez said, lifting his mug.

Chase and Hannah walked out of the bar and to his car. He opened the passenger side and let her in.

"This is quite a surprise," she said after he got in the car.

"I know it is," he said. "To be honest, it's kind of a surprise to me. I received an e-mail from Angela Cook and she told me to be over at Romano's at seven-thirty. It probably has something to do with the case."

They arrived at Romano's at seven twenty-five. There was a twenty-minute wait so they went to the bar. A few minutes later, Means entered the restaurant. He saw Chase and Hannah and walked over to them.

"I see you have to wait as well," Chase said. "I thought the editor would have a table waiting for him."

"You've got to be kidding," Means said. "Now maybe if I were a high-powered lawyer..."

They laughed.

Chase and Hannah were drinking gin gimlets.

"Could I get you a drink?" Chase asked Means.

"I'll have bourbon on the rocks, with Lucky Star"

A strange look came quickly over Chase. He took a sip of his drink and turned his head from Means.

"Is something the matter?" Hannah asked softly. "You look distracted."

"I'm not sure," Chase said.

A minute later, the maitre de came over and told Chase that his table was ready.

"I'll see you tomorrow," he said to Means. "I hope you have a nice evening."

"You enjoy you dinner," Means said before taking another sip from his drink.

Forty-two

The next morning Chase called Bennett at the police station.

"Gene, I seem to recall that a particular bourbon was found on Brett Johnson's clothing at the crime scene," Chase said.

"Give me a second and let me pull out the folder," Bennett said as he opened the side filing drawer to his desk. A few seconds later he took out Johnson's file. "Here it is. Lucky Star. Isn't that an expensive brand?"

"I believe so," Chase said.

"Why do you want to know?"

"Perhaps I shouldn't say anything."

"Don't give me that freedom-of-the-press line, Chase," Bennett said calmly. "This is about the murder of a friend."

"But I don't want to implicate an innocent person."

"It'll be off the record," Bennett said. "What is it?"

"I was dining at Romano's last night and Jordan Means showed up."

"So?"

"He ordered bourbon on the rocks."

"So what's unusual about that?"

"He asked for Lucky Star."

"That's interesting," Bennett said.

"Like I said, I thought it might be something you'd want to know," Chase said. "Please keep it between us."

"Don't worry about that," Bennett said.

"How is Riggins?"

"Mr. Riggins is doing well," Bennett said. "He's not saying much but we didn't expect him to. We're going to question him again this morning."

"If I hear or see anything else, I'll give you a call."

"Thanks, Chase," Bennett said. "I hope we get this thing wrapped up soon."

"Me, too. Then we can go back to being adversaries," Chase said with a laugh.

"One more thing," Bennett said. "We found an empty gas can in the trunk of Mr. Rhodes's vehicle."

"I suppose that eliminates other suspects?" Chase asked.

"We'll be questioning Mr. Rhodes in the next day or so and try to get a confession from him for the fires."

After finishing the conversation, Chase showered, got dressed and went to the newspaper building.

On the way to the men's room, Chase met Means, turning the corner after getting off the elevator.

"How was your dinner last night?"

"It was great. Romano's is one of my favorite places although it's a bit steep for my budget."

"I know what you mean."

"So what brings you in?"

"Since we don't have a managing editor right now, I have to take on some of those responsibilities."

"How long will that last?"

"It won't be long. I'll delegate some of the work to other editors. I've been doing a lot of this anyway since Taylor was relatively new on the job. It's a shame losing him because he had so much going for him."

"You're not expecting him back?"

"Good heavens no," Means said with a laugh. "I don't think we'll be seeing any more of Taylor around here."

Means walked to his office while Chase went to the men's room. As he washed his hands, he heard a loud pop. He ran to the hallway. The elevator door opened, and by the time he reached it, it had closed and was going down.

Chase thought of Means and ran to his office. Means was slumped on his desk, blood oozing from his shoulder. He slowly raised his head and looked at Chase with half-closed eyes. "Angela," he moaned.

Chase walked over to the Means's window and saw Angela running to her car in the parking lot. He went back to Means's desk and called security to get an ambulance. Moments later, Chase heard a siren, growing louder with each passing second. He put his hand to Means's neck and felt a faint pulse.

Chase called Bennett on his cell phone and told him about the shooting and then ran to his car to find Angela. He knew that Bennett would be putting out an all-points bulletin to track her down. While driving to her home, he noticed her car at a drive-thru bank. She was in line at the ATM.

He got out of his car and ran over to her vehicle. She saw him but couldn't move because of a car in front and behind her. He tried to open the passenger door but it was locked.

"Go away, Chase," she screamed. "I don't want to hurt you." She reached into her purse and pulled out a small handgun. He took a step back and looked at her.

"Why are you doing this?" he asked. "Why did you shoot Jordan?"

"That smug SOB thought he was getting away with everything," she said. "He didn't care about Conner and he was going to let Riggins hang out there to dry. You saw how he was acting when Riggins was arrested."

"The police aren't finished investigating," Chase said. "They are still on to Jordan."

"Jordan was there when Brett fell," she said. "He poured the whiskey on Brett to make it look like an accident."

"What do you mean?"

"Jordan and Taylor followed Brett to his home from a bar," she said frantically. "They got into an argument and Taylor shoved him. Brett fell and struck his head against the edge of a table. It was an accident. Taylor wanted to call an ambulance but Jordan wouldn't let him. Jordan had a small flask of bourbon and poured it over Brett's clothing to make it appear that he had been drinking and passed out."

"So they did this because Brett knew about Taylor's story?"

"Brett only had a hunch about Taylor's story. He didn't know more than anybody else in the newsroom about it. He found out something else."

"What?"

"He saw them kissing in a parking lot behind the bar," she said. "That's why they followed him to his house."

"What?"

"Taylor and Jordan are lovers," she said. "They were afraid he would tell others what he saw."

"I can't believe that."

"I don't care if you believe it or not," she said. "It's the truth. They went on trips together. Remember the time you followed me to the motel? I was trying to give you a clue about them."

"What about you and Jordan?"

"I was only trying to get information from him," she said. "There was nothing between us. I wanted to get back at Riggins for the way he treated Brett and it was the only way I could do it. But I found out more than I expected."

Bennett pulled into the parking lot. He approached her car slowly from the driver's side. Police blockaded the area around the bank, out of sight from Angela's view. Bennett walked to her door. Startled, she turned around and pointed the gun at him.

"Don't do anything foolish, Mrs. Cook," Bennett said. "I'm here to help you."

"It's too late to help me now," she said, holding the gun in the air.

"Jordan isn't dead," Bennett said. "He's probably at the hospital now."

"Is that supposed to make me happy? I want him dead."

"Please put down the gun," Bennett said. "Everything is going to be all right."

Angela looked at Bennett and then turned her head and stared at Chase for a few seconds. She smiled beneath her teary eyes. She put the gun to her head and pulled the trigger.

The gun jammed.

Bennett broke the glass on the window with the butt of his gun, reached in and unlocked the door and grabbed Angela's weapon. She slumped against the steering wheel. He took a cell phone out of his coat pocket and called for assistance. Within minutes, the area was sealed off by police. She sobbed while being taken away in handcuffs by a police officer.

"Why did she do that?" Chase asked Bennett as they moved away from her car.

"She must have thought everything was getting out of control after Conner was shot," Bennett said. "She felt guilty because she didn't come forward with what she knew from the beginning."

"But why didn't she?" Chase asked.

"Why didn't a lot of people?" Bennett said. "I guess she was an opportunist and hoping to gain some leverage at the newspaper from Jordan and Taylor."

"Did you know about Jordan and Taylor's relationship?"

"Conner alluded to it in his journal but it was something we were still checking on."

"I guess this will make a nice ending to Bernie and James's article."

"Probably so," Bennett said.

"If anyone believes it," Chase said with a wry smile.

Forty-three

Chase sat back in his recliner in the quiet surroundings of his living room. He closed his eyes and thought about the events of the past few months – the lies, deceits and senseless death. It unraveled as matters of confidence and rippled into other's lives. He became teary-eyed. The silence was broken by a knock at the front door.

"Are you at home, Chase?" Hannah asked.

Chase wiped away the tears from his eyes with his sleeve as he went to the door. She hugged him and rested her head on his chest.

"Oh, honey," Hannah said. "I've been so worried. I saw the story about Angela Cook on the news tonight. Are you all right?"

"I'm fine," he said softly.

Hannah took a step back and saw his reddened eyes. She hugged him again.

"I could have stopped all of it," Chase said, choking back the tears. "All of it."

"What do you mean, honey?"

"I mean that I'm responsible, too."

"How can you be responsible?"

"I knew about Taylor's fabricated story. He told me in confidence. I should have said something to someone about Taylor's story from the very beginning. Brett would be alive."

"You didn't know what would happen when Taylor told you," Hannah said, softly patting his back. "We don't know how those things are going to turn out."

"But I knew it was wrong when he told me," Chase said as they went to the couch. "I wanted him to confess the story to someone at the paper. I tried to make it happen. I let everyone down. More than anything, I let myself down."

"But Taylor let you down and everyone else," Hannah said soothingly. "He trusted you and knew you wouldn't break a confidence."

"To a fault," Chase said as he held Hannah in his arms as a cold darkness enveloped the room.

Hannah snuggled closer to him as they sat without saying a word for several minutes. Chase squeezed her hand softly.

"You know we all try to be trustworthy," he said quietly.

"No sweetheart," she said as her head lay against his chest. "Only a few can be truly trustworthy confidants. Most people are selfish and try to look out for their own needs. It's a special person who can keep things to themselves and not betray a trust."

"I suppose that's a weakness in me."

"No honey, it's a strength. It's something people admire in you. And it's one of the reasons I love you."

The phone rang. Chase turned on the lamp on the end table before answering the phone.

"What are you doing at home?" Bernie asked against a noisy background of chatter and music. "Why don't you come over to Pappy's? We're having a celebration party."

"Thanks, Bernie, but I can't say I'm in the mood for celebrating."

"Don't be that way. We ridded the newspaper of some bad people. Some would even say evil, especially Taylor Riggins."

"Well, I hope you have fun. I'll see you at work tomorrow."

"Well, if you change your mind, we'll be here for quite a while."

"They're having a party at Pappy's," Chase said to Hannah after hanging up the phone.

"That's what I could gather. And you don't want to join them?"

"I don't see this as a time to celebrate. It's a sad day. And I don't want to spoil their evening."

"I understand how you feel."

"Do you want to leave? I know I can't be the best company in the world."

"I want to be with you." She kissed him softly on the cheek.

"I'm glad you're here with me."

Chase reached up and turned off the lamp. Hannah cuddled next to him as they sat silently in the stillness of the dark room.

Meet Michael Embry

Michael Embry is the author of three nonfiction sports books and three novels, including *Foolish Is The Heart* for Wings ePress in 2008. His career includes more than 30 years in journalism as a reporter, sportswriter and editor. He lives in Frankfort, Ky., with his wife, Mary, and Yorkshire terriers, Baxter and Bucky.

Other Works From The Pen Of
Michael Embry

Works From The Pen Of Michael Embry

<u>Shooting Star</u>, Jesse Christopher finds out that it's not easy being the new kid in school, no matter how well you play basketball. When discovered shooting hoops at a school playground by a high school coach, Jesse seems to be the missing piece to the puzzle for a team that aspires to win the Kentucky state championship.

But Jesse faces an array of problems in his new environment as he tries to make friends in the classroom and become part of the school's close-knit basketball team. Can Jesse overcome the obstacles and lead his team to a state high school basketball title?

<u>A Confidential Man</u>, Sports columnist Chase Elliott has earned a reputation around the newsroom of being a person that others can confide their deepest problems. What happens when someone goes over the line? And what if a fellow worker dies from mysterious circumstances?

Elliott tries to deal with all the rumors and innuendos circulating around the newsroom while coming to terms with his own sense of trustworthiness and high ethical standards. Can he discover the truth without betraying confidences?

Foolish Is The Heart, Brandon Wilkes is a 45-year-old sports columnist who has never settled down to the point of marriage. At first it was his career that caused him to go the bachelor route. He became a respected and successful sportswriter. As he grew older, he seemed content to be single the remainder of his life. That's not to say that he didn't have relationships or that women didn't pursue him. He just didn't want to make a permanent commitment to a woman.

He was content with the way things had been in his life. Going to work, meeting friends at the local pub and covering various sports events for Kentucky Sports Weekly. His easy-going lifestyle undergoes changes as some big events happen in his personal and professional life. Brandon tries to come to terms with the direction his life is heading and trying to deal with those things he believes to be important.

A Long Highway, Micah Stewart is in the throes of a mid-life crisis. He's bored with his job as a sports writer. While he maintains a good relationship with his ex-wife and children, he feels unfulfilled in many areas of his life.

A random act of violence in the workplace forces Micah to hit the road in search of meaning to his life. Will he find enlightenment? Can he find happiness again? Can he find contentment at the end of the long highway?

The Touch, A woman in an abusive relationship finds strength and romance from a single dad.

The Bully List, Two boys get fed up being picked on and decide to come up with a list of things to get even with the bullies.

Old Ways and New Days, John Ross discovers there are many adjustments he has to make as he moves from the ranks of the employed to retirement, or as some refer to it, the pajama club.

Darkness Beyond the Light - Retirement plans are put on hold for empty-nesters John and Sally Ross when they discover a dark side about their son.

New Horizons - John and Sally Ross take a long-overdue vacation to Budapest to get away from it all but encounter headaches and heartaches on their journey that make them wish they were back home.

A Message to Our Readers

Enjoy this book?

You can make a difference.

As an independent publisher, Wings ePress, Inc. does not have the financial clout of the large New York publishers. We can't afford large magazine spreads or subway posters to tell people about our quality books.

But we do have something much more effective and powerful than ads. We have a large base of loyal readers.

Honest reviews help bring the attention of new readers to our books.

If you enjoyed this book, we would appreciate it if you would spend a few minutes posting a review on the site where you purchased this book or on the Wings ePress, Inc. webpages at:

https://wingsepress.com/

Thank You